"What happened to us last night, Lou?" Johnny asked softly.

She took a deep breath but could say nothing.

"What happened?" he prompted, more softly still, his voice running up her spine like warm velvet.

She closed her eyes for a moment. "I don't know," she whispered. Her heart was beating so hard she thought it would kill her, and the air between them was shimmering.

They looked at each other through the waves of heat. "What now?" asked Johnny, so quietly he almost mouthed the words.

She shook her head helplessly, and Johnny took a breath and stood up.

"Lou...."

Now that it was upon them, she was frightened. A lifetime of friendship hung in the balance. "God, Johnny," she whispered.

He said her name again, and there was something in his voice she had never heard before. He stepped toward her, large and dark, and when he put his hands on her arms, she rocked as though struck by a shock wave and fell into his embrace.

Dear Reader,

For years, Silhouette Intimate Moments has worked to bring you the most exciting books available in category romance. We were the first to introduce mainstream elements, to make our books themselves something out of the ordinary for romance publishing. Next month we'll take another step in that direction when we introduce an extraordinary new cover design. At last our books will "look as big as they read." Our commitment to quality novels hasn't changed, but now we've come up with a package that we think does our stories justice. I'm hoping you'll think so, too, and that you'll share your thoughts on our new cover with me just as, all along, you've been sharing your thoughts on our books themselves.

But let's not forget the excitement this month in the middle of anticipating next month's big change. Veterans Jennifer Greene, Alexandra Sellers and Kate Bradley are in this month's lineup, along with talented newcomer Joyce McGill. Actually, Joyce has written young-adult novels before, but this is her first foray into adult fiction, and I know you'll be glad to hear that it won't be her last.

That's it for now, but keep your eyes open next month for the newest look in romance—only in Silhouette Intimate Moments.

Yours,

Leslie J. Wainger
Senior Editor and Editorial Coordinator

The Best of Friends

ALEXANDRA SELLERS

Silhouette Intimate Moments

Published by Silhouette Books New York

America's Publisher of Contemporary Romance

SILHOUETTE BOOKS
300 East 42nd St., New York, N.Y. 10017

ISBN: 0-373-07348-8

First Silhouette Books printing August 1990

Printed in the U.S.A.

Books by Alexandra Sellers

Silhouette Intimate Moments

The Real Man #73
The Male Chauvinist #110
The Old Flame #154
The Best of Friends #348

ALEXANDRA SELLERS

used to force her mother to read to her for hours. She wrote her first short story at ten, but as an adult got sidetracked and didn't get published until she was twenty-seven. She also loves travel; she wrote one book in Israel, and began another in Greece. This one was written in London, where she now resides.

Author's Note

I have tried to be as accurate as possible about the history and geography of Vancouver and of British Columbia. The Victoria fire mentioned is an invention of my own, but the 1924 death of Janet Smith, the young Scottish nanny, is a real Vancouver mystery.

With thanks for their help to
Staff-Sergeant Kerry Burleigh, RCMP;
Detective Bjorn Bjornson, Vancouver
Police Department; and Richard Bourne,
Private Investigator

This book is dedicated to:
Tom and Dorothy Muurimaki;
And the Bikini Beach Bums.
And to Judy Frewing,
Who knows who she is,
And where she is.

Chapter 1

Get away from me!'' said Johnny Good. ''I haven't got time for any of your lame ducks right now! I mean it!'' He was propped against his battered desk, hunched forward, his hands on either side of his hips, gripping the thick, dark-stained edge of wood that formed its top. His legs were crossed at the ankles where his tight blue jeans flared slightly to accommodate a familiar pair of scratched, worn cowboy boots. He was smiling in a way that said if she didn't leave his territory soon he would bite her.

Since he was a pretty big, dangerous-looking man, Johnny didn't often have to bother to look mean to ward off attacks. It was a sign of how vulnerable he felt that he was bristling with all these threatening keep-away signals, and he knew Lou knew it.

''I wish you'd sit down,'' she said, although she actually kind of enjoyed all that menace hanging over her, the same way she enjoyed thunderstorms while lying snug in bed. For her, Johnny had the unique talent of being both the danger and the comfort, the threat and the protection, all in one. "Julie isn't a lame duck. She just needs help."

"Where have I heard that before?" Johnny Good asked with heavy sarcasm. He straightened, moved around the desk and dropped heavily into his chair, which protested loudly at the abuse. He raised his arms. "Babe, I am telling you, I don't care how much help she needs. I haven't got time. Why does it have to be me?"

Lou laughed. There was something about a man playing the stock role of the helpless, put-upon male that struck her suddenly as race-memory evidence of the original matriarchal structure of human society.

"You're the only detective I know," she said. "I promise I won't take much of your time. Can't we—"

"You're not going to take *any* of my time. Go to the cops, if it's a missing person. That's what they're there for, remember?"

This was a setback she hadn't quite counted on, him rejecting her plea so out of hand. For a moment, playing for time, she concentrated on trying to find a comfortable position in the stuffed walnut and red leather chair, whose skeleton seemed to get more prominent every time she came in contact with it, like a woman falling into the grip of anorexia. "I tried that," she said at last. "They wouldn't listen."

"I feel for them."

It was another very bad sign that he did not ask why the cops wouldn't listen. "They said," Lou supplied anyway, as though he had asked the question, "that she had probably gone back to him voluntarily because some women really want to be beaten by their lovers and she is one of them. Isn't that about what you'd expect?"

"Uh huh." Johnny nodded, pursing his mouth thoughtfully. "No reason not to take a report, though. Reason not to act on it very urgently, maybe."

"Yeah, well, they didn't trouble to be diplomatic." Lou slipped off a shoe and shifted her weight to bring one leg up under her long skirt, resting her foot on the edge of the rock-hard leather seat and clasping her arms around her knee. It was a long, generously full skirt in blue cotton, and it fell well over her knees, keeping her decent. She rarely wore short or tight skirts; she had never learned the discipline required to sit normally in a chair for any length of time, and she dressed accordingly. "This chair must have died ten years ago, at least. Why don't you have a comfortable client's chair in here?" she complained, then, unconsciously hoping to catch him off guard, "Johnny, can't I have a couple of minutes just to tell you about it? If you could give me a few ideas . . ."

He leaned back in his chair and suppressed a yawn that quivered in his neck and chest muscles. When he opened his eyes again, he made a face at her.

"I want people to be uncomfortable so they'll remember where they are. If they get too comfortable they start to think they're in their shrink's office," he said. "Besides . . ." He shrugged and looked around his small office, and her eyes obediently followed his, taking in the general mess. Every available surface was stacked with papers—his desk, the battered credenza behind him, and the black-painted metal shelves that leaned just enough off true to look as cheap as they were. Today there were papers even on the floor around his chair. His point was that the chair was consistent with the rest of the decor.

And it was, with the exception of one item: an antique Persian silk carpet hanging on the wall behind Lou's head. It was there for his own pleasure, not as part of the decor and not to impress clients, and it hung on the wall that faced his desk, hidden from casual view by the open door. Superficially it didn't match up with the tough, hard man behind the desk in denim and well-worn cowboy boots, but then most people hardly noticed it. Those who did were first surprised, then subtly more respectful, a fact that didn't do much to raise Johnny's estimate of human nature. To some people, and Lou was one of them, it was the one personal note in the office—the only thing that expressed any part of Johnny's inner self. It was very beautiful, a collector's item. She knew it had cost a lot more than he could afford.

She saw his eyes come to rest on it, and there were subtle signs of relaxation in the muscles around his mouth. She felt as though she were watching an animal drink at a spring.

She opened her mouth as his gaze shifted back to her, but he put up a hand to forestall her. "Look, Babe. I am up to my butt in crocodiles here. Peter Tang quit on me last week, and everybody is working overtime. I don't have time to do it for you. I don't have time to *sleep*. A missing person case can be time-consuming as all hell. Go to the cops. They've got the manpower. I don't."

"They say I'm not closely enough related to her even to make a *report*, Johnny," she told him. "They want her mother or her husband to do it. I don't even know where her family *is*."

"Ah." Johnny nodded as though he had been waiting for this piece of information to come out and suspected that she had been deliberately withholding it, which perhaps she had. Technically it justified the police in their refusal to go looking for Julie, and she wanted Johnny indignant and on her side. But he had been a cop himself, and it was a waste of time to try to snow him on something like that, even unconsciously. "Well, what the hell, Babe? You aren't. You're not even a friend, right? She's just a waitress at your favorite greasy spoon. What do you expect them to do?"

"Just what they're doing—nothing!" She shrugged. "After all, what's a human life when there are rules at stake?"

Since Johnny had quit the Vancouver police force after eight years with a deep-rooted loathing against procedure, this was a pretty blatant attempt at manipulation. Even all these years after going private, it was still easy enough to get him into a burn against the system. As Lou well knew, he reflected now, feeling the old frustration seep up inside him.

He resisted the anger and her subtle invitation to charge in on his white horse and put to rights the injustice that the city's guardians of law and order had ignored, and leaned back in his chair, a knowing grin on his face.

"Nice try, Babe," he said. "But I don't have the time right now to prove a point."

She laughed, acknowledging the unspoken accusation.

"Anyway, they're probably right. The rule's there for a reason. For all you know, she went home to her mother."

"No," she said flatly. "Come on, can't you just listen? It's nearly one o'clock. You have to eat sometime. They're wrong. You know they're wrong. Women don't go back to men who beat them because they want to be—" She let it hang, shaking her head. "You're my only hope, Johnny. If you don't help me, there's no one else to ask," she said instead.

This was a powerful conjuration. At a rough guess, Johnny Good had been saving Lou Patch from herself for eighteen years or more. Habit, if nothing else, made him feel responsible for her.

"Damnation," he said irritably, feeling this instinctive response stir in him. "What makes it so important? There must be ten thousand women in this city whose husbands are beating on them. Why do you want to get so exercised about this one?"

"Because I know her," she said, as he had known she would. "Besides, Julie's got something special. She was planning to go back to school, go on to university.... I can't stand to think of all that potential being bashed around by a bully without enough brains to come in out of a hurricane. That cop could say I don't know her well enough, Johnny, but *you* can't. Friendship isn't dependent on time," she said, to the friend she had known all her life. "Besides, wherever her family is, they don't seem to be asking any questions. Who's going to care, if I don't?''

He was spinning a pen on the desk under his fingers, the urgency of work that awaited him irritating him physically, making him tense. ''You know the odds are she went with him willingly.''

Lou felt a quick surge of anger, because she knew he was right, on the odds. Julie wouldn't be the first battered woman to go back to a brutal man because life seemed too frightening on her own. But what men never seemed to understand was that that didn't mean she didn't need help. ''That's the old cop talking, that's all. *You* know if she went with him *willingly* it's because she was scared to death of him, and she has to pretend she's okay whenever the cops come to the door.''

''She has to pretend the same thing when you do. What are you going to do? Kidnap her?''

''Yes. Well, no, of course not. Talk to her, anyway. Show her she's got a way out. I don't like to pressure you, Johnny, but I have this feeling that it's urgent. She had a scar over her eyebrow. He's big and she is *tiny*. She hardly comes up to here.'' She indicated a spot on her upper arm, just on the curve of her deltoid, where the casually rolled cuff of her white T-shirt lay against lightly browned skin. As she bent her head, her long, streaky blond hair, frizzed into charming disorder, fell forward over her face. Shaking it back, she looked into his eyes. ''Next time he beats her she could be crippled or something. I don't want to wait for that.''

The pen stopped twirling and Johnny stared off into the distance over her shoulder for a moment. He was annoyed to find himself making an automatic mental note that the missing woman was something under five feet, but the information, once fed in, couldn't be obliterated from his detective's memory. If Lou managed to suck him into this when he had no time for it . . .

He said, "I haven't got one hour of one agent's time that I can spare for at least a week. After that—" He shrugged. "I'll do what I can, but I don't promise you it'll be much. This kind of thing doesn't take much skill, but as I said, it can take a lot of time and a lot of legwork, and it's just gonna have to wait. I'm sorry, Babe, but the paying customers come first." Again he forestalled her with a show of his palm as she was about to speak. "And don't offer to pay. I'm not taking on any clients, we're too busy."

But that wasn't what she had been going to say. She said, "Is that true? That it just takes legwork? Because what I was thinking, if you would only give me the chance to say so, was that I might be able to do a lot of it myself. I didn't expect you to take it on as a case, you know. I was hoping for some help, but if you're really so busy, how about just a few pointers?"

He cocked a sardonic eyebrow at her. Lou said, "Hey, I'm serious. I don't suppose it's all that different from my kind of research, is it?"

"I always thought your kind of research took place in dusty archives." Lou made her living writing about local topics in Vancouver and British Columbia, from children's history books of the native tribes of the province to a popular column rehashing old crimes for a city newspaper.

"Not all of it. When I was doing that book on the Kwakiutl I stayed at Alert Bay for two months. And what about the Janet Smith book? Don't you remember how many people I had to talk to for that?" Johnny remembered it well. He had been called on for a great deal of advice and information during her investigation of Vancouver's famous 1924 death of a Scottish nanny that had been covered up in high places and was still unsolved.

It was that work that had given her the idea that she could track Julie down herself, with a little of the same sort of help. She'd known Johnny couldn't take on the finding of

Julie. A little advice and backup support was what Lou was looking for.

"Well, this will be different from Janet Smith," he said, happy to capitulate to the lesser demand out of relief at not hearing the greater. "But I don't see anything to stop you trying."

"All *right*!" she said, raising two fists in the winner's salute. "So, are we going to lunch?"

Johnny sighed, nodded, dropped his hands on his desk, pushed back his chair and stood up. "Yeah, I guess I can handle that. I suppose I have to eat sometime, though God knows I manage without when you're not here."

"I'm buying, I bet." She grinned, getting to her feet. "Since this is such a favor."

"You better believe you're buying," he responded, slipping his arms into a denim bomber jacket that somehow emphasized the hardness around his jaw, so that an observer might have been forgiven for assuming that he had just swung his leg off a big, ugly motorcycle. "You can break my heart with the bare bones *only* of the story of your friend Julie while we eat," he continued, opening his office door and waiting for her to precede him. "I will, from my position as expert, give you pointers—back in forty-five minutes *exactly*, Celia—" he called to the dark-haired beauty in reception as they passed the door, but Lou knew the message was meant for her "—and you, sweetheart," he finished, opening the outer door and pointing a finger and cocking his thumb at her as she passed through, "are going to do *all* the legwork yourself. And I do mean that."

Easy enough to say, but Johnny knew damned well that if Lou got into any kind of a mess he'd be sucked in right along with her, whether he liked it or not.

Chapter 2

Lou glanced around the interior of the restaurant, at the familiar red-checked tablecloths and soft wood panelling, and smiled reminiscently. "I haven't been in here for ages," she exclaimed. "We used to spend half our lives at Nick's! What happened?"

"We got old," Johnny said succinctly. "Now I spend half my life in parked cars keeping insurance fraud suspects under surveillance, and the other half doing paperwork. Thank you," he added, as the waitress handed them two large plastic-coated menus.

Lou laughed. "Funny how different life is from what we thought, eh?" She looked down at what she had automatically accepted from the waitress. "They've got a printed menu now? Is there anything that doesn't change?"

"Be grateful they haven't torn the place down."

"I liked the blackboard. What was wrong with the blackboard?"

"That depended on what table you were at, and how good your eyes were."

"I'm sure I've sat at every table in the place, and my eyes were always good enough," she protested.

"As I said, you're older now. It might not be so easy anymore."

"Ohh, Cruella de Ville!"

"I'm not saying anything you don't know, Babe," he said without remorse. "Anyway, I've aged at the same rate."

"I'm not so sure you have. Your hair's longer, but otherwise you look the same." It wasn't true. Johnny had changed a lot. She had a sudden vision of him as he had been eighteen years ago, with his square, fresh, farm-boy face, the clean, neatly cut hair falling into his eyes. He had been a very good-looking young man, though his looks had certainly not, in those long-haired, grubby days, been in the current style. It wasn't that he had lost his looks. He had gotten hard.

He grinned. "Ah, you hated my short-back-and-sides. You wouldn't take me seriously, and I knew damn well it was because you'd be embarrassed to admit to your friends that you were going out with someone so straight. But I couldn't do anything about that except apply for under-cover work. They let you grow your hair for that—just. But I was way too junior to get that kind of assignment then."

She reddened. It was true, but she'd never realized he knew it. It embarrassed her. Not because of seeing how she had followed the group, blindly conforming to a "noncon-formity" that was just as confining as any other dogma; she had recognized that youthful hypocrisy long ago. What shamed her was that Johnny had known her reasons all along. She had refused to date him seriously because he was a cop, and in its own way that was as nasty as if she had done it on a question of race.

Out of embarrassment, she protested, with truth, "We went out together all the time!"

Johnny grinned. "Yeah."

In the face of that determined knowing, she could only grin back and shake her head. "What a jerk I must have been."

"Well..." They laughed together with ease. Whatever disappointment Johnny had felt at being assigned the role of friend nearly two decades ago had long since disappeared in the comfort such a long-standing friendship had brought.

"Do you remember Alan?" she demanded, suddenly remembering him herself. "I cried over Alan right at this very table—no, it had to be the one beside us! It must be seventeen years ago now. Remember that?"

Johnny's brow furrowed. "Which one was Alan?" he asked, as though his memory were stuffed cheek by jowl with men she had cried over on his shoulder.

She made a face at him. "Come on, Alan was the first. My draft dodger, remember?"

"Oh, was that Alan? Poor fool," he said. "Feel like a salad today?"

"Yes, please." "Poor fool" was right. Alan had slipped back across the border into the States for his father's funeral, as the FBI had known perfectly well he would. The next time she had heard from Alan, he had been in jail, and likely to remain there for some time. Johnny had listened patiently while Lou had cursed the war, the establishment, the FBI and everything except Alan's own foolhardiness in attempting to outwit them. "He should have known," Johnny had said calmly, from his vantage point on the other side of the law. "Family funeral's the first place they'd look for him."

Johnny was always so rational about everything. It sometimes irritated Lou, but at the same time, his coolness often seemed to keep her from going off the deep end.

She glanced around the room, remembering them then. How young they had been. When she looked at photos from that time it was always the first thing that hit her—the freshness, the youth.

"Are you having the lasagna today?" she asked, as the waitress appeared beside them.

Johnny shook his head. "Too heavy, I've got too much work this afternoon."

"I'll order it, and you can have some of mine," she said.

"One lasagna?" said the waitress.

"And the salad bowl for four," added Johnny.

"Nothing else for you?" She smiled at him in the way that women often did, reminding Lou that it wasn't only in eighteen-year-old photos that Johnny was a good-looking man. Johnny shook his head, his hair, as usual, falling into his eyes. It was still thick on top, though no longer the short-back-and-sides cut of his youth. And the heavy lock that fell over his forehead now no longer made him look like a farm boy.

When the waitress had gone, Johnny rested his arms on the table and tapped his watch significantly. "Start talking," he commanded.

"Oh boy," said Lou, feeling the pressure to organize her thoughts fall on her mind like a damp wool blanket. "How much have I already told you?"

"You have told me nothing," Johnny said. "Start from scratch. You have a friend named Julie. Assume that is all I know."

"My friend Julie," she began obediently, "works as a waitress in my favorite greasy spoon. Or at least, she did until last Thursday. Last Thursday—no, but wait, let me tell you about her first.

"She's tiny and very attractive, with a working-class education and a first-class brain, which is being sadly underused at the moment, as I said."

"Red flag to a bull. You took her under your wing." Johnny grinned at her, as if it were self-evident, and it struck her suddenly that Julie's was not the only first-class brain not exercised up to capacity that she numbered among her friends. Johnny had been working for years toward a degree at night school, and she had often felt it wasn't really the degree that motivated him, but the fact that he found his work intellectually unsatisfying.

"Yes, well," she continued, wondering if Johnny and Julie might be attracted to each other, if she could only get them to meet. "Julie works a split shift at the Pacific Café, and she spends afternoons down at Bikini Beach with me sometimes. We've done a lot of talking for having only known each other a few weeks. I know *a lot* about her, and that cop was wrong when he said...never mind." She grinned, interpreting the look that had come over his face. "You're right. Chronology is everything. So, here goes."

The fact was, she had noticed Julie right from the first day she'd started work at Lou's favorite café. Julie had courage and native intelligence, two things that always attracted Lou to people. The kind of person who had had enough hard knocks from life not to be afraid of taking a few more if necessary.

But Julie had been taking a few too many just recently. Involved with a man who beat her, she had managed to save up enough money to get away from him, find a new apartment and a new job, and was making plans to get out of Vancouver entirely.

She had been nervous that Butch would find her before she could get away, and afraid that Butch might kill her if she refused to go back to him. Butch, she had confided to Lou, had spent two years in Oakalla Prison for assault after he had nearly beaten his wife to death a long time ago, and she was pretty certain that he had spent spells in prison on other charges since.

On Tuesday, ten days ago, Julie had arrived at the beach shaken and upset, certain that she had seen Butch in a car outside her apartment building. On Thursday, Lou had gone into the Pacific Café to discover the Chinese owner waiting on tables himself. Julie had not turned up for work. She hadn't called in.

"And I think Butch came and got her, and I want to find her, Johnny. So how do we go about that?"

He grinned the grin that told her he was immune to crude sales tactics and fired his finger at her again. "*You're* going to go about it, remember? I'm merely going to suggest how to you. Got a notebook, got a pencil?"

Lou always had a notebook and pencil, and she pulled them out of her bag and looked attentive. "All right, you didn't give me many details. Do you know any? Know Julie's last name? Know her most recent address?"

"Yes. Both."

"Go to the manager of her building. Find out how she left. Did she give notice, had she paid an advance and did she get it back? Did she remove her things from the apartment? Is she still a tenant as far as he's concerned? Will he let you into the apartment to have a look around? If you can, check with some of the tenants. Did they see her leave? Did she drive a car?"

It was a second before Lou recognized that this question was directed at her. "Oh—I don't think she had a car."

"If she had a license she'll have to notify them of her change of address. You can try there. Go back to the Pacific Café and talk to the boss again. Did she leave any salary uncollected? Do you have her phone number?"

Intent on scribbling down everything he was saying, Lou nodded.

"Call B.C. Tel. Find out whatever information they'll give you about that phone number. The phone company gets references before they give anyone a phone. See if they'll give you the names of Julie's references. Find out if the last bill had been paid. If there's a referral to a new phone number. You usually can't ask these questions straight out, by the way. This is where it gets to be very different from the research you're used to." His eyes twinkled at her. "You have to use a little finesse."

"You mean, tell lies?"

"I mean say whatever will get you the information. You have to play it by ear."

"All right, what else?"

"Do you know anything else about Butch?"

"I know his real first name is David. And I saw his picture. She showed it to me."

"That's not a whole hell of a lot."

"Oh—she said once that he sometimes worked for Jerry Mandala."

Johnny's mouth formed a small O of surprise and he raised his eyebrows at her. "Did he? Well, well!"

"Why are you surprised at that?"

"Legitimate businessmen should never have small-time hoods on the payroll. It's the sort of thing that makes cops curious." He paused. "And journalists." He looked at her speculatively, but Lou missed the significance of it.

"Why do you call him a small-time hood?"

"You told me he's been in and out of prison."

"But that was for beating up his wife."

"And the other times? How many wives does he have?"

"You think the other times it was for...for..." She couldn't think of a word.

"For criminal activity?" Johnny supplied, sounding very much like a cop. "Yes, I do."

"Why?"

He touched his nose. "Because that's what Nellie here says."

She looked at him with an innocently blank face. "Your nose?" she asked. Johnny nodded. "Nellie? Your nose is called Nellie?"

"When it's working." His lips twitched.

"That's a girl's name, Johnny. Why does your nose have a girl's name?" She asked with mock carefulness, as though she were a shrink sitting with a deviate.

He scratched his head, making a rueful face. "I hate to have to point this out to an old feminist, Babe, but that's a very sexist comment. Nellie, as anyone whose consciousness has been raised will tell you, isn't a girl's name. It's a woman's name. And the reason my nose has a woman's name is that she has terrific intuition. Right now she intuits that your boy Butch is not only a wife-beater but a petty criminal."

"Because he's been in prison?"

"And because he works 'sometimes' for Jerry Mandala."

"Wait a minute. You suspect Jerry Mandala because he's got Butch on the payroll and you suspect Butch because he's on Jerry Mandala's payroll? That's a tautology."

"I always wondered what that word meant. It means intuitive genius?"

"No, it means specious reasoning."

"Ah, then you're wrong. Nellie never reasons. She knows. The Nose, as they say, Knows."

"Are you telling me there's something questionable about Jerry Mandala?"

"I'm not telling you anything."

Lou gave up. "All right, so—do I go and ask Jerry Mandala if Butch is still on the payroll or if he's disappeared, too?"

He pushed out his lower lip. "You can try, I guess. You don't know Butch's last name?"

"No. But I was wondering if your friend on the police force might be able to find him through his record at Oakalla. I know exactly when he was there the first time, because Julie told me he went in at nineteen and came out at twenty-one, and he's thirty-seven now. And there can't be that many guys named David whose nickname—"

She broke off because Johnny was holding up his hand. "Suppose we forget about me asking my friend for a year's supply of favors in one till we've—you've gone over the ground a bit to see if it's necessary? Not that I'm not willing, in the name of friendship, to blow—"

"Yes, all right, all right, I'm sorry. I didn't know, Johnny. You've told me you still have a friend on the force who does you favors from time to time. How was I supposed to know—"

"Hey, it's okay," said Johnny. They looked at each other and laughed. "I'll ask Brent for you if it gets to that. But it'll help if you have a little more than you've got right now. There are laws protecting information in this country, and a cop isn't allowed to pull up some guy's criminal record and pass it around to his friends. See? He might do it. But he'll do it a lot faster if we have a little something to offer."

"Like what? A bottle?"

"You know what, Babe? You're mellowing." He grinned. "Not a bottle. What you find out in your investigations."

She looked at him. "I suppose you mean that if I find blood on the carpet they might be willing to listen to what I tried to tell them yesterday," she said sarcastically.

But he was immune to sarcasm. He smiled at her as if she were a particularly bright student. "That's exactly what I mean," he said approvingly.

"There is something. Maybe," she said hesitantly. She hadn't really wanted to tell him this, but if it would serve to enlist the help of his friend, it would be foolish to withhold it.

Johnny raised an eyebrow.

"Julie wasn't afraid of Butch just because he beat her. She was afraid he was a murderer."

It had been gnawing at the back of her mind ever since the day on the beach when, in a low voice, Julie had told her what really scared her about Butch: she half believed that he had raped and killed a woman four months ago.

It was a celebrated case that had been all over the front pages at the time it happened, and it was still mentioned now and again as it continued to remain unsolved on police files. A housewife, the mother of two young children, had been raped and left for dead beside her car in a Burnaby shopping mall. She had died in hospital later without regaining consciousness.

Julie had heard about the murder on the television news the day after Butch had come home late with blood on his shoes and on the knee of his jeans. She had already laundered the jeans, cleaned the shoes. Butch had a foul temper; he was always getting into fights. Blood on his clothes was not unusual. But there had been something odd about him that night. . . .

Whatever evidence there had been was gone. She had nothing but her suspicions, and the certain knowledge that if she went to the police with them and he found out about it, Butch would exact a terrible revenge. She had already been saving money secretly; she was a waitress and could lie about her tips. From that day on she put away as much money as she dared. "If he'd found out what I was doing, he'd have killed me," Julie told Lou, and if Julie's suspicions were right, that was probably literally true. If her suspicions were right.

Johnny sat in silence for several minutes under the onslaught of this new volley of information.

"It hasn't struck you," he said at last, "that your friend might have gone to the police and that they are holding her incommunicado for her own protection while they check out her story?"

"I tried to get her to do that. But she was so afraid. Anyway, wouldn't she have told her boss? I mean, notified him that she wouldn't be available to work for a while?"

Johnny shrugged. "Hard to say."

"Could you ask Brent about that?"

"Information on a secret witness in a major crime comes very high on the list of no favors possible. Suppose there was a leak that damaged their case? Suppose I was working for someone who was a cover for Butch himself? Brent couldn't afford to trust me, in the circumstances."

"I don't think Julie went to the cops. And if she were just running farther away from Butch I think she'd have gotten in touch with me by now. She's with him, and now you know why I want to find her so badly."

"Yeah. What I don't know is why you didn't tell me this from the start. You know damn well you can't mess in this thing yourself. It's too dangerous. Damn it, go back to the police and tell them everything."

"You think I didn't tell them this?"

"Did you?" Johnny frowned in surprise.

"Yes, I did. They seemed to think I was dressing it up just so they'd let me file a report. I thought you might think the same thing." But she had also known that if he did believe it he would try to stop her finding Julie herself. Two very good reasons not to have mentioned it at all.

"Who the hell did you talk to down there? Who's running Missing Persons now?"

"His name was Goldring."

Johnny cursed once and shook his head. He pulled his ear for a moment, thinking. "Look, let me check around and see if there's someone else you can talk to without actually going over Goldring's head. Almost anyone else would have taken you seriously."

"Okay, if you can get someone interested. If it'll cause your friend Brent to check out Butch's record for us, I'll be grateful. In the meantime, I'm going to do a little checking."

"Lou," he said, and she knew he was serious, because he always used her old schoolgirl nickname unless he was very serious or a little drunk. But when he was drinking he called her Looby. "The possibility now looks very good that your boy has killed Julie. It will be very dangerous for you to cross his path if that is the case.''

She hated hearing that. ''I don't believe she's dead, Johnny. Not yet. And I won't cross his path talking to B.C. Tel, will I? I'll go back to the police when I've found some blood on the carpet. We'll see if that will interest Staff Sergeant Goldring.''

''Lou.''

''I won't do anything dangerous.''

''You don't know what will be dangerous and what won't. That's what makes it dangerous.''

''And *you* don't know how important this is to me. I want to help Julie. I want to get to her *before* he kills her. How long is it going to take you to interest your friends down there on the force?''

He couldn't answer that. ''If you get into trouble with this, Lou, I may not be able to get you out. I'm not a cop, remember. And I don't carry a gun like all those tough guys south of the border. The law doesn't let me.''

''Ah, Johnny, one look at you looming up on the horizon would scare off Scarface himself.''

He was shaking his head. ''Babe—'' he began, but she put her hand on his arm and smiled at him, cutting him off.

''Johnny,'' she whispered hoarsely, in a poor imitation of some ill-remembered film scene, ''I'm on a mission. A mission from God.''

But he refused to laugh, and she sighed and looked down in resignation at the salad on her plate. ''All right,'' she said, ''all right, all right. I'll stay out of it till you see what reaction you get from the cops.''

Out of his line of vision, her left hand lay in her lap. Childishly, as she spoke, she felt the fingers move to cross over each other in a ritual as old as time, averting the evil eye from her deliberate lie. She set down her fork and let her right hand fall into her lap. It wouldn't hurt to have double protection.

Chapter 3

There was no blood on the carpet. Or, if there had been, Lou didn't get to see it. The apartment that Julie had spent three weeks in, in a large, rambling old building on Haro Street near Stanley Park, had already been cleaned and rented, and the new tenants were moving in on the weekend. The suites were all furnished, the manager informed her, and they were easy to rent.

"Did Julie ask for her advance back?" Lou pressed, mindful of the notes she had taken at Johnny's rapid dictation.

"Oh, I'm sure she did. I can check the records if you want. We wouldn't refund for the last week, of course, because the suites are rented by the month." She was turning over the pages in a large ledger, and at the last page of entries she stopped and put a large forefinger on a notation.

"No, I remember now, I told him we'd have to keep the advance in lieu of notice unless the suite got rented by the first of the month. He said they'd send an address for us to send the check to."

Lou's stomach swooped a little. "She left with a man?"

The building manager, a large woman, looked up and squinted out over Lou's shoulder into the past. "Yup," she said, reassuring herself of the accuracy of her memory. "Oh, yeah. Little fella," she added, just as Lou began to speak.

"Was he a big man?" Lou couldn't stop herself from continuing. "Dark reddish hair, good-looking?"

"Well, he was dark, all right, but I wouldn't call him big. Good-looking, I don't know. Pointed little face he had. If he was the fella who was beating her, he wasn't much bigger than her. And she didn't weigh no more than a drowned kitten."

Lou had thought of using her writing as a cover for her questions, telling people she was after a story or doing research, but confronted by a woman, she had felt the truth might serve her better. The woman who remained unmoved by the prospect of another woman escaping from a man who beat her, only to be found and dragged forcibly back, could scarcely exist in the 1980s. Johnny might find it expedient to tell lies if he were searching for a woman, but Johnny was a big and somewhat dangerous-looking man, with the old traces of authority not quite obliterated from his essentially maverick soul. For Lou, lies might prove unnecessary.

"Isn't it a dreadful thing?" said the bent but lively old woman who lived in the apartment next to the one Julie had rented. "But they say that's what happens. I only saw your friend once in the hall, and a very pretty little creature I thought her. But he was big, you say."

"I believe he was over six feet tall, and about two hundred pounds," Lou said, not unmindful of the fact that the old woman presiding over the tea tray opposite her had undoubtedly once been "a very pretty little creature" herself, and would feel all the threat inherent in Butch's size.

"Well, you do hear about that kind of thing nowadays, don't you?" said the old woman, whose name was Winnie, in the mild tone of one who has seen it all and has not much indignation left to spend. "We thought there wasn't a lot of that in my day, but now they're saying people just didn't talk about it." She clucked her tongue. "Someone his size to pick on a tiny little thing like your friend. No wonder she was afraid of him. A man as big as that could have broken her in half with one hand. Can I pour you another cup, dear?"

Her mouth full of cookie, Lou could only smile and hold her cup under the steaming spout of the big brown earthenware teapot that looked like one her grandmother used to swear by. She washed the cookie down, and said, "Did you see or hear anything unusual before she left, any noises from next door?"

"I can't say that I did, dear. Not if you mean anything like screams or beatings. Sometimes she played her television rather loudly, but all the young ones do that, nowadays. I sometimes wonder what's happened to their ears, but then my hearing has gotten more sensitive as I've gotten older, which isn't the unmixed blessing you might think." She laughed gently.

"The only unusual thing I noticed last week," she said abruptly, "was that limousine outside in the alley." Her soft pink and white skin, which must have been like silk sixty years ago, and was like a baby's now, though of course much more wrinkled, turned a little pinker. "I don't suppose your friend went off in that, but I remember seeing it there with the engine running one morning. I noticed it particularly because the license plate said MONEY. I didn't like that, I'm afraid."

Lou didn't think Julie had gone off in a limousine, either, but she dutifully asked, "Do you remember what day you saw it there?"

"No, not exactly. Late last week, though."

Lou said, "I wouldn't call a limousine in the West End unusual, myself. Was there something..."

Winnie smiled awkwardly, as though she wished she hadn't mentioned it. "It was so early, you see, and the engine was running. It was only about four-thirty."

Lou glanced absently at the window, wondering if Winnie was the kind of old woman who filled her days by spying on her neighbors. "I didn't realize you had a window that looked out on the back lane."

"No, I don't." Winnie turned even pinker. "Well, I can tell you, because I'm sure you're an understanding young woman.... I'm an old-age pensioner, you know. My husband's pension stopped when he died, it was the old-fashioned kind of pension, when nobody cared what happened to widows of pensioners. The government was supposed to look after us," she said, without heat. "If anyone can live decently on what the government pays, I never heard of it.

"Well," she said briskly, indicating a change of subject with her tone, "you don't want to hear all of that. But I wanted to explain—you see, I'm one of those people—though I hope you wouldn't think it to look at me—" she laughed "—who make their living in this city by going through my neighbors' garbage. I have to get up very early in order to stay ahead of all the others who try to make their living through the same means." She smiled shyly, but now that she had confessed it, she seemed almost eager to talk about what she did. "It's very competitive, I can tell you. You would be surprised by what some people throw out."

She lifted a gnarled hand. "And what other people will buy. I don't mean I keep what I find. I clean it up and sell it. I run a little table at garage sales whenever there's one in the area. Nobody minds if I turn up. The more junk the better. Nothing is so uninteresting to a passerby as a garage sale without much to offer," she said, with matter-of-fact

ood humor. "So I'm usually welcome with my little
oread."

She paused, a bent forefinger curled over her lips, as
aough waiting for Lou's reaction.

Lou set down her empty cup, gazing at the old woman in
ascination. "And you can really make a living that way?"

"It makes the difference. Sometimes I depend on that
aoney for food. On the pension, you know, you often have
a choose between rent and food.

"The summer is best, there are so many garage sales.
'here are always fewer in winter, of course, but there's
sually the odd craft fair to keep me going. Would you like
a see my little business?"

She stood up on the word, and led Lou to a room scarcely
ig enough for a double bed. But there was no bed in it. A
ack ran from one wall to the next at head height, half filled
ith mostly outdated, used clothing. Underneath, boxes sat,
acked and labeled, and two tables against the walls op-
osite were spread with every conceivable kind of artifact.
nives, brooches, staple guns, old wallets, belts, books. A
aird table, with a chair in front of it, was relatively clear
xcept for instruments of cleaning and repair. It was a very
usinesslike workplace.

Lou stood openmouthed in the middle of it all. "This is
mazing!" she said. "You're running an industry!"

Winnie nodded. "Cottage industry," she said, with sat-
faction. "Well, it was this or the poorhouse, except of
ourse that there is no poorhouse anymore. The truth of the
aatter is, that it was this or the streets. What do you do for
living, dear?"

Lou was still mentally gaping, though she had managed
a close her mouth and look calm. "I'm a writer," she said.

"Ah, now that's a good occupation, I'm sure. That can
ake you right into old age. You keep it up. I was a dancer,
ou see. When I married, I retired, though we didn't have
ny children. When my husband died, I really had nothing.

You stick with writing." She patted Lou on the arm. "You stick right with it. Believe me, pensions will be no better when you're my age."

"I believe you," said Lou. She picked up a wallet that was lying on the repair table and bent to examine it.

"Now, there, you see," said Winnie eagerly, taking it from her grasp and opening it. "This is a good quality leather, and there's almost nothing wrong with it. Perfectly serviceable, but probably someone bought him a new one for his birthday, so he threw the old one out. There was a hole here in the bottom of the change purse—can you see where I've stitched and glued it? You can if you look closely."

There was a difference in the quality of the thread for about an inch along the bottom, which Winnie's finger unerringly pointed out. Lou nodded. Such tiny stitches must have meant painstaking work.

"I had to clean it, of course, and throw out all the papers he didn't think worth transferring to the new one. People are so careless about personal information. Now I'll buff it up with a little leather polish, and it'll look very nice. Someone will buy it for three or four dollars and get years of use out of it still. It's very good leather, it was probably expensive to begin with."

"What about this?" Lou held up a piece of clunky, rather ugly broken jewelry that might have been an old earring or brooch or the pendant from a necklace.

"You wouldn't think that's much of anything, would you? But the young girls like that sort of thing nowadays. I'll take off the broken bits and paint it with gold glitter and put it on a pin—or maybe it would be better as an earring, and someone will buy that. That'll go very quickly, because that kind of thing costs so much in the shops."

"Winnie—"

Winnie straightened and turned, smiling. "Yes?"

"Do you—pardon me for being so rude, but do you happen to go through the trash from *this* building?"

"Oh, of course. This is a big building, you know. Not a high rise, of course, but there are a lot of suites, and a lot of the tenants are temporary. They sometimes throw out very good things."

"Do you think you might have gone through this building's trash the day Julie left?"

The gnarled hand came up and held her delicate, pointed chin. "Oh yes, I think so. The weather's been so fine this summer, I believe I've been out every morning for the past two or three weeks. Yes."

"How do you keep it sorted? Would there be any way of knowing what had come from this building?" It was a ridiculous idea on the face of it—what could Julie have thrown out that Winnie would have saved that could be at all in the nature of a clue to where she had gone? But Winnie was right—people throwing out garbage were often careless about personal information. Lou was herself. And Lou had a powerful if irrational feeling that Winnie had a clue to Julie's whereabouts. It would be foolish to pass up the possibility.

Winnie crossed to the other worktable and pointed out the row of plastic bags that sat on the floor beside and under it.

"I'm afraid the morning's take all goes into the same bag. That's what I've collected that hasn't been sorted through for repair yet. I can let you look through those bags, if you like. I don't remember anything in particular, but of course you might recognize something. This bag here at the end is this morning's. I take fresh bags each day, though I usually don't fill more than one. I don't take anything except what has real potential, you see. There are others who come after me, and I leave the junk for those who can find a use for it. And the food, of course. I try not to disturb the food trash, because there are one or two who feed themselves that way. Mostly the natives, I'm afraid. But whatever I find goes into the same bag, from all the buildings.''

"Still . . . there might be something," Lou said, excited in spite of herself, because even if there were something there that was Julie's, how could she expect to recognize it? She'd been in Julie's apartment only once, very briefly. And if she did recognize it, what significance could it have? "Do you know which would be from last Thursday?"

"Now, let me see . . . That would probably be this one or this one. I'm about a week behind in my sorting. With the weather the way it is, there's no hurry. There's always time to do rainy day work in Vancouver, isn't there? And I like to get out for a good walk on the sunny days. Would you like to take these with you, dear?"

"That's very kind."

"Are you sure it's Thursday you're interested in?"

"The manager said that was the day her things were moved out."

Winnie was pretty quick. "But of course, she might have done her packing and cleaning on the Wednesday, mightn't she? I always did, even when I was on tour and living in furnished digs. Most people like to pack up the day before, don't they? It gives you more time to think of things you may have forgotten."

"I suppose that's true," said Lou, who hadn't moved more than three or four times in her life.

"Why don't you just take this bag as well?—that'll most likely be Wednesday's pickings, though I'm sorry to say I can't be sure. I don't label the bags as I collect them, but I will from now on. It never occurred to me before that my collections might be useful to someone else, you see, and it won't hurt me to label those bags with the dates.'' She looked up at Lou from the slightly hunched position her back forced on her.

"Oh, please don't go to any—" Lou began, but she was interrupted.

"It never hurts to take a little trouble for other people," the old woman said astringently. "You remember that, dear. These days people seem to think we're put on this earth for ourselves and no one else—I've heard them say it. That's a very dangerous philosophy, you take it from me. That's as dangerous as anything Hitler ever said, and I heard most of that, believe me. If we were put on this earth for our own sakes alone, we'd all have been snails."

Lou laughed, not that she disagreed. "Snails?"

"We'd be able to reproduce without having to bother anyone else about the matter," Winnie explained, turning off the light in the workroom and following Lou down the hall to the door. "Now, you keep those as long as you need them, because I've got plenty of work to keep me busy. If there's anything else I can do, you let me know because I'd like to be of real help in finding your friend."

"Thank you," said Lou, awkward in the face of so much charity.

"And come and visit me again. I enjoyed it."

"Thank you, I'd like to."

"I mean that, you know, about wanting to see you find your friend. I think it's a shame the police won't do anything. I want to help."

Lou held up the bags. "Maybe you already have."

She didn't have a nose named Nellie, but she had the strongest gut feeling that Winnie had given her a clue to Julie's whereabouts—all she had to do now was find it.

Chapter 4

Lou always told people she had met Johnny during the infamous Gastown Riot, when she was a protester and he was a cop and she hit him with a stone. It was true enough as far as it went, but it implied that he had arrested her, which wasn't true; and it left out the reason he hadn't arrested her, which was that they had known each other as kids, having gone to the same public school until grade seven.

Johnny had moved then—she didn't know why—and Lou never saw him again until that hot summer afternoon in an alley off Water Street when she threw something hard at the cop who was chasing her and it hit Johnny Good on the cheek.

The Gastown Riot was a very ugly incident in the otherwise calm, tolerant sixties in Vancouver. Draft dodgers who arrived fresh from the confrontational policies of their own government were amazed at what they found in B.C.: no one was being busted for marijuana or psychedelic drugs. No police descended on the hippie havens in Gastown or on West Fourth in regular harassment raids. This was, after all,

Trudeau's Canada, the Just Society; and the FLQ were at the other end of the country, on the other side of the mountains.

So Lou, for all her radical political ideas, had never been in any confrontation with police before, and she was terrified. Panic-stricken young protesters who had been running down the alley ahead of her had been brought up short by the discovery that it was a dead end and had turned at bay to face the advancing police. Some had begun to throw stones, and Lou, as panicked as any, joined them. Suddenly a cop with a riot stick and a plastic shield was advancing on her. The mild "pot demonstration" had turned into a nightmare from TV news. She could see people running and screaming a few yards away at the mouth of the alley, the dust they stirred up making the scene look unreal; and then suddenly Johnny Good had her by the arm.

He was bleeding from the cut on his cheek where her rock had hit him. He said her name in a hoarse whisper, and suddenly instead of seeing the uniform she was seeing the man. "Johnny!" she whispered, her mouth so dry she could hardly move her lips over her teeth. Behind him the crowd abruptly swelled into the alley, and, seeing their mistake too late, joined the milling, frightened group already there.

Dragging her with him, Johnny pulled her along the lane and in behind a small, protective, brown painted brick wall that shielded the back door of a shop. Smashing the lock with his riot stick, he pushed her into a dark, dusty storeroom, where they stood breathing, panting heavily, listening to the pounding of running feet and the panicked screams of the crowd.

"I gotta get out there," Johnny said after a few moments, as the noise increased. "Wait here for me. Don't go out there, Lou. Wait till I come back for you. Probably be a long time."

When he had gone, she stumbled through the darkened storeroom to the store in front, which turned out to be a plumbing supply shop. Through the dusty windows she could see mayhem. Police on horseback were riding down the protesters, who, running, falling, screaming, had almost nowhere to go to get out of their way. They were boxed into the four tiny streets that led to the square where the "smoke-in" had been taking place. Behind the horses were riot police, shoulder to shoulder, their plastic shields terrifyingly anonymous as they advanced. Every shop doorway was crammed with people trying to get out of their path. Across the way, she could see that a restaurant bar was jammed with people, packed in like a bus in rush hour.

The doorway of the plumbing shop was similarly jammed. The people were all facing her, their arms up to protect their heads if the police attacked.

All this she took in at the first stunned moment of her arrival in the front of the shop. Then she ran down the aisle to the doorway and, turning the lock and sliding a bolt, opened the door.

A dozen people instantly swarmed into the shop, crying, screaming with fear and relief. As the sinister police line moved forward, they were followed by others who joined the silent crowd in the darkened shop with a whispered word of thanks for the door that had opened so opportunely. There they all stood like silent sentinels, appalled by what they saw out the windows. Every now and then someone cursed, but mostly they were quiet and afraid, watching as the police line broke up again and a full-scale street battle ensued.

It seemed hours before Johnny came back for her. The others had already left, going at intervals as the riot calmed down, but Lou waited. He didn't come back until it was all over, and she had been waiting alone for half an hour. She was sitting on the floor against one wall, crying in the reaction to two hours of terror and disillusionment, when she heard the heavy, police-booted footstep in the storeroom.

"Johnny?" she called, at the same moment hearing her own name, and she ran to the open storeroom door. "I'm here."

He had taken off the riot gear and was in simple uniform, and he had a padlock in his hand. Outside, in the shadowed alley, she waited while he used the butt of his gun to pound in the screws his riot stick had half uprooted, and fastened the door with the padlock. The door no longer caught properly and the shopkeeper would know he had been broken into—but the padlock would protect him against casual thieves until then.

"But how's he going to open it?" Lou had asked Johnny quietly. There was still an edge to the air that made the darkness seem dangerous.

"What?" he turned, puzzled.

"It's not his padlock, is it? How's he going to get the key to open it?"

Johnny frowned, as though this element of the thing hadn't struck him. Then he shrugged. "He'll have to break it off," he said. "I'm in enough trouble without admitting to break and enter. Come on."

"Where are we going?" she demanded, in sudden fear that his policeman's code would now force him to arrest her. That was insane, but then, so was everything Lou had seen in the past hours. Nothing in her life, not even the infamous War Measures Act, had constituted such a betrayal of her unconscious convictions of what her country was. She had been through an enormous crisis of trust in that plumbing shop, and she would never be quite the same again.

"I need a drink, but I can't drink in uniform. You want to go for a coffee?"

In the bright lights of the café, she saw the cut on his cheek for the first time. It had bled freely, and there were traces that the blood had been hastily wiped off, then had welled up again and dried in an ugly, oozing bulge of maroon and black that didn't disguise the raw edges of the gash or the purpling bruise across his cheekbone and around his eye.

Lou was horrified. "My God, why didn't you have that looked after?" she demanded. "It needs a bandage, maybe even stitches."

"Yeah, well, I wanted to get back to you. I'll go back to the station in a minute. They've got a doctor down there tonight, and he's got enough to do to keep him there for a while."

"I'm sorry," she whispered. Johnny might have a scar on his cheek for the rest of his life because of her.

"It got pretty ugly out there," was what he said by way of forgiveness.

"Thank you for—" she smiled self-consciously "—rescuing me, Johnny."

It wasn't the last time she would say something like that to him. Johnny seemed to have the knack of being there when she needed him, as the following years had proven. She had good reason to listen to him, and especially to any warning that suggested she might be getting mixed up in a danger bigger than he could handle.

But she had to do it. Because of what Johnny had said, she was going to be very careful. But she was going to find Julie Hastings.

As soon as she had eaten dinner and washed the dishes, Lou spread newspaper over the tabletop, carried the working lamp from her study, screwed its leg to the table edge, and set the first of Winnie's three plastic bags in the circle of its light. She sat down and rolled up her sleeves, resisting the sense of unreality with which this kind of preparation suddenly seemed to imbue everything. She was beginning to feel like a television detective.

The first object out of the bag was a battered black plastic bow that had almost certainly fallen off a cheap shoe. It was covered with something gritty that might have been tea leaves, and after a moment Lou got up, went to the kitchen, washed her hands and slipped on her rubber gloves.

Second out of the bag was a gold colored ballpoint pen with much of its gilt worn off. It looked cheap and worn out, and it occurred to Lou that she was probably going to be less surprised by "what people will throw out" than by what Winnie considered it worthwhile to salvage. She set it to one side with the bow.

There followed a small black-lacquered box and lid from India, very like one she herself used for paper clips. She had been told the box was hand-painted when she bought it from a market stall on Granville Island. She examined the crudely drawn gold birds on a gold branch that adorned the lid. Hand-painted they might be, but mass-produced, nonetheless. Hers had cost her three or four dollars new. Even if she managed to polish it up, Winnie could hardly expect to get more than fifty cents for it.

Lou took a sudden echo-sounding of the future, and shivered. And she was a baby-boomer. When she was old, half the population would be old. There would be even less to go around.

She opened the little trinket box automatically, but she didn't expect to see anything inside, and didn't.

Her hand closed next on a used deck of tarot cards encircled with a thick elastic band, a dried half slice of tomato adhering to the wand over The Fool's shoulder. "The subject of the reading is a dreamer," Lou recited automatically from memory, gazing at the card. "He has the desire to accomplish a great goal." The resonance of it made her laugh. She bent the deck with a thumb and riffled through it, remembering old times as the familiar pictures flipped by. Out of a lingering respect, she carried the cards to the kitchen and carefully scraped off the tomato, wiping the card afterward with a damp sponge. They were well-worn, she noted, setting the cards aside. No one who had used the tarot deck so thoroughly would have disposed of it so cavalierly. Unless they had suddenly "seen the light" and discovered the face of evil in these relics of ancient religious knowledge.

Life must be full of other people's little mysteries, if you only knew where to look.

There followed a cracked teacup with a very pretty painted design, that looked irreparable to Lou's inexperienced eye. A disgustingly dirty hat that made her glad she'd put on gloves. A stained wooden spoon. An empty plastic bankbook, brand new, the kind every bank gave away free. A small framed picture of nothing in particular, in a brass frame that looked reclaimable.

A bridge scoring book, half the pages still intact. A frayed scarf. A green plastic container with a warped white lid. A box of individually plastic-wrapped condoms, half full. Lou held it in her hand and looked at it for several moments. What was the story behind that? A decision to have a baby? A renunciation of sex? A new couple whose AIDS test had come back negative? Or just a variation on the drunk's attempt to put on the plastic wrapping while he tossed the condom?

Next came a gilt filigree-and-rhinestone bracelet with a broken clasp. Winnie had to be pretty handy, if she expected to fix that. Or perhaps she sold such things to girls who were happy to do the fixing themselves.

She was nearing the bottom of the bag now. Next to last was a blouse that, though she did not recall ever seeing it before, reminded Lou of Julie. It was pretty and feminine: a blue cotton-and-polyester blend, V-necked, with a broad collar edged by an inch and a half of white eyelet that also trimmed the three-quarter sleeves. It was finished with tiny blue buttons and delicate tuck-work down the front.

It looked like Julie, and it was the right size, so small it might almost have fit a ten-year-old. It was torn along the seam under the underarm, the top button was missing, and a waist dart had frayed open to show the faintly deeper blue the blouse had originally been. All signs of normal wear. And no proof that it was even Julie's.

After a moment Lou set the blouse aside. Then, her hands shaking, she reached for the object she could see in the bottom of the bag—a tiny cat, no more than an inch high, with hideously cute glass eyes, a red wool bow on the back of its neck, and in its outstretched paws a little red heart on which was etched in white, I Love You.

This she remembered. It had sat on the old white-painted wooden mantelpiece in Julie's apartment, in front of the small inlaid mirror that surmounted it. Lou could clearly see in her mind's eye the hairline ridges of white paint running along the mirror's edges, where a less than careful painter had overswept the target, and, in one corner, a picture of Butch. The little cat had stood guard in front.

"He's gorgeous," Lou had said, staring at the fleshy good looks of the face in the picture for signs of what he was and why.

"Yeah, he's really good-looking," Julie said calmly. "Women always like him."

He didn't look dangerous. Johnny Good looked a hell of a lot meaner, and she couldn't imagine Johnny hitting a woman, let alone raping and killing one. As far as she knew, Johnny had never killed anyone, though he had told her once that he had shot an escaping robbery suspect in the leg and the bullet had destroyed the man's knee.

The cat in her hand, Lou leaned back in her chair and gazed vacantly in front of her. That the cat was special was indicated by the place of honor it had occupied on the mantelpiece. Did that mean some hand other than Julie's had tossed it? What else had been thrown in the trash from Julie's apartment that day, and by whom? The ferrety little man who'd talked to the super? Had the photo of Butch been thrown out, too? If only Winnie had saved that! That would have been worth something, if only she'd known. Lou would have paid almost anything she asked for it.

She cast an eye over the oddments on the table. No telling which, if any, had also come from Julie's place. Slowly Lou picked up each item again, examining it thoroughly without knowing what she was looking for. When she got to the ballpoint pen, she unscrewed it, dumping out the dried-up refill and a little metal spring. Holding up the top portion, she looked through it at the light. Nothing. The thought of Julie leaving a message inside a dead pen made her snort in amusement. She screwed the two halves of the pen back together and was about to toss the refill when it struck her that Winnie might want it. She couldn't imagine any purpose it might be put to, but she opened the pen again and carefully rehoused the refill nevertheless.

Then she carefully put everything except the blouse and the little cat back in the red-and-white Shoppers Drug Mart bag and set it on the floor.

There was no point in going through the other bags, but the distaste for sloppy work that caused reviewers to laud her "painstaking research" in her writing now forced her to examine every item in every bag. In the end, she was left with the same two items. She rolled up the dirty newspaper and trashed it, took off the rubber gloves, washed her hands, and sat down on her sofa with the little cat.

It was firmly glued to a small square of cardboard that was signed Josef Original, JAPAN in the lower right corner. Its large glass eyes were blue with black centers, and it had the sweet look on its face that was endemic to such creatures. It was made of molded plastic that had somehow been covered with a kind of fuzz in a tabby design. It was absolutely ordinary—you could find such things in tourists shops and in train stations by the hundreds. It might not even be Julie's.

But she sat staring at the thing as though it were capable of giving her a message, if only she knew how to read it.

Why had it been thrown out? Because Julie no longer wanted any memento of Butch, or because someone other than Julie had been packing up her apartment? Or even, that in her haste she had left it behind and the building manager had thrown it out while cleaning the apartment?

Why was the blouse there? Assuming it was Julie's, too, had there been a lot of other clothing that Winnie had simply not bothered with? Or had someone else found the clothes before her? Lou went into her study and got a notepad, making a note of the questions she wanted to ask Winnie when she took her loot back to her, not least of which was, could she keep the cat and the blouse for a while?

She sat thinking for a long time, but thinking didn't help much. In fact, she knew no more now than when she had begun: that Julie had moved, for reasons unknown.

The knock on the door broke into her reverie, and she had to suppress a guilty start when she saw Johnny in the doorway grinning down at her. For one wild moment she imagined that he was here because he knew she wasn't keeping her promise, but of course that was only her guilt talking. She wished he'd buzzed from downstairs, but Johnny had ways of bypassing such things.

"You offering coffee, Babe?" he asked wearily. "I'm whacked."

Lou carefully led him past the three plastic bags on the floor without glancing at them, swept up the blue blouse and tossed it into her bedroom as though embarrassed to be caught with the house in a mess, and set the little cat on the windowsill behind the sofa as he sat down.

"Have you just finished work?" she called from the kitchen, as she set the coffee maker to work. "It's so late!" Johnny hated instant coffee, though he often drank it. But never in her house, if she could help it.

She heard him grunt an affirmative—which no one but herself would have understood to be one—as he relaxed on her sofa. There was the clunk of his boots against the coffee table as he put his feet up. "We're really missing Peter," he said.

She came back into the living room to find him sitting, arms outstretched along the back of the sofa, the little cat in his hand. He was gazing absently at it, and Lou's heart slid down into her stomach. He turned it around and examined the cat's back with its little red bow.

"You got a new admirer, Babe?" he asked.

She laughed uneasily. "Not exactly."

"Better tell him from me that cute little cats aren't your style," he said. "I give him a week."

This time she really laughed. "And you know so much about me, of course!"

He looked at her, setting the cat back on the sill. He grinned. "I know what bores you, anyway."

Lou sat down and relaxed. The cat was already out of his mind. "Oh yeah? What bores me?"

"Over the long haul? Anybody but me."

She laughed again, not because it wasn't true. "Well," she shrugged, "I don't bore you, either, so we're even."

"You irritate me all to hell," Johnny agreed, mock pointedly. "But I have to admit—"

"—I never bore you. What a pity you never made a pass, Johnny. So—what's irritating you tonight?"

"What a pity you turned me down when I did. My ego never recovered. What's irritating me tonight isn't you, but your friend Goldring. I checked around, and there doesn't seem to be any way to get around him at the moment. An old buddy of mine just got transferred out of Missing Persons, and another's on holiday. Until he gets back, I can't get the scoop on the setup there. Sorry, Babe."

"Your ego would recover from a steamroller, Johnny. Who are you trying to kid?" she said, not to let him have the last word by burying her in detail, and wondering why the atmosphere seemed a little charged. She and Johnny had engaged in flirtatious banter all their lives. It meant nothing. "So what does this mean? My hands are tied? I have to leave Julie to the wolves?"

"Look," said Johnny, seriously. "I understand your feelings, but there's nothing I can do right now. Can you just leave it till next week? I should be wrapping up a case this week that's been taking a lot of time. If I can't get anybody down there interested, I'll do some looking around myself as soon as it's tied up."

Lou said, "People can go a long way in a week."

"Yeah, I know they can, Babe, but I don't want you messing in this thing. There's something about it I don't like. I'm sorry I couldn't get Goldring interested for you, but I promise you something'll be done one way or the other. Just not immediately."

Lou didn't like lying to him. She said, "I'm going to do a little checking, Johnny. I don't see any reason to wait."

He sighed. He looked exhausted. "How about because I am telling you to? That a good enough reason?"

She jumped up and went to the kitchen, thinking hard as she arranged the coffee tray. He was tired. It made no difference if he knew what she was doing, except that he would worry. She didn't want him worrying about her. And as soon as his work calmed down, she would tell him what she had done. If he still thought it was dangerous, he could take it from there. And, of course, if she did find Butch and he seemed threatening, she could just withdraw until Johnny or the police had time or the inclination to deal with him.

When she returned, she poured the coffee in silence. Johnny seemed almost asleep. "You sure you want this stuff?" she asked. "Wouldn't you rather get some sleep?"

"If I could be sure of waking up," he admitted. "I have to be on the road in another hour."

"What?" demanded Lou. "Aren't you finished for the night?"

He shook his head. "Babe, I told you, I'm up to my ears. You think that was just talk?"

She moved to stand over him. "If you've got an hour, forget the coffee. Put up your feet and get some sleep. I'll wake you."

He shot his cuff. "At exactly ten-thirty, okay? Can you keep the coffee hot till then?"

She eyed him sternly. "I'll make you a fresh cup in an hour, if it's all the same to you."

He slung his feet up, and pulled a cushion under his head. He grinned slowly at her. "Ah, I love you when you're being the proud housewife, Babe. You wanna get married and take care of me forever?"

"We-ell, I'd have to think about that," she said. For about two seconds she furrowed her forehead to indicate deep thought. "No."

"You see? And you complain because I never make a pass."

"You want to sleep, or argue?"

"Snore," he said, closing his eyes. Lou leaned over him to turn out the lamp, feeling suddenly warm and maternal. It wasn't often she had the chance to take care of Johnny. There was an unfamiliar sweetness to it.

Chapter 5

What's your name, please?"

"Lou Patch. I won't take much time. If Mr. Mandala could see me for five minutes I'd be very grateful."

Jerry Mandala was the latest in the crop of brash B.C. millionaires who sprang up from time to time in the odd economic and political climate of the province. He was an entrepreneur. He had apparently started out in used cars, where he made his first small fortune, and had then branched out into real estate where he continued to prove that he had the Midas touch.

Lou had never heard any suspicion that Jerry Mandala was anything except strictly legitimate. He was a kind of favorite son of the avowed free enterprisers in both government and community: look what a little dash and conviction can do, when government doesn't stand in your way and tax you to death. Only thirty-six, Jerry Mandala was already many times a millionaire, through nothing but his own hard work.

Lou almost believed it. The current government in Victoria was certainly not dedicated to putting any picayune difficulties in the way of men like Jerry Mandala, in the name of protecting the environment from the worst excesses of their pillaging, or their tenants from excessive rent increases. She assumed that things stood as the government said they did: a man with unlimited greed had the opportunity for unlimited acquisition in the province.

So she was skeptical of Johnny's assessment of the situation vis à vis Butch. Julie had never given her any indication that Butch was the "small-time hood" Johnny thought him to be, and surely there must be any number of part-time jobs in the burgeoning Mandala empire.

She had, in fact, little hope that Jerry Mandala would be able to help her in any way. Butch might try to impress Julie by saying he sometimes worked for Mandala, but that didn't mean it was true, or even that Jerry Mandala knew every employee in each of his enterprises. Especially by their first name.

Mandala Enterprises had their offices in the Concord Building, Vancouver's newest prestige address. Just off the downtown core, near the waterfront, it was almost within walking distance of the West End, where Lou lived next door to Stanley Park, but Lou had driven. She hadn't phoned first, because she felt unequal to the task of explaining her mission over the phone, but she had told the building's parking attendant that she had an appointment with Jerry Mandala, had shown her press pass, and he had let her park her little car in amongst the limousines and take the elevator straight up without phoning.

Now the receptionist smiled nervously. "Oh yes, Miss Patch. I read your column. Are you going to be writing about us?"

Many people might be disturbed by a visit from a journalist, but Lou wasn't used to such a reaction: she was rarely interested in any crime committed after 1965; she wasn't an investigative reporter at all, and didn't want to be one. She raised an eyebrow. "I doubt it," she said. "Unless Mr. Mandala confesses that it was his grandfather who killed Janet Smith." She smiled. "I'm interested in finding out about a man who may work for Mr. Mandala. His nickname is Butch, and I know his real first name is David—"

She broke off there, because the phone was buzzing on the receptionist's desk, and with an apologetic smile, the woman answered it. Lou watched her idly as she spoke into the phone. She looked the sort of young woman who had been chosen for her looks rather than her skills—a beautiful, very slender girl with deep brown hair who almost certainly was trying to break into modelling.

"They do?" she was saying into the phone. The call had been for her. "Oh, Mary, isn't that wonderful! What are the shooting dates?" She spoke breathlessly, in instant confirmation of Lou's guess. She made a note on the pad in front of her. "Look, I can't talk now, I'll phone you back in a few minutes, okay?"

She hung up, smiling breathily, and turned back to Lou. "I'm awfully sorry about that. I shouldn't be taking personal calls, really, but Mr. Mandala doesn't mind. He understands what it's like. He lets me take off all the time I need, too."

Lou smiled sympathetically. "A job?"

"A commercial! Modeling Leo Chevalier jeans. And there were so many of us up for that part!"

"Part," Lou noted. She privately thought that she wouldn't be an actress for any money in the world, but she tried to keep the pity out of her face. "Congratulations!" she said. "I'll watch out for you."

The girl laughed shyly. "Oh, well—but you aren't interested in me. You were asking about David Stockton, weren't you?" Her face lost a little of its glow. "I think I'd better ask—"

Picking up the phone again, she buzzed someone. "Oh, Margaret, Lou Patch is here. You know, she writes that column . . . well, she was wondering if Mr. Mandala would talk to her about David Stockton. She says she only needs five minutes. . . . Yes, all right."

She hung up the phone. "Mr. Mandala's private secretary will come out to get you, if you wouldn't mind taking a seat?"

She had gotten the name for free, Lou reflected, taking a seat in the sofa grouping a mile or two away from the reception desk. That might be a very big help indeed. For a start, Johnny's friend would have no trouble looking Butch up on the police computer now. It wasn't a "year's supply of favors any more"—just a simple check.

But wasn't it very odd, in a reputedly large and expanding business empire, that the name should be so readily on the receptionist's tongue?

"Miss Patch?"

Lou looked up. Ah, here was the real weight. Jerry Mandala might dress up his reception with attractive staff, but his private secretary had been hired for very different reasons. She wasn't much older than Lou, but she was every inch capable and intelligent.

And wary of Lou. "You wanted to see Mr. Mandala?"

"Yes, I was wondering if he could tell me anything about a man named David Stockton, who I understand works for him. I'm not sure in what capacity."

The private secretary looked at her oddly. "I see," she said, as though Lou were trying to put one over on her. "Yes, well, he will see you, but I must stress that it can only be for a minute or two. You'll appreciate that Mr. Mandala is extremely busy and preoccupied with all this, but he does like to cooperate with the press wherever possible."

Lou blinked at her. She felt as though someone had turned over two pages of a book she was reading, and she had missed a crucial bit of the plot. "Yes," she said. "It's very kind of him."

"This way, please."

She walked beside the woman down a long, wide corridor with large double doors at the end. They walked in silence for a moment, then she decided it might be wiser to probe for a little more information before meeting Jerry Mandala.

"I take it Mr. Stockton is still in Mr. Mandala's employ? He hasn't left recently?" she asked.

The woman's head turned, and her gray eyes were cold with suspicion. "I hope you're not going to try to make a mystery out of this, Miss Patch. Believe me, it is quite enough of a disaster without that. As you must be well aware, David Stockton was in Mr. Mandala's employ right up until he was killed. *If* he was killed. I'll have to ask you not to quote me on that."

There were three men in the corner office as she entered it, none of them behind the massive desk that sat at an oblique angle between two walls of window, in front of a magnificent view of the mountains. There were the kind of clouds brushing around the tips that might mean rain later, but at the moment the sky was a bright, clear blue, and Lou was struck with the Vancouver compulsion that said she should be on the beach right now, in case the sun didn't shine again for two weeks. Getting serious work done in the summer in Vancouver was a hazardous undertaking: every instinct called the city's inhabitants to enjoy the sun while it lasted, and many of them did. "Do that when it rains," was the true Vancouverite's battle cry. The problem was that some summers, and this looked like one of them, it never did rain. The people of Vancouver, as a statistical fact, work fewer hours in the week than the workers of any other Canadian city. But not everybody considers this a bad thing.

Current events weren't Lou's strong point, and she didn't for a moment know which of two men was Jerry Mandala. The third man looked Chinese. But as one of them spoke she half remembered a front page photo of this face with the province's Premier at the unveiling of some public-minded project.

"How do you do, Miss Patch?" he said, as the secretary disappeared behind the closing door.

She was surprised by what she saw. He was a large, blondish, handsome man. He looked like someone who had been a high school football player without ever being the team hero, and as though that fact still rankled with him. He had none of the obvious signs of animal cunning, shrewdness, or even intelligence that the name "Jerry Mandala" conjured up in her mind. She doubted if she would have bought a used car from him, though by all reports she was nearly alone in that judgment. He had all the surface air of self-importance she had expected, without the deep inner conviction of worth that people who made money usually had. It was extraordinary.

"Mr. Mandala?" They shook hands and exchanged courtesies and the obligatory Vancouver weather report, while Lou searched her mental picture file for the other two faces. She didn't find them, and she wasn't introduced. "Now, how can I help you?" said Jerry Mandala.

She wished she knew what she obviously ought to know. "It's about David Stockton," she began.

"Ah, yes, Margaret said you were interested in him. May I ask what your angle is going to be?" He smiled at her with a spurious air of businesslike firmness painted over a sad attempt at little-boy charm. This man a multimillionaire? Well, it just went to show: money-making obviously did not require the more brilliant talents. "Or is that a journalistic secret?"

"Well..." Lou began, uncomfortably aware that the other two men were watching her with close attention. What on earth had she got into here? Why did the name of Julie's "small-time hood" boyfriend make them all so wary?

"Maybe we should invite Miss Patch to sit down," said one of the other two men, who had been silent up to now, and there was another delay while Jerry Mandala led her to an armchair and sat on a sofa opposite her. The other two remained standing by the window. One of them lit a cigarette.

"I understand that David Stockton is dead?" Lou began at last, on a querying note, because she could think of no way of disguising her ignorance of whatever facts these men had in their possession.

Jerry Mandala laughed without mirth. "Well, your guess is as good as anybody's, till the plane is found, isn't it? We certainly are still hoping that he is not."

By the window, one of the men spoke. "Do you know something we don't know, Miss Patch? Has there been a police report in the past few minutes?"

At last that triggered a memory, and suddenly she understood what they were talking about: the plane that had been flying the Solicitor-General of the province up to the Queen Charlottes that had been reported missing last week. She had picked up the news by subliminal means—she had certainly never consciously read or listened to any report.

She said with a gasp of mingled enlightenment and amazement, "Do you mean David Stockton was on that plane? The one that's missing?"

Jerry Mandala asked, "Isn't that why you're here, Miss Patch?"

"No!" she exclaimed. "I'm just looking for a friend—I heard that he sometimes worked for you. David Stockton, I mean."

"Well, the mystery is solved, I'm afraid," said Jerry Mandala. "Though not in any way that will relieve your mind. Your friend was on the plane that is missing. No doubt that's why you haven't heard from him." He moved to stand up.

"No, David Stockton wasn't my friend. Isn't. Wasn't." She gave up. "It's David's girlfriend I'm trying to find. I thought she might have gone away with him, and I was hoping you could tell me..." She paused. "The Solicitor-General was flying to a fishing vacation on somebody's private island. Was that *you*?" What brilliant deductive reasoning, she told herself dryly. Of course it was him! What else do you think he's so worried about?

"You say you think—" Jerry Mandala began.

At the same moment as Lou suddenly exclaimed, "But of course! He *did* come for her! She must have been on the plane, too!" She gazed at Mandala. "Is that possible? That David Stockton's girlfriend was with him on that flight? Oh my God, is Julie *dead*?" They could talk all they wanted about there still being "hope," but Lou knew, as anyone sensible knew, that a plane lost in the mountains or over water for ten days was a plane whose passengers were dead.

Jerry Mandala glanced toward the two men by the window. "Ah—" There was an odd moment of silence, as though no one could think of what to say. "Ah, yes, Gordon Harrison was on his way to my fishing camp. I—uh, doubt very much whether David would have brought a personal friend along. No, no, I'm sure there was no one on that flight except David and Gordon. No, no. Don't upset yourself, Miss Patch."

One of the men by the window cleared his throat. "I don't like to be the one to say it, but if your friend is missing—I suppose it is possible he wanted to give his girlfriend a thrill by taking her along for the ride, Jerry."

There was an odd tone in his voice, almost of warning, and another little silence followed, that she did not understand.

Lou said desperately, "Wasn't there any kind of flight manifest? Doesn't the pilot have to report all his passengers for any flight over the interior or something? Her name, I know her name," she added stupidly.

"There was no other name on the manifest, Miss Patch. No woman's name at all. What I'm suggesting is that David might have deliberately avoided filing it, if he didn't want Jerry to know he was smuggling his girlfriend aboard."

At last it sank into Lou's brain what she was being told. She said, "Are you telling me that Butch—that David Stockton was *piloting* the aircraft?"

All three men nodded in unison. "But that's impossible," she protested. "He wasn't a pilot!"

She was unprepared for the instantaneous, shocking reaction of all three men to her words. They were motionless, their eyes going cold in a watchful stillness, alert to any breath she might take.

"What exactly do you mean?" The Chinese man spoke for the first time. He had a heavy accent.

"The David I'm looking for—I don't actually know him—but I'm nearly sure he couldn't have been a *pilot*. I think I'd have known if he were. Was his nickname Butch?" She remembered suddenly that she had gotten the last name from Jerry Mandala's own receptionist. What a fool she was. Of course, hearing the name "David" in such circumstances, the receptionist's mind had automatically leaped to this disaster. Lou only wanted to get out of the room—and yet, if there were any faintest chance...

"I'm afraid I don't know," said Jerry Mandala briefly.

"I'm awfully sorry, but I really would like to— Had he been working for you long?"

"Ah, yes, for a—for about six months. He was my standby pilot, though this was the first time he'd ever had to fly for me."

Maybe it was possible. How much did she really know about Butch, after all? Maybe Julie just hadn't bothered to say what it was Butch was doing "sometimes" for Jerry

Mandala, or maybe she herself hadn't known. If Julie had been on that missing airplane, Lou wanted to know.

"Do you happen to know what David Stockton was doing between approximately 1972 and 1974?" she asked, and suddenly remembered a time when her mother had said, "Don't poke sticks through the bars, Louise! You'll get bitten, and serve you right!"

"Why do you ask?"

She said, "I was wondering if he might have been in Oakalla Prison on an assault conviction."

She seemed to have found the knack for stunning the men as many times as she opened her mouth.

"What?" exclaimed Jerry Mandala harshly. "Absolutely not. What are you suggesting? That I would let a convicted criminal pilot the Solicitor-General around the province? Where do you get your information from, Miss Patch? Let me advise you strongly against publishing any such speculation. For your information, though I really see no reason to tell you, according to his personal record, David Stockton was in Vietnam for two years during that period."

An air of real hostility, of danger, was now tangible in the room. It shocked her. "It must be a different man," she said stupidly. "I do know that Julie's—that the boyfriend of the friend I told you about was in prison at that particular time."

"And his name was David Stockton?"

She thought of the fate in store for the receptionist if she told the truth. "I believe so," she said awkwardly.

"And you thought he was working for me?"

"That's what Julie said once. Perhaps I misunderstood? I may have gotten the name wrong. Or I suppose there aren't two David Stocktons on your payroll?"

She was confused by the atmosphere. They were so hostile, so wary. Was it possible that it *was* the same man, and they were desperately trying to cover up a possible scandal? And what a scandal it would be!

"It's most unlikely. But I'll have someone check out the possibility."

"It's so odd," said Lou. Logically, she had to accept that she had blundered. She should never have pretended that she knew Butch's last name. And yet the coincidence was so strong. . . .

"And the plane went down in the mountains?"

"As you will be aware if you listen to the news, Miss Patch, no one is very sure of anything with regard to this plane. We have no knowledge of where it went down. It's quite possible it got completely off course and for some reason flew out to sea, or back across the mountains, before going down. At this point I'm more concerned with the fate of the two men I know were on the plane than to start speculating on whether there was someone else on it. And frankly, I don't think the police will be any more interested in this girl confusing matters right now than I am. They have enough on their plate with a full-scale air-sea search that is still going on."

It was a pretty long speech. Lou almost congratulated him. No doubt you had to be able to talk fluently to make a success of used car sales and real estate. Or maybe his friendship with politicians was causing something to rub off. It made her mad. She certainly wasn't stupid enough to go to the police with what amounted to groundless suspicion, and it irked her to be spoken down to.

Lou stood up. "That's two warnings I've been given already," she said, not bothering to hide her irritation. "Or should I say, two pieces of friendly advice?"

One of the men by the window cleared his throat. "Don't get us wrong, Miss Patch. It's not that we aren't concerned about your friend," he said. "We just have some other very important worries on our minds, as I'm sure you understand."

"Yes, I do," she said. "To me, of course, Julie is just as important as the Solicitor-General. They are, after all, both human beings."

"And she is your friend. If we hear anything that suggests there was anyone else aboard this aircraft, we'll let you know."

She allowed it to pacify her. Her instinct was telling her to get out.

"Thank you," she said.

Jerry Mandala said suddenly, "Did you say you've never met your friend's boyfriend?"

"No, never," she said. She turned to the door, and then back again, struck by a sudden thought. "Do you have a picture of your pilot?"

"Why, Miss Patch? How can that help you?"

"I've seen a picture of Butch—of David. I thought..." Her voice trailed off questioningly.

"I'm sorry, we have no picture of the pilot. Naturally the police asked us that, to help in their investigations. But for some reason his picture was never taken for the employment file. Somebody in Personnel apparently overlooked it."

"Thank you," she said.

"I wonder if we could have your card, Miss Patch? In order to be able to get in touch with you should we have any news?" That was the Chinese man by the window.

It was impossible to refuse, and she had no logical reason for the feeling that she should. Lou pulled out her card case and placed one of her cards in Jerry Mandala's hand. He was still looking at it thoughtfully as she said her goodbyes and left.

Something nagged her all the way home until she worked out what it was: the picture. For some reason she wished she'd never said she'd seen Butch's photograph.

Chapter 6

Johnny, I think I know Butch's last name after all," Lou said tentatively. "Do you think your—"

"*Damn* it! Damn it, Babe, I told you to leave this thing alone!" Lou's phone was a cheap one, and his shout jammed the crystals and nearly fried her ear.

"Ouch," she said mildly.

"Ouch, hell! What are you trying to do? I told you I'm too busy! If you start getting into a mess—"

"I'm not getting into anything, Johnny, will you calm down? I just think I remember something Julie said, and I wondered if your friend might make that search on less than a year's supply of favors if you had the whole name."

He wasn't taken in for a moment. "No blood on the carpet, eh?" said Johnny, dryly angry.

Lou's determination to tell him nothing collapsed. "Look," she said, "something very weird has happened. I hate to ask, but is there any way you could give me ten minutes?"

"I knew it," Johnny muttered to himself. He breathed in, and she heard the rasp of his palm against his rough cheek.

"You haven't shaved for two days, by the sound of that beard," she said. "Don't you think that's a little too *Miami Vice*?"

"Three days," he said absently. "My shaver broke and I haven't had time to get it fixed. All right, Babe, I'll pick you up in one hour from now. Don't drink any tea or coffee, we won't be near any gas stations. Oh, and bring a jacket."

His battered truck pulled up in front of the apartment building fifty-five minutes later, and Lou, waiting in the lighted lobby, waved and ran out to the curb.

Night had settled softly on Vancouver, cool but not chilly. She could hear the ducks squawking and the other familiar cries of night from the park. There was a strong ocean breeze; altogether a night for a stroll along the sea wall, or a drive through the park.

"Hi," she called softly, climbing into the truck and turning to lift her tote bag onto the back seat. Johnny violated all the tenets of good detection by driving a big Ford Bronco that Lou personally could have identified half a mile off, and he never bothered to clean it out. Lou shook her head as she found a spot for the tote bag amongst the old newspapers and paper cups and loose tools. "What happened?" she asked. "They wouldn't let you land at New York? You have to drive around forever with this stuff?"

Johnny ignored that, eyeing the tote bag with exaggerated interest. "What's that?"

"Midnight snacks," Lou said. "We are on a stakeout, right? We may never see Nick's again?"

"Damn, I'm starving," Johnny said fervently. "What've you got in there?"

She dragged the tote bag back into her lap and rooted in it as he pulled away from the curb and down into the darkness of the trees at the edge of the park. "Your favorite," she said, holding it out. "Mushroom and bacon. Still warm."

Johnny carefully opened the little bag and sank his strong white teeth into the toasted sandwich. "Mmm," he grunted in satisfaction. "Ah, Babe, I should take you with me on every job. Terrific."

"Coffee?"

"Terrific," he said again.

He was driving down to the main road that ran through Stanley Park to the bridge. "North Van?" Lou asked. "West Van?"

"Out near Horseshoe. Father's got the kids for the week. Mother thinks he may be planning to run with them. The scoop is, he's a ferry boat captain and she thinks he might try to take them over the U.S. border by sea."

"And what will we do if he does? Stop him?"

"Well, we've really got no authority to do that, so I have to be careful." There was little traffic so late at night; they drove quickly through the darkness of the Douglas firs toward the bridge. Johnny was an obvious expert at maneuvering the wheel with one hand while he alternated the sandwich and coffee with his right. Lou held the coffee for him between sips. "There are a few options. One, we try to stop him. Two, we alert the U.S. immigration at the border and hope they'll turn him back on grounds of suspected kidnapping. Three, we follow him all the way to his destination and then get in quick and grab the kids back again."

A little burst of startled laughter escaped Lou. "Really? Have you ever done that?"

Johnny glanced over, caught off guard by her surprise. "Oh yeah. It's the only way that doesn't take months. Or years. Grab 'em back quick before he runs them down to Greece or Saudi Arabia and really makes it impossible."

"But isn't that breaking the law? You told me once you don't take on anything illegal."

"It's a gray area. If the mother has custody, she has the right to ask her appointed agent to take the kids wherever she wants, right? Anyway, what kind of charges can the father bring without admitting to kidnapping himself? The big problem is not to lose him. It's a helluva lot harder to find them than to grab them."

As they hit the bridge and left the trees behind, she saw the moon for the first time: full, heavy and golden, low above the blackness of ocean on their left.

"Isn't that breathtaking!" exclaimed Lou, who never took Vancouver's natural beauty for granted.

Johnny finished the last bite of his mushroom and bacon sandwich, scrunched up the bag and tossed it over his shoulder into the back, where it fell immediately among friends. He reached for the coffee Lou held. "Yeah, beautiful. You can appreciate a full moon when you're not on the police force. Thank God it's not my job anymore to think about all the nutcases at full moon."

"You're thinking about them right now," Lou pointed out.

Johnny raised his eyebrows and nodded. "Yeah," he said. "Yeah, I guess so. Well, it's a beautiful moon."

"You have to be there any particular time?" she asked.

"Eleven. This would have been Peter Tang's gig. We're going crazy putting all his time in between us. Don't let me fall asleep, okay, Babe?"

He finished the coffee and handed her the cup. "High Road or Low Road?" he asked. "I've got time."

She had been going to ask for the low road, which was their own name for the road through the residential district of West Vancouver. But down amongst the tree-filled streets they would see little of the ocean or the low-hanging moon. "High Road," she said. "I want to get as much of that moon as I can."

It was a pleasant run; they had made it many times together over the years. Lou loved being in a car at night, for the feeling of softened voices and being in her own little world.

"I didn't realize your life was so cops and robbers, Johnny," she said once. "What else do you do besides kidnapping?"

"Not a lot that's exciting, Babe, and no, you can't write an article about me." He pulled off the road and jumped out into the night. The interior lights didn't come on when he opened the door, and in the darkness he groped behind the driver's seat for a minute before pulling out a large flat oblong board. He closed the door and she heard a bang as he slapped something against the side of the door. As he walked around the truck toward her, Lou caught sight of what he was carrying: a sign. She rolled down her window and called out as he came up to her, "What on earth is that?" He held up the sign in the moonlight. "Johnny's Towing And Repair," she read, and then he slapped it against the metal of the door and stood back.

"Good enough," he said to himself.

When he was inside again, and they were back on the road, she said, "Is that effective camouflage?"

"Ah, a truck is invisible anyway. Cops never drive 'em, and nobody except a gangster worries much about anybody but cops. But it never hurts to have an excuse for being somewhere when you don't really know the neighborhood. We're looking for a ditched car somebody called us out on. If anybody asks."

Shortly afterward he drove down off the highway and into Horseshoe Bay. After a few minutes of slow driving through the streets, he killed the lights and then the engine, and glided to a stop beside the row of cars parked along the street. As he rolled down his window, a car door ahead of them silently opened and silently closed, and a face appeared by Johnny.

"It's like a tomb," said Mark Crowder, in a low voice. She recognized him as a man who had been working for

Johnny for several years, and whom he considered not one of his best agents. "You sure won't miss it if anything does happen around here."

"Everybody inside?"

"Yeah. Some guy turned up a couple of hours ago and hasn't left yet. I didn't get much of a look at him, except from the back. Didn't see him till he was going up the walk. Tallish, balding, late thirties, maybe."

They talked for only a minute, and then Crowder pulled out and Johnny maneuvered the truck into the space Crowder had left.

It was companionable, sitting together in the darkness. Lou slipped off her shoes and curled her legs up onto the broad seat, her head falling back against the headrest. Johnny shifted the steering wheel and wedged his back into the angle between the seat and the door, where he was at a direct angle to watch the house on Lou's right.

"Okay, so tell me what you've been doing."

"I just realized something—are we here for the *night*?" Lou demanded suddenly, the pieces having finally fallen together in her head.

"Yup," said Johnny.

"I don't believe this! I have to sit in this truck till dawn?"

"Hell, no. Sun comes up at five-thirty. We'll be here till eight. At least." Johnny was grinning, as though at a private joke.

"Johnny!" she protested. "You might at least have told me!"

"Yeah, see, Babe, but you didn't ask. And when you do ask, you don't listen to what I say, do you?" His arm was resting along the top of the steering wheel, and the strength of his hand was outlined by moonlight and shadow as he gestured. He bent a knee and lifted a booted foot onto the seat between them, resting his right arm on his knee. "See, this gives me a chance to hear exactly what the hell you've been doing and how much trouble you've already gotten yourself into, and with a little luck it also serves as a powerful deterrent to ever disobeying me again when I tell you something. See?''

Lou began to laugh. "You creep! That's nothing but an excuse! You just wanted some company for the night!"

Johnny lifted his hands and grinned. "Yeah, it's been a long time since I did the surveillance work myself. It helps to have company, 'cause then you can go into the bushes when you have to, without worrying about losing your quarry while you're at it. Otherwise you have to use a bottle, and it is a fact of nature that whatever bottle you bring is never going to have enough capacity. One of the lesser known laws of perversity. And on the other hand, you needed to be taught a lesson. Now, tell me what you've been doing."

She thought his position looked more comfortable than her own, and she shifted her back against the door till she mirrored Johnny, tucking her cast-off jacket, which she didn't yet need, behind her head. "Well," she began, "there's not really much to tell, except for one very interesting coincidence yesterday that I don't know what to do about."

"No such thing as coincidence," muttered Johnny. "What?"

The atmosphere in the truck suddenly seemed very pleasant, nostalgic almost, as though the years might have disappeared under cover of darkness, and they were two adventurous teenagers with most of their lives still ahead of them, and so much will to live it.

She told him about her interview with Jerry Mandala, and the receptionist's slip of the tongue, in a quiet, night-in-a-parked-car voice. There had been a time when they discussed "issues" in just such voices, such places—nighttime overlooking the ocean or the strait, with lights flickering on the ships out in the water, their steady gleam broken up by distance and the air currents. Lou felt a sudden stab of passionate regret for those lost days, for the time when she knew she would be young forever, would do something important in the world. She had the sudden powerful feeling that she had let something go, had given up what must never be given up. Somehow she had wandered from the mark, without ever really knowing what the mark was.

When she stopped speaking, Johnny sat in silence for a while, as though sharing the feeling. "Well," he said at last, "there's really no reason to imagine that David Stockton the pilot is the same man as your Butch, is there?"

"No, except that—you remember Nellie?"

"Of course I remember Nellie. What's she got to do with this?"

Lou rubbed the tip of her nose reflectively. "I'm beginning to think my nose—his name is Herbert, by the way—has undiscovered talents, too. I think, in retrospect, it was the way those men reacted—there was something there, something they knew and I didn't, and they kept wondering if I knew or not."

"Hmm," grunted Johnny, as he processed this information.

"And—I don't want to seem alarmist, but—I was sorry I mentioned I'd seen Butch's picture almost the second the words were out of my mouth. You think I'm being too imaginative?"

"Noooo," said Johnny thoughtfully. He yawned. "Damn, I wish you'd left this till I had a little time. Tell me again what happened in Mandala's office. From the beginning. This time I'll stop you."

"I stepped off the elevator. The receptionist's desk is right there. I said, I want to ask about a man who's nickname is Butch. His real first name is David. The phone rang. It was her agent."

"Stop there. You told her the guy's nickname was Butch? Are you sure of that?"

Lou nodded. "Absolutely."

"So you said Butch *and* David, and she came up with the dead pilot."

Lou thought a moment. "That's right."

"I don't like the smell of this," said Johnny, absently tapping his fist against his upraised knee. "Babe, I wish you'd leave it alone. This is a cabinet minister we're talking about here. And whether it does or doesn't have any connection with your missing friend, but for sure if it does, it's not something you should mess with."

"Why—do you think there's something about it Mandala isn't telling the Mounties?"

"Maybe, maybe not. But you've as good as told the guy that his pilot is known—by you—to have a criminal record. Whether that's true or not, he's got a good reason to hope you don't publish your suspicions, right?"

"I suppose so."

"More than suppose. And people with as much clout as Jerry Mandala aren't usually satisfied with just hoping about things. They can take steps to get what they want, and they mostly d—Kee-rist!"

With no warning, and unbelievable speed, the hand that rested on his knee snapped out and grabbed Lou's wrist, while he leaned forward and with the other hand grasped her waist to drag her across the seat and into his arms. He buried his face in her neck while Lou lay stunned, her body pressed against his, his leg along the length of hers.

"Put your arm around my neck," he ordered. "Quick! I know that sucker!"

Gasping with shock and surprise, she obediently raised her arm to shield his face from view. After a moment in which she listened to her pounding heart, she whispered, "Who is it?" Her face was pressed against his, her lips brushing his cheek as she spoke.

She could hear the sound of footsteps on the pavement now. Johnny's arms tightened around her, and he slid down a little farther. His eyes followed whoever it was as the man neared the truck. "Harry Thornton," he muttered, mostly to himself. "Where the hell did he come from, and what's he doing here?"

By now his eyes were at the level of the seat back, and he watched the passing man through the gap left by the raised headrest. Lou could see nothing, but she heard the sound of a car door slam. "Third car behind us!" said Johnny. "I'll have Crowder's butt!"

"Who's Harry Thornton?" There was the sound of the car engine starting up, and then there were lights pouring through the window onto them.

"Free-lance," he said. He slid down to a fully supine position on the seat as the other car pulled out and its lights flashed past them. "I've used him once or twice. He wasn't available this week, he said he was on a job. I sure hope he doesn't have those kids in the trunk! Hey!" he finished with a grin, "to hell with him, Babe! You think we been missing something all these years?"

She was lying on top of him, cradled in his hips, his arms still wrapped around her. His face lay in the moonlight that poured through the window above their heads; her hair blowing in the breeze caused a rippling moonshadow across it. She could smell ocean, trees, her own perfume and Johnny. Her heart still hadn't slowed its crazy thudding. She thought distantly that she'd be happy if neither of them moved again for the rest of time.

She laughed then, to dispel her mood; and Johnny laughed, and then, as she moved to draw out of his hold, he jackknifed up, half lifting her back to her own seat, and swung his legs under the wheel. He leaned over her to snap the glove compartment open, pulling out his portable phone.

As he dialed, Lou busied herself with dragging her jacket out of the space down beside the seat, where it had entangled itself with the seatback mechanism. She pulled it on, trying to still the nervous reaction that now had her visibly shaking.

Johnny would think it was the surprise, she hoped, or the cold; but she wasn't worried as much about Johnny's reactions as her own. It was the knowledge she now had about herself, and wished she didn't have, that consumed her: the knowledge that for the space of one atom's leap in time, her stupid brain had imagined that Johnny was reaching for her out of need.

And that was all it had taken to release the demon. Because what was making Lou tremble wasn't shock, or the cold: it was the aftermath of desire. As powerful and sweeping a rush of physical need as any she had felt in her life.

Chapter 7

"Can I get out?" Lou asked softly, just as Johnny spoke into the phone.

"Celia? Johnny here." He looked up as he spoke and nodded. "Don't slam the door," he murmured.

Lou slipped gratefully out into the cool air and shrugged into her jacket. There was a fresh ocean breeze blowing and she breathed it in, her eyes closed, head back, trying to sort out confused feelings and calm them down.

She leaned against the truck, the quiet drone of Johnny's voice vibrating through the metal into her flesh. After a moment his voice stopped; then she heard the phone buzz, and it started again. He laughed softly.

Well, **this** was a new one on her. As far as she knew there weren't many precedents for falling in love with your best friend eighteen years on. *Women Who Love Too Much* was one thing, but as far as she knew *Women Who Love Too Late* was still unwritten. Lou laughed to herself, shaking her head, but actually she felt a kind of sinking despair. She couldn't see any way out of this one. What on earth would she do?

The drone of Johnny's voice stopped, and she heard his door open quietly. A moment later he was standing beside her, putting a small cigar between his lips. "Truck lighter's broken," he said softly. "Can you shield the flame so they won't see it from the house?"

She wordlessly turned her back to the house and held her jacket open, and Johnny bent his head down into the lee she created in the wind and flicked his lighter into flame. His head was at the level of her breasts and she felt a painful mix of many feelings: the urge to cradle and protect him against her breasts; a wild compulsion to pull him against her and fall backwards on the grass; a need to cry; but perhaps strongest of all, a wish that he would crack a joke and snap her out of this awkward, ridiculous, impossible mood.

He stood up, puffing on the cigar and absently pocketing the lighter. "Nice night," he said softly. He sank down till he was sitting on the chrome footboard, and after a moment Lou followed suit. Their shoulders touched, and it seemed a moment of perfect companionship.

"Did you find out anything about Harry Thornton?" she asked in a low murmur.

He laughed briefly, soundlessly. "That was Harry phoning from his car," he said, nodding backward toward the truck. "He recognized the truck and called to give me the horselaugh. Turns out he's the kids' uncle. He told his sister to call me for this job, because he didn't want to get involved professionally. He's been in there trying to talk some sense into his ex-brother-in-law."

Lou laughed softly. "If I've told you once, I've told you a dozen times, this truck is too obvious for a private detective."

"Yeah, Babe, but I hardly ever do the surveillance work these days. I leave that to the drones."

"I guess it's just as well." She was joking as usual, a small fraction of her mind managing to carry on normally, in spite of her confusion.

Johnny looked over at her in the moonlight, and opened his mouth to say something. Lou froze, waiting for it, but he abruptly dropped his cigar to the pavement, ground it out with his shoe, and got to his feet. "We better get back inside," he said. "One of these good citizens will be calling the cops soon, if we're not careful."

She was both relieved and disappointed. Part of her wanted Johnny to have made the same discovery she had. But another part was almost frantic in wanting nothing in this friendship to change, in wanting Johnny to be always what he was right now—the best friend she'd ever had.

One of the things that came out of their conversation during the long, bittersweet night that followed her moment of truth was Johnny's suggestion that Julie might have gone to one of Vancouver's homes for battered women, and that was what Lou busied herself with during the next few days.

It wasn't easy. The whole point of battered women's shelters was that they needed to be secure, and that the women there needed the safety of anonymity. But whereas Johnny or any other man would have found the going very tough, she found he had overestimated the difficulties she would encounter. Johnny had advised her to tell people she was researching a magazine article, but something in Lou rejected the dishonesty of that, and again, she found that the truth, in the end, surmounted the obstacles.

If Julie had sought the refuge of such a home, it was almost certainly not one in Vancouver. Lou fell back on the less likely avenues, and sat down one afternoon to phone the license bureau, the electric company, and B.C. Tel.

As she expected, Julie Hastings had had an unlisted phone. Her name appeared nowhere in publicly available records. Butch would have to have a friend on the inside to get even the minimal information that Julie had a phone.

Lou wondered if he did. The speed with which he had turned up at the apartment argued some kind of connections not available to the average citizen.

Lou, however, didn't have that problem. She already had Julie's number. Calling the business office and asking to speak to the service rep for that number was a shortcut into the system.

Even the B.C. Tel service rep was not immune to her description of Julie's situation. Lou had been used to considering the telephone company authoritarian and monolithic for so long that she almost blew it with an assumption that she would get nothing out of them.

She was wrong, or else she was just tremendously lucky with this one employee out of thousands, who didn't even mention to Lou that she was breaking regulations in giving out confidential information, and gave her, in the end, everything the file had to yield.

Julie had given two names as references—both women. The service rep gave Lou the names and phone numbers, and mentioned that both women were listed as "friends," which must mean Julie had no family in or near Vancouver.

The final bill had been paid at the B.C. Tel office on Davie Street, on Thursday, July 18. It had been paid in cash.

"Hi," said Lou, who was finding this easier to do with every phone call. "Is that Rosa Carbonari?"

"Yes."

"My name's Lou Patch. This might sound a little odd to you, but I'm a friend of Julie Hastings, and I wonder if you've seen her lately?"

"Not for a month or so. Why?"

"Well, she's sort of disappeared. I'm worried because—well—did you know Julie's boyfriend Butch?"

"Where did you get my number?"

"Julie put you down as a reference for her new phone."

"Look, I didn't know Julie very well. She worked with me for a while in the restaurant, and then I never saw her again. But I remember that guy she was going around with."

The tone of voice said she hadn't thought much of him, and Lou said, "Well, Julie ran away from him and came down to the West End and got a job here. And now she's disappeared. I'm afraid Butch just came and got her. Is there anything you can tell me about him?"

"Nothing except that he was a pretty frightening man. Yeah, it wouldn't surprise me—he was really jealous. He scared me, I didn't know why she let him near her."

"Oh, God," said Lou, who found this confirmation of her mental image of Butch depressing.

"What makes you think he came and got her?"

"She thought she saw him in a car in front of her house one day. Two days later she was gone. I'm trying to find them and help her if I can. Rosa, is there anything you can tell me—anything at all that might help me guess where to look for her?"

"Honestly, I hardly knew her. And he was so jealous of everybody, you know, she never stuck around after work for a cigarette or anything—she went straight home. Oh! I just remembered—somebody came in, some guy, a few days after she left, and said he was from the income tax office and he had this rebate check for her and this was the only address he had for her. He wanted to know if I knew where he should send it. I thought it was a bit weird at the time."

"But you didn't tell him anything?"

"I didn't know anything. I'm glad now I didn't. Well, except that I wish I could help you. I really hope you find her. Butch was a big guy. And he was mean. You know what I mean?"

"Yeah, I know what you mean," said Lou, feeling both depressed and encouraged by the fact that someone else thought she was doing the right thing in trying to find Julie. "I know what you mean."

The conversation contributed to her determination to find Julie, but, like all the others, told Lou nearly nothing new. She was beginning to think that being a detective might be one of the world's more tedious occupations.

"Hi, this is Lou. Sorry I've missed your call. I'll be at the Pacific Café for lunch and then under the tree down at Bikini Beach. So if you want to join me, I'll see you there."

Lou didn't belong to the "We're either not in, or not answering" school of answering machine thought. She had friends in Toronto who would have died rather than let anyone know for certain that their apartment was empty at any given moment, but this was Vancouver, her apartment building was a secure one, and besides, much of her daily social life was carried on between the Pacific Café and the beach during the long summers. She liked her friends to know where they could find her. Many of them, of course, would already be on the beach. Lou had a large number of "summer friends" who mostly met there.

This was shaping up to be one of those long, hot summers that meant most Vancouverites got little work done. Lou, of course, had the sort of work that she could often do at the beach, and she took advantage of this good fortune, leaving the research for mornings and rainy days, and spending sunny afternoons scribbling on the beach.

Her machine was getting fractious, and would no longer record a new outgoing message. She had a note on the door reminding her to, "take ans. machine in for repair," but it would be ages before she got around to it. Meanwhile, last Tuesday's message would have to serve, though she wasn't stopping off at the Pacific Café this afternoon.

She tossed her beach dress on over an emerald-green bikini, swung her beach bag over her shoulder, put her sunglasses on her head, and let herself out.

Downstairs she saw a card in her mailbox and pulled it out just as two other tenants came in the front door. In the rush of saying hello, stuffing the card into her pocket and grabbing the open door, she forgot all about it until she was halfway down the path that skirted the park en route to the beach. She pulled it out and wrinkled her forehead over the picture of sunset and the black outline of a sampan.

Hong Kong. Who on earth did she know in Hong Kong?

In the middle of the beach path, shaded on one side by trees and on the other by perhaps the tallest and ugliest high rise in the West End, Lou stopped dead as she read the card.

"Sorry I didn't say goodbye. I got the offer of a job here. It's really strange, but an interesting place.

Yours truly, Julie"

Relief rushed through her in a torrent. "Oh, thank God!" Lou cried aloud. Not dead, after all, or in a shattered plane somewhere in the mountains dying from hunger and thirst!—a possibility that had been worrying at Lou's peace of mind more than she knew. "Thank God!" A man was passing with what had to be the tiniest dog, in this city of small dogs, on a leash.

"Good news?" he asked in friendly interest. The West End had more than its share of nuts, but most were harmless. A woman saying "Thank God, thank God!" to herself was unlikely to be a danger. Besides, he'd seen Lou around, and most residents of the West End pride themselves on the small-town atmosphere they create in the tiny space that is one of the most densely populated areas in the world.

"You bet!" Lou told him, smiling, and bending to pat the little dog. "Thank you, the best."

Her friends Dorothy and Tom were on the beach, as well as several others, and she breathed a sigh of relief as they called their hellos. There was nobody she'd rather have seen right now, and she settled her blanket beside their beach beds and mentally scuttled the afternoon's tentative work plan in favor of a friendly afternoon and lazy chat.

"What about your little friend? Have you heard any news?" Dorothy asked, as Lou was getting settled.

"I just this minute got a postcard from her! Would you believe she's in Hong Kong?" Lou stood up to get her dress from where it lay on a rock and pulled the card out of the pocket.

"Well, that doesn't sound as if she's in any trouble, does it?" said Dorothy, reading it. "Tom, did you hear that? Did you hear that, everybody? That little Julie's in Hong Kong! Lou's got a postcard."

"Mmm," said Tom, from the depths of the racing form, while two or three of the others ambled up.

"Read this." Dorothy handed it up to him and he read it carefully, then surrendered it as someone reached for it over his shoulder.

"Who's Julie?" he said, with the glint in his eye that meant he felt the moment right for a little leg-pulling. Behind him, the others were chatting happily.

"Now, Tom. She's that nice little girl Lou's been bringing down here, the one that went missing. Don't you think that sounds as if she's all right?"

"Uh huh." Someone handed the card back to Lou with a brief word. "Pretty quick work. I didn't know she spoke Chinese."

"Now, Tom, she doesn't have to speak Chinese! We don't, and we've always talked about going to Hong Kong!"

"Yup, but we weren't going to work there. Girl says she's got a job. What kind of job?"

"Oh well, anything, I guess," Dorothy said, but even though she knew he was joking, Lou gazed at the postcard with a frown.

"No, he's right, Dorothy. She's a waitress. Who would bother to offer a waitress a job in Hong Kong?"

"She's a very attractive girl," Dorothy said practically. "If somebody offered me something like that, I'd have taken it, when I was her age. Why not, with a chance to travel to the East?" The great thing about Dorothy was that that was no more than the truth. She had been devil-may-care in her youth, from all Lou could gather, and she still was.

"Why not?" agreed another woman.

"I suppose so," said Lou doubtfully. "You know, I've never seen much of her handwriting. I wonder if she really wrote this."

"Now, there you go, Tom, you see what you've done? Now she's going to start to worry all over again. Of course she wrote it, Lou. If she didn't, who did?"

Lou nodded slowly. "Yeah," she said. "That's what I'm wondering. If not Julie, who, and why?"

Chapter 8

Lou spent a fair bit of time over these few days thinking about that extraordinary moment in the truck. At the time, it had seemed a moment when her eyes had been opened to something that had been lying dormant within her for a long time. She had felt a burst of understanding, a kind of "so *that's* what it is!" that had shocked her through and through.

That such a possibility might be the truth now dismayed her. She played the scene over and over in her head, each time with a greater determination to find her reaction a simple, silly aberration, only a temporary madness, with no real foundation.

"All women like to think that all men want them," she said out loud to herself. It was a habit she hoped wouldn't increase with age, or ever happen in public, but one that often helped her clear her thoughts. "Johnny's never shown the least sign of wanting me before, so of course it excited my feminine ego when I thought he was finally caving in."

It was not quite true that Johnny had never before shown any sign of wanting her. When they were younger, she knew, he had hoped for a while to get serious with her. It hadn't happened, however, and he had never seemed to regret it. There had been another moment, too—years ago—that she couldn't help remembering again. It had often haunted her in the past, because it was the only time in his life that Johnny had asked her for something, and she had failed him.

Except for two long suspensions in their friendship, once when Johnny simply disappeared from the neighborhood without warning during the summer after grade seven, and once during Lou's unfortunate attempt at marriage, Johnny had been perhaps her best friend throughout her life.

That summer of the Gastown Riot they had both been surprised by how glad they were to meet up again after five years. They had walked down the alley in the silence of deep mutual understanding, Lou wiping the tears that wouldn't stop. In the little café, her eyes had finally dried, and she could talk.

"Johnny, where have you been? Where did you go?"

"We moved," he answered shortly. "I live over in the East End now."

"Oh." The East End was a poor district. Lou had spent all her life up to that moment in Kitsilano, a most comfortable middle-class neighborhood in Vancouver, and she couldn't understand why Johnny's family would move out of it. "And now you're a policeman." That was a mystery, too, but not one she wanted to delve into very deeply. She supposed he had not gotten the marks to go on to university, as she would do in the autumn. Johnny had failed grade five—up until then he had been a year ahead of her in school, but after that he had been in her class for three years. He had done well in his marks during those three years, but that was only to be expected, really, when he was a year older than everyone else. "Did you finish grade twelve?"

"In June," he said.

"So did I." And Lou had gone on to talk about her plans for university and a future as bright and straightforward as her past had been.

Johnny was a great listener. Unlike most of the boys she knew, who tended to lecture her on Marxism and the futility of war as though she were not reading the same books herself, he seemed interested in what *she* thought, what she had to say. So Lou talked and Johnny listened, and that had been the pattern of much of their friendship during that time, though Lou hadn't seen it quite that way then. She only knew that Johnny seemed to understand everything she said, and all about her dreams, and if there was a small tinge of disappointment in her attitude toward him as a young man with no dreams, he never challenged her on it. After all, someone who would choose the police force, in those days when the sixties seemed likely to go on forever, was nearly beyond the pale. Yet she couldn't help liking him.

They had dated, but as Johnny said, she had never taken him seriously. She hadn't yet had any serious boyfriend, and the thought of sex made her nervous, though she never said so to anyone. It was important to seem sexually sophisticated, to "assume a virtue, if you have it or not"—virtue, in this case, being experience. So it was easy to keep Johnny at bay without even knowing that she was doing so: on the one hand she talked a lot about sexual freedom, and on the other, she always shied away from any move he made. Johnny drew the obvious conclusion that he just didn't "turn her on," which, though she was hardly conscious of it, suited her nervous fears, and eventually they had a *fait accompli*—a friendship that was solidly platonic.

Johnny married early, but Lou didn't make friends with his wife. Marianne was a nice girl, but her interests were so far from Lou's that they seemed to have nothing to talk about. New kitchen curtains were the sort of preoccupation that Lou and her new feminist friends were laughing at in those days. And Lou didn't want to laugh at Johnny's wife, so she avoided her. Johnny and she saw less of each other, but they still had regular meetings, if not dates, and there were still problems she couldn't discuss with anyone else. But she could hardly introduce Johnny to her friends— after all, he still called her "Babe," her old nickname from elementary school days on the baseball team. The name commemorated a fantastic home run at a crucial moment, but now sounded sexist, a fact that affected Johnny not one bit; even worse, he was still a cop. So their friendship remained a separate thing in each of their lives. Lou never admitted to anyone then, least of all herself, that Johnny was the best friend she had. Johnny didn't judge, didn't label, didn't try to force her problems into a preconceived structure. He just listened, and sometimes advised.

His wife died in childbirth. An extraordinary, unbelievable event for the year 1979. An incompetent obstetrician had missed the signs of toxemia until it was too late and then tried to mend matters with an emergency caesarean. There had been a nightmarish twenty-four hours while Lou had kept Johnny company in the hospital waiting room and the news came down, first that his newborn daughter had died, and then her mother. It was the first time she'd seen Johnny cry since grade six, and although she felt inadequate to the task, she had sat and comforted him as best she could through that night and the painful weeks that followed.

For once, the tables were turned in their relationship, and Lou provided the comfort and the strength—it had brought them closer, deepened the bond. It was a few months later, when Johnny turned to her for another need, that the moment had come that later haunted her.

She had had no way of understanding the depths of loneliness that he was going through. Intellectually of course, she did know, but nothing in her own life had ever hit her as deeply as Johnny had been hit by his tragedy. Emotionally she simply did not understand what it was that drove him to want her—to want a warm, loving, female body—in his bed that night.

"Lou," he had whispered, as, standing up to go home late one night, she had given him their usual warm hug. His arms had tightened around her in a fierce kind of desperation. "Lou, don't go, please don't go. I need you, I need someone, Lou. Please."

She was shocked. Not, she supposed now, because there was no sexual chemistry between them. It had just been made manifestly clear to her that there was *something*. She hadn't consciously thought about anything so honest as whether it might actually be a relief to break through the barrier of habit and mistiming and consummate the friendship with physical intimacy. She had contented herself with being righteously shocked because Johnny should still be mourning Marianne. She had been too young to understand that he was.

But it would have been one thing to have understood his need and refused him. The simple failure that lay in not making love to him when that was what he needed from her didn't bother her much. It was the lack of compassionate understanding of his need, the condemnation of him that had been in her tone of voice when she refused, that she had later seen as the real betrayal.

Years later, when she at last understood something of what he had been suffering during those months, she was ashamed to remember her reaction: she had thought him just another male chauvinist missing the "free sex." "I need someone," had seemed to her to explain it all. His wife had been dead only a few months and in Lou's narrow view he was being unspeakably disloyal. She hadn't said so in words, but of course Johnny had seen it. "Sorry," he said, but she could read a tremendous disappointment in his face—disappointment in her as a person. She did not understand it.

If he had to have sex, why didn't he pick up someone in a bar? Why was he asking this of her?

Johnny had not let it damage the friendship, though at the time, she had felt it was *she* who was being noble. He left the police force shortly afterward, "going private," as he called it; and then Lou got married, and her husband was jealous of the closeness he saw between them, and the second long hiatus in the friendship ensued.

It was only when her own marriage failed after three years that she came close to understanding that night: it wasn't the sex Johnny had wanted so much as the memory of intimacy—the comfort of a loving body, someone he could hold and love, someone not a stranger. A woman picked up in a bar was the last thing he could have coped with. It was loving closeness he had asked her for, and she had turned him down.

Lou never said anything to him about it directly, but one night, during the period of desperate loneliness that struck a few months after the euphoria of "being free" of her marriage had worn off, they had talked about it obliquely.

"It's not the sex so much, is it?" Lou said. "It's the intimacy. It's just the—being able to be with someone without explanations or having to talk...it's just the ease of...the intimacy."

They had looked at each other, and he had known that this was her apology for that dreadful night.

"You get through it," Johnny said gently. "It's hell, Lou, but you do get through."

She had gotten through, and the breakup of her marriage had matured her as nothing else had done. It was perhaps the first time in her life that Lou had really suffered, and suffering is the great growth-producing factor in life. Slowly but remorselessly, she was now examining all the values that had made up her life up to this point, and many of them were being turned on their heads. The years since she had kissed Solly goodbye in a blaze of self-righteous glory had been filled with more deeply felt emotions than she had ever experienced before—pain and suffering first, but then, increasingly, the joy and content that came from understanding and a new inner strength.

She had, of course, stopped beating her breast about her betrayal of Johnny that night, but now she involuntarily found herself looking at it from another point of view entirely. Now she thought, though she tried not to: suppose that moment in the truck was real? Suppose I've been blind to what I really want?

Because Johnny may have wanted her then, but he had shown no sign of ever wanting her again.

"You want the scoop on your friend Butch?"

"What scoop?" Lou demanded excitedly. "Johnny, what did you find out?"

"He's got a record that begins in juvenile court. Assault, sexual assault, resisting arrest...." She heard the sound of a paper being shuffled. "Not the petty criminal I'd imagined. He's strictly violent. Lou, I want you to get off his case right now."

"Oh God, I knew it," she said in despair. "Oh, poor Julie! What about his last name—is it Stockton?"

There was a long pause while the telephone spat in her ear. Lou thought absently that she would have to stop buying five dollar phones before her hearing was destroyed. "Johnny?"

"Babe, I want you to quit looking for your friend, you hear me?"

"It *is* Stockton! It is, isn't it?"

There was the breath of a pause. "No, it is not Stockton."

"What is it? Who is he?"

"Do you promise to leave this alone till I have the time to do something about it?"

"Johnny," she carolled warningly. "This is Lou, remember? She's a human being. One who can make her own decisions."

"Yup, I remember," said Johnny flatly. "And so is Johnny, and so can he, and he is damned well not telling you anything else unless you give me your word—and I mean your *word*, without any crossed fingers this time—not to move a muscle in this guy's direction until I have some time to give you on it."

"Johnny, don't try to run my life, okay?"

"Nope, I only run mine. Maybe you haven't noticed that this is information that is not yours by right."

She could hear her own building irritation reflected in his voice. "To hell with you," she said softly. "Julie's my friend."

"And you're mine."

"Then please tell me Butch's last name."

Her blood was buzzing with anger. She couldn't remember when she'd last really fought with Johnny.

"Read my lips, Lou—no. This is no game. We are not talking about 'Crimes of the Past' here. This guy is a real live perp, and he's dangerous."

"I don't intend to walk up to him in the street, Johnny!"

"You won't get a chance to walk up to him in the street. This is a guy who comes up behind you. Are you listening to me?"

She said, "I got a postcard from Hong Kong today, signed Julie. I don't think she wrote it. If she didn't, he already knows I'm looking for him, doesn't he?"

"Yes, and I guess he'll know if you quit. Are you listening to me?"

"I think Julie's in danger, Johnny. I think this postcard was sent to get me off the trail."

"Unless she wrote it herself. Why do you think she didn't write it? You must know her handwriting."

"Yeah, as long as she's scribbling TBLT and Cof. It's hardly the same thing."

"You still eating those things, Babe? Don't you know all that fried bacon is bad for you?"

But for once Lou refused to laugh. "Anyway, it says she got a job offer. How likely is that?"

"Depends on the job. Maybe somebody took a fancy to her."

"The kind of men who can afford to take women off to Hong Kong don't eat in the Pacific Café, Johnny. And Julie wouldn't go off that suddenly with a stranger. At the very least I'd have heard a suggestion that she'd met someone interesting." She was convincing herself as she spoke. Up till now she had been in two minds about the postcard, but fear and anger were doing their job of turning vague suspicion into fact.

"Stop talking yourself into it," Johnny ordered flatly, with an insight that infuriated her and drove her further into certainty. "You think she spent twenty-four hours a day in the Pacific Café? Besides, you don't know who goes in there. Use your sense."

Reluctantly, she remembered that the owner was himself Chinese. For all she knew, he had partners, and one of them had propositioned Julie somehow.

"I don't believe that postcard came from Julie!" she said anyway. "I think the fact that I'm looking for her is worrying somebody."

"Yeah! Me! Will you stop being so damned pigheaded and listen to what you're saying? If you're worrying anybody, it's a guy with a history of violence as long as your arm, Lou! Now, leave it alone!"

She was beyond stopping to wonder why she was so irrationally furious with him. Not in a million years would she have admitted to herself that it had anything to do with the moment in the truck. She only felt that she was angrier than she had ever been in her life at Johnny, and that the anger was a kind of relief.

She said, "When you're through trying to run my life—"

"I'm not trying to run your life! What the hell is bothering you?"

"At the moment, you," she said, with perfect truth, and hung up the phone.

Chapter 9

Lou awoke next morning with several certainties having crystallized in her mind. The first was that Johnny had lied to her. Butch's last name was almost certainly Stockton. There had been something in Johnny's voice, and her brain had analyzed it overnight: he'd been lying.

The second was that if his name *was* Stockton, it would be one hell of a coincidence if he were not also the missing pilot.

The third was that the one way to be absolutely certain about it was to get a description of Mandala's pilot somehow, and see if it matched her memory of the photo she had seen.

The fourth was that if he were the missing pilot, and had kidnapped Julie, then Julie might have been aboard the missing plane.

The fifth was that if Julie had been aboard, and the postcard *was* really from her, the plane couldn't possibly have crashed.

The sixth was that it might be a good idea to find out exactly when that plane had first been reported missing, and where and in what direction it had been flying. Suppose, just suppose, that Butch had flown the damn thing to Hong Kong, with Julie aboard?

"Hi! How's the acting business these days?"

The receptionist looked up from her sandwich with a breathtaking smile. "Oh, hi! How are you?" It was obviously taking her a moment to place Lou, and Lou used her momentary confusion to set her tray down on the table. "Mind if I join you?"

She had decided that this was a case at last that called for a certain amount of Johnny's "finesse." She had parked herself in the lobby of the Concord Building at a quarter to twelve, and had waited till the receptionist emerged from an elevator, then tailed her into the building's small restaurant where the outdoor tables were crowded. The patio was set down slightly from street level, surrounded by trees, and cut off from the offices by a waterfall that ran down over the windows and formed a small pool between it and the main building. It had not been hard to keep out of sight.

The receptionist had sat at a small table and pulled out a book to read while she ate. Lou had bought a light meal and approached the table as if about to pass, then pretended a start of recognition.

"Oh no, please do," the receptionist said, evidently placing her at last. "It's very crowded, isn't it?"

Lou sat down and unloaded her tray, continuing to chat in a friendly way that meant the other woman had to put her book down.

"How did the filming go?" she asked.

"Oh, that! Oh, I haven't done that yet. That's right, you were there the day I got it, weren't you?"

"Mmm," agreed Lou. "So you haven't met him?"

"No," she said ruefully. "I don't think we will. They never said anything about him being there."

"That's too bad. Didn't I hear that he's supposed to be really good-looking or something?"

"I don't know. I never heard that." Well, that made two of them, Lou reflected.

There was a pause, but the receptionist didn't seem up to contributing anything further. She chewed comfortably, and watched her sandwich between bites.

"Maybe I'm thinking of someone else. I keep asking my editor to let me do a column on Canada's ten best-looking men, but he keeps saying no." This was an appalling lie. Lou would have resigned before she'd have done a column on Canada's ten best-looking men. "It's not the column so much as the research I'm thinking of."

That at least raised a small laugh. "I know what you mean." The girl sighed. "I wish you'd do a column on Canada's ten best-looking women, and put me in it." She looked aghast at herself and apologized hastily. "Not that I think that, I was just thinking it might get me some work."

Lou sighed inwardly over this sidetracking of her gambit. It was never this difficult in books. "Well," she said, "I know a man who does interviews for a small arts magazine. He often does unknowns. I could certainly put you in touch with him." It was pretty well the first thing she'd said that wasn't a lie. But it was horribly blatant. She hoped the girl wasn't any brighter than she seemed.

"Oh, really?" That excited her. "Who is it?"

Lou named the man, and the girl's face fell. "I haven't heard of him."

"Well, if you give me your number, I'll get him to call you, at least."

"All right, but I haven't done very much work, you know."

"Listen, my friend has a thing about beautiful women. If you smile at him, he'll be putty in your hands." God forgive me, God forgive me. "You think your boss should be on my list of Canada's ten?" She leaped at it, because the girl's sandwich had disappeared and there was no dessert in sight. Subtlety would take too long.

The beauty considered it, her head tilted on one side. "He's all right. But he's a bit old, isn't he?"

"Not for a millionaire," Lou said dryly, and they both laughed.

"I know a man I'd put on the list, if only he were rich or famous—your boss's pilot. You think he's attractive?"

"Well, not very." Jenny wrinkled her nose regretfully, as though not being very good-looking was an incomprehensibly malign fate. Lou reflected that for Jenny it would be incomprehensible. "Don't you think he's kind of small? He's balding, too."

Lou swallowed as her heart thumped. What a crazy world it was. "Oh, I must have made a mistake," she pressed, determined to be sure. "I'm thinking of a really big, gorgeous guy named Butch. I thought he was—"

"Oh, you mean *David*! Oh, I thought you were talking about Mr. Mandala's regular pilot! Oh, yes, Da—Mr. Stockton is *very* good-looking."

"That's the one," said Lou. She smiled again. "Tall and well built, with reddish hair."

Jenny smiled, but said nothing.

"I didn't realize Butch had been on that plane," Lou continued, after a moment of silent eating. "He was a friend of mine's boyfriend. I was really shocked to hear he'd been killed. Well, reported missing."

Jenny's eyes widened. "Really? You knew David?"

Lou opted for Johnny's "finesse" again. "Not very well. I was looking for him because my friend disappeared. I thought he might know of her whereabouts. Now I keep wondering if she could have been on the plane with him." For two pins she'd have asked Jenny what the plane's maximum flying distance was, but the idea that it had gone to

Hong Kong seemed too ridiculous, and anyway common sense told her the girl wouldn't know.

Jenny looked horrified. "Oh, that would be awful!"

"Yeah, it's horrible, not knowing. Mr. Mandala says there's no way she could have been on it. But I keep wondering." She laughed without mirth. "I had no idea Butch was even a pilot. It was such a shock."

Jenny nodded, engrossed. "I didn't, either. I didn't even know he could fly till Sandy called in sick that day and Mr. Mandala said David had been on the flight. I always thought he was just a chauffeur."

Lou stared at her, her brain racing with confusion. There was something very odd here.

"That's weird," she said, without thinking. "Why on earth would a guy with a pilot's license take a job as a chauffeur? There must be all kinds of high-paid jobs going with the timber companies."

The receptionist's face abruptly went white, and she lifted a hand to her mouth. "Oh, golly! I just remembered Mr. Mandala asked us not to talk to anybody about all this till it's over. Oh, golly, you're not going to write about what I said, are you?"

Lou smiled and shook her head reassuringly. "Trust me," she said. "I write a features column, and children's stories. This is strictly personal for me. My friend is missing, and I'm trying to find her."

Jenny sighed. "Gee, I hope you find her."

"So do I," said Lou.

They stood up together, and Lou turned toward the short flight of stairs that led up to the street just in time to see that the limo had pulled up and Jerry Mandala was walking down the street toward it.

There was no reason she shouldn't be lunching with his receptionist, but instinct told her it would be better if Jerry Mandala didn't know about it. Without mentioning that she had seen him, Lou waved goodbye and turned to the exit on the opposite street.

"Oh, Miss Patch! Miss Patch!"

The girl's voice was clear and ringing. Lou shrugged, turning in time to see Jerry Mandala's head move to search through the tables. It was obvious that Jenny had still not seen him.

"You were going to take my phone number to give to your friend," she said breathlessly, coming up to Lou between the tables.

"Yes, of course," Lou said. She waited while the girl scribbled on the back page of her novel and tore it out and handed it to her.

"I hope he'll want to meet me," Jenny said earnestly.

"Believe me, he will when I get through with him," Lou said lightly, aware all the time that Mandala's eyes were on her, that he had seen her when she'd seen him, and that he was leaning against the limousine, very obviously waiting to speak to her.

The receptionist didn't notice her boss as she ran past the gently rushing waterfall toward the door of the building. Lou moved slowly through the tables and climbed the stairs from the pleasantly treed enclosure to the pavement.

"Hello again, Miss Patch," Mandala said, straightening and smiling at her.

"Hello. Any news yet?"

"No, I'm afraid not. Do I assume you're going to be writing a story?"

She smiled. "Oh, no, it's not really my turf. I'm a columnist, you know. I'm only interested in ancient crimes."

"Ah. But I think that was my receptionist you were talking to."

She felt she was on very thin ice, without knowing why. "Oh, we just bumped into each other. She was hoping I might know someone who would give her a bit of publicity," Lou said, as casually as she could. She wished to hell this hadn't happened.

"I see. And have you found your friend?"

Lou laughed. "Yes, as a matter of fact, I have! I just got a postcard from Hong Kong, of all places!"

"Ah, well, then at least one of us is happy."

"Oh, yes. She'd have saved me a lot of worry if she'd said goodbye," Lou added, for something to say.

"Miss Patch, I wonder if you'd have dinner with me one night?"

It nearly knocked Lou over backward. "What?" she asked helplessly. "I mean, why?"

He grinned at her disarmingly. "Because I find you an attractive woman and would like to get to know you. Why else?"

She'd never felt so gauche in her life. "Well, why not?" she said. "You have my card, I think."

"I'll call you then. May I call you tonight?"

"By all means."

They smiled at each other with two of the falsest smiles she'd seen outside of Ottawa, and he climbed into the limousine and it started off. Lou watched it drive out of sight, then strolled down the sunlit street, lost in thought. He didn't in the least find her an attractive woman, and she knew it. He found her... her brain sorted through the unconsciously absorbed clues... some sort of danger? A threat? It seemed ridiculous. In what way could she be a threat to Jerry Mandala?

There was another piece of information her brain had taken in almost unconsciously, too, and this one staggered her. The license plate on the car Jerry Mandala had driven away in had read MONEY.

Chapter 10

Lou was ashamed of herself. She had absolutely dismissed the limousine in the back alley when Winnie told her about it, had let it go completely from her mind. All because she couldn't imagine that Julie had any connection with a limousine.

At the very least, she ought to have run a check on the license plate. And even worse, why hadn't she thought of that limo when she got the postcard? Everybody said a rich man had probably made Julie an offer she couldn't refuse—at least *then* Lou should have made the connection.

And none of this beating her breast was any help in working out what had really happened to Julie. If she had been picked up by Mandala's private car, and had been on the plane, the plane had to be in Hong Kong. Along with Butch and the cabinet minister. None of it made sense.

She remembered that odd certainty she had felt, that Winnie had given her a clue to Julie's whereabouts. If only she'd followed up this information before going to see Jerry Mandala.

"Damn it!" she said aloud. What on earth would the Solicitor-General be doing in Hong Kong? Yet how could Butch have kidnapped Julie if his plane had crashed? Could he have got her and locked her up and *then* flown into oblivion?

She needed a few hard facts about that plane's disappearance. Lou climbed into her car and turned it in the direction of her newspaper office. There she went into the library and read the front pages of the past couple of weeks.

Later she went to see Johnny.

"I'm sorry," she said as he opened his apartment door. "I'm really sorry, Johnny."

He stood for a moment looking down at her. "If you ever hang up in my ear again, I will strangle you," he said.

She was astounded by the wave of feeling that swept over her. It was the first time she had seen him since that long night in his truck, and she had almost convinced herself that what had happened was a temporary aberration. But now his presence was nearly overpowering, so that it was all she could do not to grab him. Just standing beside him made her want to cry. She couldn't believe it.

She thought, What would you do if I hugged you, and the hug turned into a kiss, and you discovered I meant it? For a moment she was nearly sure she should try it and see. But the thought of his embarrassment if she were wrong, the thought of how it would strain the friendship if they learned that she wanted him but he didn't want her, stopped the possibility at the thinking stage. She simply didn't have the courage, or the confidence, that such a move required. The mere idea of it scared her silly.

They always did hug when they met, but now Lou side-stepped, looking past his shoulder as though she hadn't noticed his instinctive movement and asked, "Are you alone? Could we talk for a minute?"

He closed the door and followed her into his sitting room, and she nervously threw off her jacket and sat down.

Lord, he was big. Why had all her boyfriends, and her husband, too, been such small men? Tall, sometimes, but always slim and wiry. Now she thought nothing could be so attractive as Johnny's half intimidating, half protective, sheer masculine bulk.

How long had she been fooling herself? Since a lot longer than a few days ago in the truck, she had to assume. This seemed a form of discovery of what existed, not the birth of something new. Well, it was easy enough for friendship to blind you to the existence of something more potent, especially if you were convinced that the something more potent would wreck the friendship. In a way she wished she had continued blind.

"What is it?" asked Johnny grimly. "Finally realized you're in over your head?"

She gave him a startled glance. "What do you mean?" she asked stupidly, wondering if she had given herself away, fighting for time to clear her head if she had.

He said, "I take it you're still messing in that Mandala business."

"Oh!" she said. "Yes, listen, Johnny, I've found out something really weird."

He sighed. "All right," he said. "Want a drink? Shall I open some wine?"

She said yes before she thought that wine might end up sabotaging whatever protective coloration she could muster. "Oh...uh, no thanks," she mumbled, but he was already in the kitchen, and she let it go.

He came back with the open bottle and two glasses, sank into the chair opposite her and tossed down the small cigars that he smoked. He leaned to pour out the wine and handed her a glass, then sat back and lit a cigar.

Lou stared into the red liquid through the heavy cut crystal. Johnny liked fine things; he always had. The Persian carpet was the only sign of it in his office, but his apartment was full of treasures. She thought, suddenly and irrelevantly, other men would spend the money on a new car every two years. Johnny's been driving the same truck for ages.

"Well?" he prompted.

She said, "As far as I can tell from the receptionist's description, the pilot David Stockton and Julie's boyfriend were—are the same man."

Johnny's eyes were hooded. He watched the smoke trail up from his cigar. "Yes?"

"*Was* his name Stockton, Johnny?"

"You're telling the story."

"I was nearly convinced Julie was on the plane and had crashed with it, and Jerry Mandala got someone to send me a postcard from Hong Kong to cover up something, or maybe that they'd all flown to Hong Kong and the Solicitor-General was doing a disappearing act."

Johnny closed his eyes in what seemed like resigned irritation, then looked at her again. "You'll get yourself killed," he observed. "But of course that didn't stop you."

"I can't stop now. You don't know what I've found out."

"All right, I'll bite."

She shook her head. "It's so weird. On Tuesday that week, Julie came down to the beach and told me she thought she had seen Butch outside her apartment building, watching her."

"Right. I remember."

"Jerry Mandala's limousine has a license plate that reads MONEY. His receptionist told me that Butch Stockton actually was hired as a chauffeur. It's reasonable to assume, then, that he would have access to that limousine, right?"

Johnny shrugged. She could tell he wasn't going to help her along with this reasoning at all.

"A woman, one of Julie's neighbors, saw that car in the alley behind Julie's building at four-thirty one morning around the day that Julie left. According to the building manager, Julie left on Thursday."

"I'm with you."

"So—Julie tells me she thinks she's seen Butch outside her apartment building on Tuesday the sixteenth. On Thursday, the eighteenth, she disappears, possibly in Jerry Mandala's car. Follow?"

"I follow."

"Right. Now—the plane carrying Gordon Harrison was reported missing on Monday the fifteenth."

Johnny's head jerked forward. "Say what?"

"Got it?" said Lou. She took a sip of wine, and waited.

"Good God," Johnny breathed, sinking back against the cushions, his eyes narrowed.

"There's more. One, the postcard I got was postmarked the day after I saw Jerry Mandala in his office. Two—" she was holding up fingers now, and sipping her wine between each point as she watched him take the information in. "There were two other men in Mandala's office that day, and one of them was Chinese and spoke English with an accent. He kept chiming in on things, although how it was his business was never explained. Three, the postcard was from Hong Kong." She set down her glass. "Are you following this, Johnny? If Butch Stockton was on that plane and it really went down, it couldn't have been Butch, but Jerry Mandala who snatched Julie in Jerry Mandala's car. If Butch snatched Julie, that plane didn't really go down. So then, where's the Solicitor-General?"

Johnny was staring into his wineglass, the cigar smoking between two strong fingers. "I'm following you. Anything else? I mean, any more facts you've unearthed?"

"Julie's phone bill was paid in cash on Thursday the eighteenth. That's as far as I've gotten."

"And it's as far as you're going to get." He finished off the wine in his glass at a swallow. "I don't know what this is all about, but I know one thing—your messing in this is likely to worry somebody a whole helluva lot, if it hasn't already."

"Don't I know it. I'm going out to dinner with Jerry Mandala tomorrow night."

"The hell you are!"

"Yes," she said airily. "He likes me and wants to get to know me."

"I'll just bet he does! You aren't going, Lou."

"I am. He bothers me, thinking I'm so stupid I can't see through a ploy like that. You should have heard him on the phone tonight, sweet-talking me. I'd like to—"

"Yeah, well, what you'd like to do and what it is prudent to do are two entirely different things. How about we just go to the cops with this?"

"With what? They've already had their chance with my suspicions, and look how they reacted. We haven't got a shred of evidence except for one old woman thinking she's seen a license plate, and—"

"We have got David Stockton's criminal record."

She noted in passing that he had admitted it. "And who's to say they'll believe it's the same man? What Julie told me about Butch working for Jerry Mandala is hearsay, isn't it?"

"Don't be stupid," Johnny said flatly. "Once they make the connection, the proof will be there."

"Will it? Yes, perhaps. You can tell your friend Brent if you want. That should pay him back the year's supply of favors. But they won't be concerned with where Julie is, will they? They're going to be all wrapped up in Gordon Harrison's whereabouts. I'm looking for Julie." She drank her wine and held out the glass as he refilled it.

Johnny said, "If I thought you meant that, Babe, I'd..." He broke off, shaking his head. Lou took a quick gulp of wine. When Johnny was menacing, he was really menacing.

"You'd what?" she demanded, thinking crazily, now why does that turn me on?

The atmosphere seemed to thicken. Johnny stood up abruptly. "You're being a fool, and you know it. Have you actually said you'll have dinner with this guy?"

Lou nodded. She wouldn't have believed that sex could enter the room like that, like a third party, just seeping in from the walls, up from the floor, clouding her brain and making her tongue too clumsy for speech.

"I think I might find out something useful. I know how to play a stupid female, you know, and that's what he seems to be expecting."

Johnny was staring out the window at mountains that were invisible in the darkness, except for the lights of the cable car that lay like a small bracelet near the top. "You know how to play a stupid female, all right," he agreed, with deceptive mildness. She could hear the irritation under the surface. "Like, right now." He turned and looked down at her. His jaw was tight. "But I doubt if that's what he's expecting. You have to stop," he said slowly, spacing his words. "Don't mess with me, Lou. You have to stop this."

She said, "Anyway, I like Jerry Mandala. Why shouldn't I marry a rich man?" She was drunk. One glass of wine, but she was drunk. For two cents she'd turn on him and start giving him hell for being blind to what she'd been blind to for so long. For two cents she'd tell him what she was feeling and shout at him for not feeling the same.

"Marry whomever you want, once this is over," Johnny said, his blandness infuriating her. "But leave this alone."

"You think he doesn't fancy me, don't you?" she demanded. It seemed as though the only protection she had was anger. "You think he's got something else besides sex on his mind, don't you? You think—"

"Yes, and so do you," said Johnny, getting steamed himself. "Don't be such a bloody fool. God knows what's going on, but we're talking about the Solicitor-General of the province! Do you realize what a scandal this could be?

Can you imagine what lengths Mandala'd go to to prevent it leaking out? Whatever it is?''

She stood up and set down her glass.

"I have to go. Good night, Johnny."

"Lou!" he commanded.

Her back to him, she stopped. She said nothing.

"Don't go out with Jerry Mandala."

"Why not, Johnny?" she asked, knowing she wasn't going to get the answer she wanted, but waiting for it all the same.

"Because it is dangerous. You know why not."

Lou exhaled steadily. She swallowed. "Good night, Johnny."

She closed the door gently behind her. There was really no reason to slam it, but that was what she wanted to do.

Chapter 11

There were three hang-up calls on her answering machine early the next afternoon when she got back from Winnie's. It was unusual—most of her friends identified themselves, because Lou hated hang-up calls, and she made sure everybody knew it.

She had been to visit Winnie, to take back the blouse and the little cat and to drink a cup of tea. "You keep that little cat," Winnie had told her. "I wouldn't get anything much for it, and besides, it's your friend's."

"It's cute, isn't it?" Lou said, holding the little creature up. It *was* sweet. She supposed that was the worst of this stuff—that you could react to it in spite of yourself. Somebody had done a lot of market research on wide eyes and gentle mouths and open arms. All the signals said the little cat loved her, accepted her totally, needed her. It made her heart soften toward the inanimate object, and that was lunatic.

She stared at it absently, and the thought rose in her mind: These are obviously pretty potent signals. Suppose I looked at Johnny just like this—he might respond before he knew it.

That made her laugh a little, and Winnie went on, "Maybe he'll encourage you to carry on when the search gets difficult."

She meant the cat, not Johnny. "A mascot," Lou agreed, thanking her and tucking the little cat away in her bag. As Winnie refilled her cup, Lou said, "You remember telling me about that limo in the alley?"

"Yes," said Winnie calmly. "Is it important? I did wonder, later."

"It might be. Is there anything else you remember about it, or about the morning you saw it?"

"I don't think so. Do you mean you think your friend did actually go away in it?"

"I think it's very possible," said Lou, unwilling to explain too much. The fewer people who knew she was beginning to suspect Jerry Mandala of involvement in something sinister, the better. "You didn't happen to see the driver?"

"It had tinted glass, as far as I remember." Winnie closed her eyes briefly. "It seems to me the engine was running. And the license plate. Did I tell you about that?"

"Tell me again," said Lou softly.

"Ah, I can see you're a real detective," said Winnie with a smile. "I read your crime column, you know. 'Patch's Patch'—it's very interesting, the way you reconstruct those old murders. I remember some of them, of course, from the time they happened, so it's particularly interesting to me."

Lou was immediately sidetracked. "Do you happen to remember the Janet Smith case?" Most people Winnie's age did, if they'd been living in Vancouver at the time, and there'd been a time recently when that was the question most on Lou's lips.

"Oh, yes. Yes. I was just a young girl at the time, but oh, that was very big. Very important. The whole city was in an uproar. Have you written about Janet in your column? I don't think I read that."

"I wrote a book about her," Lou said. "Or half of one."

"Oh, yes—I remember reading that—but was that yours? I thought a young man..."

Lou smiled wryly. "Yeah, he beat me to it. I'd no idea he was even there." A couple of people had told her they'd already talked to someone, but Lou couldn't find out who it was, and they'd said it was several years previously, so she'd let it go. After months of painstaking research and methodical reasoning, she had made her own deductions from the evidence, delivered the outline to her publisher, and was in the middle of the writing, when one day she had gazed in horror at a book in the window of her favorite bookshop entitled, *Smooth Silence: The Cover-up of Janet Smith's Murder*, by a writer she had never heard of.

"But Janet Smith is *mine*!" she had shrieked to an uncomprehending passerby, who, since Lou was in the West End at the time, had simply smiled tolerantly at her and walked on.

After five minutes' ponderous consideration, Lou's publisher decided not to publish her version of Janet Smith's murder, since the "limited market" for such a work would have been swallowed up already. Her editor didn't even try to pretend she believed what she was saying, but Lou had read between the lines.

Janet Smith's death had involved families in high places, and they were still in high places, and still, presumably, suppressing the evidence. Lou was certain in her own mind of what had happened. The publication of the first book had caught the powerful old Shaughnessy families unawares, and alerted them to the possibility of the second—hers. Amongst those Establishment families a nod was as good as a legal injunction—somebody had nodded in the direction of her publisher. In a few years, perhaps, she might try to sell the project to someone else. But it was pointless now.

Someone had offered to introduce her to the other writer, who, it turned out, was a Vietnam draft resister who had come to Vancouver in 1970 and made it his permanent home. Lou remembered her old dead fury at the Vietnam War and marveled at consequences—because France had refused to give up power over an Asian colony decades ago, her book on the Janet Smith case was not being published in Canada in 1988. Now, if time were, as some people said it was, an illusion—if it ran backward, or if everything was actually, unseen by human consciousness, happening concurrently, wasn't it possible that her anger with the Vietnam War in 1970 had been *caused* by the fact that a man who otherwise wouldn't have been able to place Vancouver on a map had come to live there, and so been given the chance to get fascinated by her Janet Smith in 1988?

As a result of this, she had written a children's book called *The Backwards Boy*, and another called *The Go-Ahead Girl*, about children who did not move through time the way the rest of the world did. Nobody had preempted her on that, and the books were having a small success as companion volumes.

"But my Janet Smith book is still on my shelf, half finished. Actually—" she finished with a grin "—it's the tragedy of my life."

Winnie clucked her tongue. "Maybe one day they'll change their minds."

"If I could solve it, they might. Even that book didn't untangle the thing, you know."

"Well, someone knows the truth. They're not all dead, not by any means." Winnie meant the people involved in the murder and the cover-up. "And you're very diligent." She sighed. "My, how times have changed. When I think of the fuss over Janet Smith, and here you are, having to find your little friend all on your own, because the police aren't interested."

That brought them neatly back to the investigation at hand. Lou was surprised at how far away her thoughts had gone.

She shook her head to clear it. "We were talking about the limo you saw, weren't we? Je—" She stopped herself just in time from saying the name. God, she had been miles away.

"And you were trying to see if I still remembered the license plate," said Winnie, nodding. "Well, I do—it was MONEY. I'm sure of it. Are you going to find out whose car it was?"

"I should have done it before, shouldn't I?" Lou said remorsefully. "But you know, it just didn't even cross my mind that it had any relevance to Julie. Isn't that stupid?"

Winnie shook her head. "No, just very human," she said. "I wonder what reminded you of it, dear?"

Lou smiled. How quick she was. "I saw it again, that limo, in rather unusual circumstances."

"And you aren't going to tell me any more than that, I can see."

"Not now. I'm sorry, you've been such a help to me, but—"

Winnie patted her hand. "Never mind, dear. But I'd appreciate it if you could find the time to visit me again when all this is over, and tell me all about it."

"That's a promise," said Lou.

The phone rang while she was in the shower, and later, while she was dressing. She answered it the second time, for some reason expecting it to be Johnny. But it wasn't Johnny. The voice that spoke to her was that of a stranger.

"Is that Lou Patch?" he said. Her heart tightened, and for no good reason she had an impulse to deny it.

"Who's calling, please?" she temporized.

"Lou, this is Max Renault. I think we've met at some press party sometime or other. I'm the west coast correspondent for the *Globe*."

She couldn't recall meeting him, though of course she knew the name. "Oh, yes," she said. "What can I do for you?"

"Well," he said, "to be blunt, you could get off the Gordon Harrison story and leave it to me."

She still had her bath towel wrapped around her—she'd been doing her makeup when the phone rang. She was so startled that the towel slipped from its moorings around her breasts. She made a wild grab for it and the receiver went flying. "Hang on, I've dropped the phone!" she called breathlessly. She let the towel slide and dragged the receiver up by the cord. "What did you say?" she said, when she had it at her ear again, the towel in one hand at her breasts.

He said, "I want an exclusive on the Gordon Harrison story. I know you're working on it. What would it take to ask you to leave it to me?"

In a purely unconscious reflex, she took the receiver away from her ear and looked at it. She put it back to her ear again. "Are you out of your mind?" she said. If he wasn't, she must be. "Am I dreaming?"

"What's wrong?" he said impatiently. "I'm not expecting you to do it for free. I'm prepared to offer you a certain—"

Lou interrupted. "Do you mind telling me what makes you think I'm on the Harrison story?"

"I've heard around," said the voice. "It's not—"

She took a breath. "I don't know who you are, mister, but let me tell you, if you ever call this number again, you'd better believe I'll find out," she said coldly.

"I told you, my name is Max Renault," said the voice urgently.

"Yes, you did. And I'm sure Max Renault would be very interested in that fact."

The tone of voice changed. "Be careful, Miss Patch," it said flatly. "The day may come when you wish you weren't so smart."

She had her mouth open to answer when the dial tone sounded in her ear. "Hello," she cried stupidly. "Hello!"

There was a harsh knocking at the door, and she jumped in sudden panic. "Who's that?" she demanded, frozen into immobility in the middle of the large plant- and sunlight-filled sitting room.

"Johnny," said Johnny. "Let me in."

"Johnny!" she shrieked in relief, darting toward the door as she struggled to pull the towel around her. But hearing her cry, Johnny didn't wait for her to unlock the door: he did it himself. As it came flying open, Lou jerked to a stop, the towel cloaking her from breast to floor in front, naked down the back.

"Johnny," she said more quietly, watching him register her presence alone in the room, and then quietly enter and close the door.

"You okay?" he asked. "I heard your voice, you sounded . . . nervous."

Her tongue was stuck to the roof of her mouth as he came closer. "Babe, what's the matter?" he said urgently.

She tried to laugh. "How did you get in?" she asked, and he held up a stiff piece of white plastic in his left hand. At the sight of it she managed to laugh in earnest. Johnny had come a long way since that first break and enter at the plumbing shop. "Your phone was busy when I buzzed from downstairs," he said. He must have been worried, she thought dimly. He hardly ever used the plastic card on her door, however much he used it elsewhere. "You look— what's the matter? Who was on the phone?"

She shook her head. "The most ridiculous thing I ever heard," she said. "Some idiot who obviously knows noth-ing whatsoever about how newspapers work just tried to buy me off the Gordon Harrison story. He said he was Max Renault. Is that bizarre, or what?''

"Buy you off?''

"Buy me off. As if I'm the only other writer in the country interested in the biggest news story to hit the province since the election. Do you credit it, Johnny? Whoever these people are, they are unbelievably stupid.''

Johnny looked thoughtful. "Maybe not quite as stupid as you think. They must think you've got information that no one else is likely to have, Babe, and that's true enough, isn't it? All they're doing is offering you money to stop investigating. Why should they care what pretext they use? Why should you, if you're willing to be bought?''

Good point. Lou nodded, suddenly aware that except for the towel she held clutched to her throat, she was stark naked. Johnny seemed to realize it at the same time, just as he was about to head past her to the sofa.

He stopped where he was standing, four or five feet away. "That's the latest fashion for trapping millionaires, is it?'' he asked with a grin. "And to think I always credited you with a certain amount of subtlety.''

Lou swallowed. "Oh, subtlety is a waste of time with millionaires.'' She was trying to keep it light, but in fact she felt more awkward than she would ever have been in a similar situation in the past. She couldn't remember when she'd last felt so tongue-tied and shy.

"I'm sure you're right,'' said Johnny lightly, but she was nearly sure he didn't feel as much at ease as he pretended. She was silent, looking at him. For a moment neither moved or spoke.

"I'm just getting dressed,'' she said then, awkwardly. "Wait here a minute.'' She sidestepped out of the room, into the bedroom, closed the door and leaned against it. She thought, if he opens this door, it'll be because . . .

Then she heard the click of his lighter, and there was the scent of his cigar smoke on the summer air. It was an odor she had associated with Johnny for almost as long as she could remember, and for a moment it was overwhelmingly nostalgic, and painful.

It was a sound that meant he wouldn't be opening the door.

Chapter 12

When she entered the living room again, it was in a mood of yearning after impossibilities. Johnny had his booted feet up on the ottoman and an ashtray beside him on the sofa. He was watching the smoke from his cigar crawl upward to the high ceiling.

Lou's apartment was on the top floor of an old four-story building of the kind that had once covered the West End, but had now mostly given way to more modern apartment buildings. It was known in real estate jargon as a "character" flat, which meant it had old-fashioned windows and high ceilings and odd bits of stained glass here and there. Her walls were painted white, but the effect was softened by the green of her many plants, the warm stain of the pine floors, the colorful furniture and carpets.

Her soft sofa cluster sat on three sides in the window embrasure, and through the open windows she could hear a softball game in progress in the school yard behind, and see the sun at the edge of the roofs opposite on its way to setting into the waters of English Bay.

It seemed so perfect—a moment out of time. If you were quiet and didn't push your memory, she thought, you could imagine that the last twenty years hadn't happened, even the last fifty. Life was carefree and innocent, made up of softball games on summer afternoons and clear water. No oil spills threatened the dwindling otter population—life was a straight line before you, not a zigzag behind . . . and everything important to you was within your reach.

She stood in the center of the room, gazing at Johnny, fighting the certain feeling that her life would never be comfortable again. She thought inconsequently, it might all have been different, the past twenty years, and yet I might still be standing here in front of Johnny, dressed to go out—this one moment out of all the others could be identical, the point where two different lives touch and match. And what I'm yearning for is that other life, the one I didn't live, without ever having recognized before that it was even a possibility.

Johnny said, "Babe, you look beautiful. I think you meant it when you said you'd decided to marry Mandala's money."

She thought, If you knew why I'd dressed the way I have, you'd probably laugh. You say I look beautiful, but I don't think it touches you, not the way even the curve of your hand around that cigar affects me.

He said with a conspiratorial grin, "Want to go to Nick's? We could be gone before Mandala gets here."

Her heart thudded so hard it frightened her. Playing for time, she said, "What are you doing here, anyway? What made you come?"

He frowned. He said, "I don't like the idea of you alone with Mandala. I came to tell you I'm going to be tailing you tonight. So if you get into any trouble, just scream."

She was immeasurably relieved, especially after the phone call, which had unnerved her more than she knew. Yet she couldn't help protesting, "Oh, for goodness' sake, Johnny, I'll be fine!"

"You will if I have anything to say about it, and I intend to," he agreed, unperturbed. "Do you by any chance know where you'll be eating tonight?"

"No," she said. She was unsettled now, and it was a moment before she realized she was wishing she'd taken him up on his offer to skip before Mandala arrived. They had done lots of crazy things in their lives; running out the back door with Johnny while Mandala waited at the front wouldn't be in the least out of character for them. She suddenly remembered a night when they had each stood up a current date to dash off and see some ridiculous old film they'd suddenly heard was in town and both wanted to see. They'd laughed over the adventure for days, the more so because the film was disappointing and both relationships, not surprisingly, had foundered immediately afterward.

Well, he'd made his offer. She couldn't expect him to do it again. She said, "Johnny, want to go see *The Manchur—*?"

She stopped because the phone rang, and she knew it was Jerry Mandala announcing himself downstairs. Johnny got to his feet as she reached for the phone. He raised an eyebrow at her. "Well?" he asked.

"We'd never get out of here without him seeing us now," she protested with a grin.

"Don't answer the phone," he said, in the moment that she picked up the receiver. She made a rueful face at him over it and said, "Hello?"

"Hi there. It's Jerry here. Ready?"

"I'm ready. Are you downstairs?"

"You betcha. Shall I come up?" He had a deep, mellifluous voice, far too calculated in its effect to grab her, but she could feel the pull that must have affected others.

"Oh, uh, no, I'll come right down. Just give me a second."

"All the time you want," Mandala assured her, with the air of a man prepared to wait forever for the woman he wanted. Lou began to think he had more charm than was visible at first sight.

"I won't be a minute."

Johnny was already at the door. "I'll be behind you in the truck. If you run into a problem, you know my car phone number. If you can't phone, flash his headlights, or just hit the horn, or wave."

She smiled at him, wondering why she was going out with the wrong man when she could be with Johnny. "What do you think he's going to do to me?"

He shook his head, his eyes alight. "Babe, the way you look, anything at all," he said, and in the next moment the door had opened and he was gone. Feeling somewhat let down, Lou picked up her bag, pulled her evening jacket around her shoulders, and followed him out the door. It was only when she saw the word MONEY on the license plate of Jerry Mandala's car that she remembered Julie, and why she was there with him at all.

Because of Johnny, she was choking back laughter all the way to Il Piccolo Mondo, a pleasant Italian restaurant that was so close to her flat they might almost have walked. The limousine, with all its ponderous self-importance, seemed too big for the tree-lined streets of the West End, and Johnny was making no bones about being right behind them. He did everything except call them "road-hog." When he saw them stopping at the restaurant, the truck peeled off from behind them and laid rubber for several yards down the street before it screeched to a halt, as though some teenage driver had gotten his father's wheels for the night and was anxious to impress the world with the importance of his journey. Lou was already choking on her suppressed hilarity, so when she gulped in a yard of oxygen for laughter that would have been irrepressible, and some saliva went down the wrong way, she was grateful for the coughing fit that ensued. At least it sobered her.

Only Johnny, she thought, preceding a concerned Jerry Mandala into the restaurant, could make me laugh at a hundred yards. Johnny always made her laugh, and it suddenly struck her that she was dating yet another man who did not. If Jerry Mandala had a sense of humor, it wasn't on the same wavelength as hers, and she knew before she began that she had sat through this dinner date a couple of hundred times, with a couple of dozen other men.

She knew she would say to Johnny later, If I have to get ponderous about the ozone layer one more time, Johnny, I'm gonna go out and blast a hole in it myself! And she had a very clear, momentary image of how they would laugh at that.

She thought, well, at least tonight I hope I'll have something of more immediate significance to report than on the ozone layer. Jerry Mandala sat with his back to the door, so she had a clear view of how Johnny dealt with the objections of the headwaiter to his battered denim. "Sheer intimidation," she would accuse him later, and he would protest, "Hey, I slipped him a twenty!" "A twenty and a very mean look," she would amend, and he . . .

I am having conversations with Johnny in my head when he isn't around, Lou realized with shock. I wonder how long this has been going on?

After that she turned her full attention on Jerry Mandala, with all the focused concentration of a spiritual initiate contemplating a *koan*.

"Like to look at the wine list?" he offered, obviously very skilled in the ways of treating career women. Lou wondered idly, not really caring, whether his actual preference was for women with a strong outside interest, or women whose central interest was clinging to him. She shook her head graciously.

"No, please choose," she said with a smile. They chatted idly about the latest massive oil spill up the coast as they chose their meal, and he told her how glad he was he'd never invested in oil or tankers, only in environment friendly businesses.

"I wouldn't have called cars environmentally friendly, myself," Lou said lightly.

He made a face of rueful acceptance. "Yeah, well, but everybody uses cars."

She wondered what he used for brains when he needed them. "I suppose everybody uses oil, too."

It wasn't her cue, she knew. She had missed her cue two lines ago, when she was supposed to ooh and ahh over Jerry Mandala's world conscience, in his own small way caring about the environment.

"Yeah, I see your point," he said, as though the point were profound, and she noted the little-boy puzzlement of the eyebrows so she could reproduce it later for Johnny—

"But of course you don't deal in cars anymore, do you?" she said, burningly interested. "You got into real estate and other things, I think? What's your latest area of interest?"

"Well, gambling's looking pretty interesting. I've got one casino ship that makes more in a week than the car lot used to make in six months." He laughed, encouraged by Lou's brilliant smile.

"I didn't know gambling was legal in B.C. except for charity," Lou stated mildly, and was surprised to see his face shut down.

"Yeah, we have to take it out beyond the twelve-mile limit. It's not ideal circumstances, for sure." He took a sip of wine and abruptly changed the subject.

"So, how are you getting on with your story?"

She had to pause for a moment of remembering if she had made up a story about working on a story for him. "Which story?" she asked, a bit belatedly.

He smiled. "You're a writer. Aren't you working on a story?"

She inclined her head. "Well, the story for this week's 'Patch's Patch' is the 1952 hotel fire in Victoria, and frankly, it's a bit boring because there's nothing to print except speculation, but I did dress up the unidentified body a bit. I mean, it *could* just conceivably have been delivered to the burning building, and the whole thing a cover-up for murder. Unlikely as all hell, but we won't tell the readers that."

He made an attempt to enjoy the wryness of that. "And that's what you've been working on this week?"

"That and a little book called *Time Out of Mind*. That's a children's book that tries to deal with the question of whether time exists within the universe, or the universe within time, without tramping on too many religious toes in the process. I'm enjoying that one."

Ever since her brief meeting with Time at the time of the Janet Smith catastrophe, she had been fascinated by its face. Less and less could she accept that the way human consciousness perceived time was the way it in fact operated. She enjoyed passing this questioning on to younger minds who, perhaps through her, might be inspired to go on asking questions, with a greater chance of getting the answers right.

"I don't see why that would run aground on religion," said Jerry Mandala with a questioning lilt.

"If the universe exists within time, it had to come into existence at some point in time. Therefore you need a creation, or a big bang or something. And if the universe includes God, then God exists within time and needs a cause. Right? On the other hand, if God is the universe, and time exists within the universe, then time is merely one of the tools God uses to manifest its will, so to speak, and our perception of time and creation and big bang is really a kind of dream, no more."

Mandala blinked. "And you're putting that into a children's book?"

"Mm-hmm," Lou said with a nod as their food arrived. The waiter poured them more wine and departed.

"And that's really the kind of stuff that you write?"

She looked up from her salad. "Yes, what did you think?"

"I thought you perhaps were an investigative journalist writing under another name."

Lou laughed. "No, thank you," she said.

"Why not?" he asked, with real interest.

"What?—chase after politicians all my life, looking for slime on their coattails? It's just not my idea of a good time. There are more important things in life."

"Like what?"

She smiled. "Like whether the human mind's perception of time is a crock."

"But crime fascinates you. It must. Why don't you investigate the criminal element of today, instead of that old stuff?"

She looked at him. He was after something, but she didn't know what. "I believe criminals have a way of discouraging the public exposure of their activities," she said. "Old crime has lost its punch. It's an exercise in research, which I enjoy, and it pays the bills."

"And what's your interest in Gordon Harrison, then?" he said, a little as though he were going to catch her out in a lie.

She looked at him straight, noticing, over his shoulder, that Johnny had registered this subtle shift in the atmosphere at their table. "Gordon Harrison?" she shook her head. "None whatsoever."

"Jen tells me you've been asking her questions about Sandy McMaster," he said, his voice losing all its chest resonance and coming out thin and hard.

She stared at him. "Somebody's got me confused with some other journalist," she said. "Who's Jen?"

He gave the look of a man unimpressed by a butter-is-safe-in-my-mouth act. "Jenny is my receptionist. You had lunch with her yesterday."

Lou's brow cleared. "Oh, right! But who's Sandy McMaster?"

He raised both eyebrows, still unconvinced. "My pi—"

"Oh, your pilot!" she exclaimed. "Of course. I never knew his name."

"I see," he said.

"While we're on the subject, do you mind if I ask you a few questions?"

"I thought you weren't interested in Gordon Harrison."

"I'm not. But I'm interested in my friend Julie."

"I don't see her connection with this at all," Mandala said. "Haven't we established that there is no connection between my pilot and this man you're looking for?"

"The names are the same, and the description is the same. How likely is it that it's not the same man?"

"Ah," said Mandala. "Jen didn't tell me that you had asked for a description of David." His voice was cold, and Lou interrupted to protect the girl.

"I didn't ask. I didn't have to, I already had his description," she lied. "I ran into Jenny quite by chance, and we mostly discussed the possibility of getting her career some publicity."

A look came over his face, and she knew she had said the wrong thing as far as Jenny's career in his office was concerned. "I see," he said, and there was no more she could say. He could see the manipulation she had used quite clearly, and he was angry about it. "Tell me again about your friend Julie."

She thought it best to comply as though he had expressed friendly interest and not a direct order. "She really is a terrific kid," Lou said enthusiastically. "She left school in grade eleven, but she's planning on going back to finish high school and then going on to university or a training college. She thought she'd like public relations. The fly in the mixture was her friend Butch.''

"That's the man you think is my ch—pilot?"

"Apparently he's a violent man. He started to beat her up, and she was afraid. She got away from him and came down to the West End, but then she figured he'd found her. It was shortly after that she disappeared."

"How did she figure he'd found her?"

"She saw him outside her apartment building one day." Lou suddenly decided to try shock tactics. "He was in a limousine with MONEY on the license plate."

Jerry Mandala knocked over his wineglass. Across the room, Johnny's eyes narrowed and he shook his head warningly at Lou.

"Is that what made you think your friend was on my plane?" he asked, when the waiter had cleaned the mess.

Lou nodded. "But I've had that postcard from her, so I'm assuming she's all right for the moment. I expect her to write soon, giving me an address where I can reach her. It's all a bit strange, really."

She knew she was poking sticks through metaphorical bars again, but Jerry Mandala irritated her with his assumptions that implied threats would frighten her, and she wanted to see how he would react to the same treatment from her. She wanted him to know, too, just in case it meant something to him, that Julie was under *her* protection. It was a territory game, and he had obviously expected to be the only one playing it. He had expected to cow her.

"What's strange about it?"

Lou shrugged and drank more wine. "Just the way it happened. I still haven't completely accepted that she wasn't on the plane with Butch, really," she said, because caution suggested that it would be wise to pretend she didn't know this was an impossibility. Wherever Butch had been, it was

Mandala's car that had almost certainly picked up Julie Hastings. Better that he should think she thought Butch alone was behind it.

He said, "Well, if she was, I wish she'd write and tell you where Gordon Harrison is." He smiled briefly to show her how stupid she was being. "Frankly, I don't accept that she had any connection at all with my pilot. David Stockton was not a violent man."

"Didn't you say he'd been in Vietnam?" asked Lou innocently.

Shutters dropped over his eyes. "As far as we know."

Lou shrugged. "A lot of men came out of that war violent. It wrecked a lot of psyches."

He asked flatly, "Are you going to be publishing any of this speculation, Miss Patch?" He seemed to have forgotten that they had established first name terms.

Lou shook her head. "My interest is Julie," she said. "If she was on that plane, or has been harmed, then I'm out for blood—David Stockton's or whomevers. For the rest of it, I don't care."

She became aware only as she was saying it that the words were a lie. She wasn't sure what had tipped the balance, but she was now absolutely fascinated by what it was about Gordon Harrison's disappearance that had Jerry Mandala frightened out of his mind. But of course, there was a long way between being interested and going out of your way to find out the truth.

"You know, my next project is to start a new Vancouver paper to go up against the *Sun* and the *Province*. One of the reasons I wanted to see you tonight was to offer you a job on it," Mandala said suddenly.

She laughed. "Well, offer away! I never said I didn't have to work for a living."

"I was thinking about asking you whether you'd like to come aboard in the early stages as adviser."

Lou set down her wineglass. "I wonder what I could advise you on. I'm a features writer, as I said, not a journalist, and I'm no expert on current events. Or how to run papers." She cocked her head. "What were you thinking of?"

He said, "I was thinking of you going on a research trip, coast to coast and maybe into the States, too, to examine the newspapers in various cities and come up with some ideas for a really new paper."

"That sounds interesting," Lou lied. It sounded absolutely boring to her. She didn't suppose a really new paper was even possible. What interested her was the fact that Jerry Mandala thought it worthwhile to get her out of Vancouver, in spite of her express lack of interest in the Solicitor-General's missing plane. She rested her chin on her hand, her elbow on the table, and gazed at him curiously, inviting him to carry on.

Across the room, Johnny crossed one strong denimed thigh over the other, raised his glass and winked at her. She was suddenly aware of her posture as that of the sycophantic female adoring the wealthy male, and hastily raised her napkin to hide a smile. The man was out of his mind—if he kept this up, Jerry Mandala would be asking soon who he was.

"Who is it?" asked Mandala, instantly proving her point, and she shot a reproachful look in Johnny's direction. "Is it your boyfriend?"

Lou choked a little. "No, not really," she said hesitantly.

"Ex-boyfriend, perhaps?" Jerry Mandala turned slightly in his seat and gave Johnny a down-the-nose stare.

"Something like that," Lou admitted, her sense of humor getting the better of her judgment.

"Want me to warn him off?" Mandala asked, ponderously confident. He obviously thought money made up for lack of bulk. On the other hand, Lou thought wildly, his eyesight might be weaker than she knew. "Does he follow you around every time you go out with someone else?"

"Not every time."

She was shocked that he actually had the gall to turn and summon Johnny with an upraised, wiggling forefinger. What wealth did to people couldn't be adequately described in words, but it was all there in the arrogant imperiousness of that gesture. For a moment Lou expected that Johnny would ignore it, because it seemed to her a no-win situation for him; but in fact he smiled and nodded graciously as if this were a commoner's invitation to royalty, slowly lifted his boot from his knee, stood up and made his easy way over to their table. If his arms swung at his sides in the posture of someone approaching a street fight, he seemed unaware of it.

Lou felt Jerry Mandala move restlessly.

"Hi, Babe, how's doing?" Johnny asked softly when he reached their table; and his hand came up and roughly stroked her cheek and the side of her head, holding it a moment before he dropped his hand again.

She almost cried out. As it was, her lips parted for an involuntary intake of air, and her heart kicked into life so hard she felt faint.

"Uh, Johnny, this is Jerry," she managed to say. "Jerry, my f—my friend Johnny."

They exchanged greetings, and Johnny's hand, larger, browner, rougher, enclosed Jerry Mandala's manicure, and what messages were exchanged with that clasp she could only make a womanly guess at, and she guessed that Mandala lost the duel.

But he wasn't going to give in as easily as that. "Do you mind telling me why you've followed us here tonight?" he asked severely.

Johnny appropriated a free chair from the neighboring table and calmly straddled it, the back between his spread thighs. He pulled out a cigar and lit it, tossing the packet onto the table, the match into the ashtray.

"You didn't ask the lady if she minded," Mandala said, fighting for points. Johnny's dark gaze was instantly on her.

"You mind, Babe?" he asked caressingly.

She shook her head helplessly. She couldn't have said yes to save her life, not even for the amusement of watching how Johnny would handle it.

Johnny nodded and turned back to Mandala, whose lips tightened. He raised his eyebrows inquiringly.

"I said, I'd like to know why you followed us," Mandala said, severely but quietly, so the other tables could not hear. "There's no point in denying it. It's been quite obvious to me from the beginning."

God, thought Lou, I never realized that. I wonder if he knew I was laughing, too?

Johnny grinned easily. He hardly ever had to look mean to score points. "Good. That's good," he said approvingly. "I was afraid you might be a little slow."

"I am not slow," said Mandala coldly, showing a few of his hackles. If they were frogs, Lou thought crazily, they'd both be puffing up now like rubber dinghies.

"Good," Johnny said again. "So I'll only have to say it once. I followed you here because this is my woman, and I look after her. I don't mind her having dinner with other men—" he raised his finger and the little cigar together "—but they don't drive her home. I'm the one who drives her home, and I'm the one who makes love to her tonight. See?" He stood up. "Now, you carry on and enjoy your meal, and when you're ready to leave, I'll be here." He inclined his head graciously, swung the chair back to its position at the other table, and left them.

Mandala stared at her in silence for a count of five. Then he said coldly, "Who is that man?"

She shook her head in disbelief. She couldn't look in Johnny's direction, because wild laughter was reaching the point of hysteria in her, and if she caught his eye, the madman, the lid would come right off.

"An old friend. He has never done that before," she assured Mandala, thinking, *and he never will again if he knows what's good for him.* She couldn't imagine why on earth he had done it now, unless somewhere along the line, without telling her, he had discovered that Mandala was a dangerous lunatic. That might excuse it, she supposed.

"I recognize him from somewhere," said Mandala. "Who is he? What's his name?"

For the first time in an evening of veiled threats, she was frightened. It occurred to her that Johnny had in some mysterious way thrown himself in front of the gun for her, drawing Mandala's attention. There was no logical reason for thinking it, but she did.

She said, "Please don't worry about him. He's an irritation, but he's not dangerous."

Mandala turned for another look in his direction. Johnny didn't nod this time, just returned a level stare.

"He looks like a bodyguard," Mandala said disparagingly.

Lou laughed. "He runs a bakery," she said, out of the blue. She was nervous. She didn't want Mandala interested in Johnny.

He nodded wisely. "Mob stuff," he said, as if filing it for future reference. He smiled. "Now, let's forget all that and finish our meal in peace."

Lou tried; she really did. But Johnny was in her line of vision, and he was watching her so obviously that nearly everyone in the restaurant seemed to be aware of it. Other women kept glancing at her with little smiles and overtly envious looks. How many women in the modern world could hope to have two men fighting over them in public like *The Challenge of the Stag King?* Especially when one of them looked like Johnny and the other looked rich?

When Mandala went off to the toilet, the entire room seemed to hold its breath, as if expecting Johnny to ride off with Lou over the pommel of his motorcycle. And when he caught her eye across the room and she couldn't look away, the moment was frankly electric, even for the maître d'.

She tried, but it was, on the whole, impossible to forget Johnny or the scene they had just played.

"It's me she'll be making love to tonight," he'd said, and Lou closed her eyes when she unexpectedly remembered it, her stomach clenching, the thought shivering fitfully over her skin like wind through a wheatfield.

It's madness, she thought. One day soon I'll wake up and find I'm sane again, and this fit will have passed. But what do I do until that happens? God, oh, God, what can I do till then?

Chapter 13

Lou closed the door and leaned her back against it, facing Johnny across the room. He was sitting on her sofa, one leg up on the footstool, grinning at her.

"Do you mind telling me what that was all about?" she said, her lips twitching. There was, in spite of everything, a bubble of laughter in her system. The kind of laughter that said that to feel like this about a fellow human being was a gift of God and she should delight in it.

"Hey," said Johnny innocently. "I only laid out the ground rules for the guy. Nothing wrong in that. I even let him break one of them."

By that she supposed he meant that he had given in to Mandala's clear determination that since he had brought her, he would see Lou home. He had been visibly prepared to do battle, but Johnny hadn't bothered to engage. "See you at home," he had said to Lou in the restaurant, winking and shooting her with his finger as she walked past him with Mandala. Out of Mandala's line of vision she had rolled her eyes at him in heavy exasperation, but he ignored it, smiling up at her as though she were blowing him a kiss.

He came out the doors of the restaurant just as the limousine drove up, jogged along the road to his disreputable truck, and wheeled it into a U-turn before Mandala's chauffeur had managed to pull out into the traffic.

Jerry Mandala was ostentatiously ignoring the whole thing. "Now, what about this job?" he began when they were moving. "I'd like to get going on that as soon as possible. When can I have your answer?"

Lou said, "I don't really enjoy travel all that much. It's not really my kind of job, frankly. Thank you for thinking of me, but—"

"I won't take no for an answer now," Mandala said. "We haven't discussed salary yet, and I expect to make that very tempting. And there may not be all that much travel. You could go to New York for a month, for example, and check out a lot of the U.S. and foreign papers right there. You'd be on expenses, of course. You could do the same in Toronto. Think of it as a glorified shopping trip."

She supposed he didn't realize that there was an implied insult there, and she decided to ignore it. Perhaps because of her sudden fears for Johnny, she was able to recognize that there might be some danger behind his determination to get her out of town. She decided to tread softly. "What sort of salary?" she asked.

He named a ludicrously high figure, and she allowed herself to look greedy and impressed. "I do still want to think it over," she said, in the tone of someone who has already decided to accept.

"All right," he said complacently. "I'll call you tomorrow."

"All right," she smiled. "And now, can I ask you a question?"

"Sure," he said easily, but she felt that he went on guard.

"Why do you have MONEY on your license plate?" she asked, smiling, because it really interested her, the mentality that could fix on something like that.

"Well, it's because of my mother, really," said Mandala, in a prepackaged tone that she had already learned meant he was out to impress. "You know, I grew up poor—we never had enough money. I used to promise her that one day there'd be plenty, and I was right. Only," he dropped his voice, "she didn't live long enough to see it."

Lou thought cynically, I'll bet the business magazine profilers love it, but she said only, "I'm sorry to hear that."

That was about all they had time for before the car drew up outside her building. Mandala said, "I suppose you wouldn't care for a drive around the Park before you go in?"

Even through the tinted glass, the lights of Johnny's truck as he pulled up behind seemed very invasive. "Well…" Lou began, and Jerry Mandala lifted his hands.

"Perhaps some other time," he smiled, "when you've dispensed with your—ah, chaperon. I suppose he would follow us?"

Lou shook her head. "I really don't know," she said. "He's—um, unpredictable. I am very sorry about tonight."

"I'll tell you frankly," said Mandala, "it's the sort of thing you'd better nip in the bud. I've heard of men getting these obsessions. It's easy to see the man's grasp of reality is borderline. How long have you known him?"

"A long time. All my life, nearly."

"Ah, well, I suppose that makes it difficult. Well! Do I dare try to see you to your door?"

Johnny had parked in the street and was already heading across the grass to the front door. She could see the square of white plastic in his hand, but of course Mandala wouldn't notice. He would assume Johnny was letting himself in with a key. They watched in silence as Johnny slid open the door and, without a backward glance, went inside.

"I'd better go," Lou had said, beginning to crack.

And now she stood and looked down at Johnny, shaking her head.

"Let him break one what?" she demanded. "One of the ground rules?"

Johnny clicked his tongue in agreement. "Man takes my woman out for dinner gotta observe a few rules."

She laughed. "While you, of course, observe none at all."

It was the kind of foolish joking they'd shared for years, and if for Lou everything was now given an edge by this crazy, crazy feeling of wishing it were all real, it in no way diminished the pleasure of laughter with Johnny. Increased it, perhaps, the way jogging in stinging rain made you colder but more alive at the same time.

He lifted his arms in mock amazement. "When did I cease to be a gentleman? When did I do one ungentlemanly thing?"

She said, "If there was one soul in Il Piccolo Mondo who didn't understand your ultimatum, they were blind and deaf and not in Il Piccolo Mondo. And it's probably the poor man's favorite place to dine and he'll never be able to go back."

"Money doesn't buy everything," said Johnny, with a faint edge to his voice. "Time the man learned it."

"According to him, he grew up poor."

"What?" said Johnny disbelievingly. "That guy *smells* of Shaughnessy."

"No, does he?" asked Lou, not that she disagreed. "A little West Vancouver in the bouquet, I thought, but that could be latter-day, you know. He says he had a starving mother who always wanted him to make good."

She had so far avoided the necessity of sitting down by wandering around the room, putting on the lamps, turning off the bright overhead, taking off her jacket and hanging it up. But when she was through, the problem of where to sit remained. She almost always sat beside Johnny on the sofa, usually leaning against the arm with her feet up cross-legged or tucked in behind his back. She couldn't sit so close to him tonight; she could feel the physical pull from here, halfway across the room. She didn't intend to make any kind of fool of herself if she could help it. Yet she felt he would think it odd if she sat down opposite him. She stood facing him, arms crossed, smiling.

"If that man had a starving mother, I'll eat tomorrow morning's *Province*, TV guide and all." Johnny snorted.

"Fried or toasted?" she asked sweetly.

He smiled slowly at her. "You gonna cook it for me, Babe?" he asked lazily, so that her heart turned over, because there had been real intent behind the words; and she had a sudden suspicion that he knew and was playing with her.

She gazed at him for a moment of silence. She thought, if it embarrassed him, he wouldn't tease me. At the very least he doesn't mind. "Of course," she said softly, her heart kicking mercilessly in her breast. "Phone or nudge?" She was actively flirting with him now, for perhaps the first time in their lives, and it was nothing like the flirting game they so often played. Lou's blood was pounding in her temples as if she had never taken such a wild leap in her life.

His head tilted back against the cushions, he looked at her from half-lidded eyes. There was a long, long moment of silence. Then, "What happened to us in that truck, Babe?" Johnny asked softly.

The heart of the whole world missed a beat while she looked at him. She felt a half smile stir the corners of her mouth, and her head shook gently from side to side. She took a deep breath, and could say nothing.

"What happened?" he prompted, more softly still, his voice running up her spine like warm velvet.

She closed her eyes for a moment. If this kept up she was going to explode out of her skin. "I don't know," she whispered.

"I'll tell you what happened to me," he said, very, very softly, such promise in his tone that her bones were melting where she stood. "I saw Harry coming out of that house, and the next thing I knew I had you lying on top of me, and that is all I remember of that night, except that I spent the rest of it trying to stop myself dragging you into the bushes. What about you, Babe?"

"I spent the rest of it wishing you would," she admitted, with tremendous relief. Her heart beat so hard she thought it would kill her, and the air between them shimmered.

They looked at each other for a long, silent breath. "What now?" asked Johnny, so quietly he almost mouthed the words.

She shook her head helplessly, and Johnny took a breath and stood up.

"Lou," he said softly.

Now that it was upon them, she was frightened. A lifetime of friendship in the balance. "God, Johnny," she whispered protestingly.

"Lou," he said again, and there was a tone in his voice she had never heard before. As she moved toward him he stepped toward her, large and dark, and when he put his hands on her arms she rocked as though he had struck her, and fell into his embrace.

"Oh, God!" she cried in surprise, because it was too much to bear. "What *is* this?" She tilted her head back to look up into his face, scarcely believing this could be Johnny.

Johnny's breath scraped his throat and he closed his eyes for a moment, then opened them to stare into hers, the pupils wide like a cat's, so that his eyes seemed black.

Now that it was upon them, they were *both* frightened.

He lifted a hand to brush her hair, and the hand was visibly trembling, whether with desire or a sense of danger, or the heady mix of both, he didn't know. He stared at it, as though it were an unfamiliar object, then laughed once in helpless acceptance. His hand slid into her hair, large and strong and trembling until it tightened into firmness, and it touched some chord within her that had never been touched before. Her whole body began to shake, and it frightened her as much as his hand's trembling had frightened him.

"Oh, God, oh, God, it's such a risk!" she said helplessly.

He looked into her eyes. "I'm willing to risk it," he said. "What else can we do?" There was a kind of pleading in his tone, but whether to her or to fate she didn't think even Johnny knew. "What do you want to do?"

She shook her head. "There's no choice, is there?" They stood for a moment in the circle of each other's arms, looking into each other's eyes, and the fact that there was no choice, there could be no saying no, was more frightening than if the passion had been small and containable and had allowed the possibility of choice.

Johnny said, "We'll just have to make a promise to ourselves that if it doesn't work we'll go back to being friends. No matter what."

"All right," she agreed, though her heart was full of *what ifs*.

He said, "I've never been this scared even facing death." They both laughed, a mixture of joy and nervous hilarity buzzing in their blood.

Lou said, "Maybe we should just neck for a while, like teenagers. Make up for what we—" She had been going to say, what we missed when we were young, but as though she had asked him to kiss her, Johnny bent his head. "Good idea," he said softly, and his mouth touched hers, gently, questioningly.

They had kissed many, many times over the years, but not with any intent to passion. Lou's skin shivered into awareness over her whole body. This is Johnny kissing me, she thought in disbelief. Johnny. In spite of all her desire, it didn't seem possible.

"I wish I knew how to do this," she whispered.

Johnny grinned at her. "You mean, you waited for me, Babe? You really don't know how it's done?"

They laughed again, with fewer nerves and much more of their old, familiar, friendly camaraderie. Giggling at the nonsense, Lou thought—but of course, he's right. The way to do this is to laugh our way through it. That's what we have to do.

And that was what they did. They opened a bottle of wine, and took it into the bedroom, and lowered the lights, laughing and teasing, and sidestepping the heat that was building up between them; two friends embarking on a strange new adventure, each more nervous than the other had ever seen them, and wildly high.

The laughter died at last when they were naked and warm under the light duvet, and the single lamp cast magic shadows over the room, their faces, and the summer night. When Johnny lifted himself into the cradle of her hips, and into the waiting heat of honey and musk, the laughing stopped at last, smothered in a torrent of feeling that shocked them both into silence.

They looked at each other in amazement, and each movement of his body in her forced a cry of too much feeling from her throat, and a grunt of uncontrollable response from his.

"What were we *waiting* for?" he said at last, and then it was all burned up into nothing: laughter, smiles, fear, hope, friendship—all were scorched into blackness, and for a moment there was only endless sensation, and the cry of the other carried on the wind.

Chapter 14

They lay on the bed in the darkness of early morning, the blind and the window open, gazing out over the street and the Lagoon beyond. The street was quiet. At this moment, the whole city seemed quiet—dreamlessly asleep under the high vault of heaven and the steady flicker of its scattered, mysterious pinpoints of light.

On the far side of the Lagoon, they watched the intermittent sweep of lights of cars along the Park highway, reflecting off the black, wind-rippled surface of the water. The breeze was cool, coming in from the mountains to brush gently over their faces and bodies. Summer's scents were soft on the wind, blossom and earth and sea in a mixture as sweet as summer love.

Lou lay naked on the sheet, the duvet lightly covering her legs and hips, resting on her elbows with a pillow tucked in under her breasts. Johnny was beside her, on one elbow, his hand propped under his ear, the other reaching out at intervals to stroke her back, for the pleasure of watching her skin in moonshadow, shivering under his touch.

They talked about Julie, and about Jerry Mandala. The world had realigned itself since midnight, but they did not know quite what that meant, or how to say so, each afraid that for the other it had only rocked a little on its axis. So they lay calmly discussing everything except what was uppermost on both their minds, as though their friendship and their lives had not been forever changed by what had happened between them.

"So what are you telling me?" Lou said softly. "The stories about Jerry Mandala's success are all a crock?"

"The used car lot certainly is. As far as I can find out from the public record, the used car lot was financially in the red, or close to it, for most of its life. And he didn't start from scratch, either, the way he likes people to believe. He started with a quarter of a million dollars."

"How on earth do you know all this?" she demanded.

He grinned. "Research, Babe. The thing that journalists do, you know?" He stood up to pick up his jeans and pulled out his cigars and a lighter.

"I thought you were really busy," Lou said.

Johnny shrugged. "The worst was last week. Anyway, now I've hired Harry Thornton full-time, so we're getting back to normal." He tossed his jeans on her trunk and returned to the subject. "That money was Mandala's inheritance when his father died," he said, sinking back onto the bed, "and he was such an incompetent businessman, as I said, that most of it went down the tube."

"I don't see how that's possible, Johnny," Lou protested. "I mean, he's very rich now, isn't he? Are you telling me he's living on—what?"

"I don't know what he's living on. But I'd like to find out. Somebody bankrolled him for his big move into real estate, and since it wasn't the car business, who was it?" He lit a cigar and blew the smoke out toward the ceiling.

She backtracked. "He can't have inherited so much money. He told me his family was poor."

"He tells everybody his family was poor. His family wasn't poor. I know that by looking at him, but in any case I checked it." He was belatedly looking around for an ashtray. "He went to Upper Canada College, and he takes a lot of trouble to hide the fact."

"What's Upper Canada College?" Lou dumped some trinkets onto the windowsill and wordlessly handed him the little china dish.

"A private school for the sons of the privileged in Toronto. I told you, the guy smells of Shaughnessy. Well, you know what I mean," he amended. "I'm not suggesting he's exactly old money."

Lou looked over at him, beautiful as a pagan god in the summer moonlight, his body marble and shadow. One strong hand held the ashtray steady on the bed between them as she moved.

"What do you mean, you can tell by looking at him that he didn't grow up poor?"

"I grew up poor. You can recognize someone else who has. He didn't."

"Can you really?"

"A lot of the time, yeah."

"But up till you were eleven or twelve—"

"Yeah, before my father died, and for a couple of years after, we were middle-class, Babe. But you can forget an awful lot at that age, believe me. By the time I was thirteen I felt as though I'd lived in the East End all my life."

"Did you ever think that the reason you failed grade five was simply because your father died that year?" she asked suddenly.

He shrugged.

"I've thought since that they should have passed you anyway. It was so obvious you were too intelligent to be repeating a grade. Amazing how little child psychology was around in those days, when you think of it. So cruel."

"Yeah, I guess so."

It was one area he hardly ever talked about, but now Lou had a courage she'd never quite had before, to push it.

"And on top of that you had to move away from all your friends…. I still don't know why the house had to be sold."

"The bank repossessed it. My father didn't believe in insurance and didn't have mortgage insurance on the house. My mother couldn't keep up the payments."

She said slowly, "You've never told me that before."

He shrugged. "When it happened I guess I was too embarrassed and hurt to tell anybody anything. Later, what significance did it have?"

"I don't know. It's part of you, part of who you are."

"Yup," said Johnny, as though he were remembering scenes in his head. "Yeah, it is that."

"It must have been hard, making the adjustment to the East End. Worse than if you *had* grown up there."

"Maybe," said Johnny. "I was a bit of a late grower, so I was smaller than a lot of the guys. But once I grew, I never had any more trouble. I could beat the pants off anybody, so they didn't mess with me much."

She smiled at him. He looked dangerous just lying there, his hair falling over his hand, his day-old beard already shadowing his chin with black. The sight of him made her breath catch in her throat. She opened her mouth to tell him that she loved him and the past didn't matter, but said something else instead.

"And it's because of that that you knew Jerry Mandala's story about his past was a lie?"

"I've always thought there was something about Mandala that stank." Johnny butted his cigar and rolled over on his stomach to set the ashtray on the wide windowsill at the head of the bed. She felt the warmth of his arm near her own, and that small breath was enough to fan the embers in the pit of her stomach into glowing life.

"That would be Nellie, I suppose," Lou said, heaving a deep sigh as Johnny rolled onto his side, facing her, and then onto his back, his arms sliding around her and easing her gently onto his chest.

"Mm-hmm," he said. She smiled down at his face, her indrawn breath a little hiss as his hand moved down her back. His leg kicked twice, and the duvet slithered to the floor. She shivered sensuously again as a gust of mountain air blew in through the window and straight down over her body to her toes.

He didn't say any more. His arms tightened around her, and as her mouth came down toward his, his hand moved to cup the back of her head.

The kiss was heartbreakingly sweet, the taste of flowers on their lips. He kissed her gently, sensuously, his lips warm and soft. When she lifted her head, his hand touched her lips and, turning her lower lip back, he raised his head to put his mouth to the soft inner flesh. He sucked it lightly, and a sensuous thrill rippled through her body, surprising the embers into flame.

Their first lovemaking had been a plain, simple, satisfying coupling, as though they knew each other too well to be so soon comfortable with any very erotic exploration of their bodies. Now, however, he began to make love to her in a pure, sensuous dedication to her body's pleasure—not intent, not demanding, but with the delicate craftsmanship of a musician tuning a fine instrument.

He asked nothing from her, not even her response. He simply gave, and gave again. He did not drink in her response, the way her husband had done, feeding on her need to fire his own passion, but only accepted her cries as soundings, his guide to the intricacies of her body and the touch that made it sing the truest note.

It sang a song of mountains and wind and sea; wild, open, and free; and whether it was Johnny or whether it was the wind that loved her she did not know: she only knew that her pleasure was the freest gift she had ever been given.

He entered her the moment she asked him to, as if his body were an instrument for her pleasure, entirely at her command; and she could allow it to be so; she could accept what he offered with gratitude, not needing his need, but only desiring his touch.

Images of pleasure flashed through her mind: statues, paintings, rich cloth, wildflowers. She saw a peach tree laden with ripe, heavy fruit, its branches low to the ground, and lightly, easily, she lifted a hand to the nearest one. The fruit touched her palm, furred and warm, and her body shook with mingled pleasure and delight, and she called out her startled joy that such richness was possible in the world. "Yes," said Johnny approvingly, on a long-drawn breath. "Yes." She felt the pleasure ripple between their two bodies then, as with no effort, no strain at all, the peach fell into her palm, and was hers.

"Here's another thing," she later said musingly, when the sky was lighter and the rising sun was painting Lost Lagoon in heavy strokes of pink and gold. "Julie never hinted that Butch wasn't Canadian. But Jerry Mandala, and all the newspaper articles about the accident, say that David Stockton was an American who was in Vietnam in the early seventies. They say that's where he got his pilot training."

"Yeah," said Johnny. "I know."

"Yeah. But he couldn't have been in Oakalla and Vietnam at the same time, could he?"

"Nope."

"Well, does it strike you, Johnny, that it's one thing if they made a mistake about his background, or he lied about it, but it's something else again when you try to figure out—if he wasn't in Vietnam, where did he get his pilot training?"

Johnny breathed deeply. "Yes, that does strike me."

"I mean he was what—nineteen, when he went into Oakalla? He sure didn't get his license before that. And you say he's got a long record since then. How likely is it that he managed to squeeze pilot training into a life like that?''

"Well, it's just barely possible, but he sure isn't likely to have gotten a lot of flying time in. Flying is an expensive habit.''

"Could Jerry Mandala possibly have been stupid enough to send the Solicitor-General up with a barely qualified pilot?''

"More likely a case of being stupid enough to take the man's word for it that he was fully qualified.''

"But it still doesn't make sense, really, does it?''

"Not a whole helluva lot," he agreed. "But I suppose guys do learn to fly without getting their license. And a man with enough ego might convince himself he could do it, you know.''

"There is something going on here, Johnny. There really is. I'd really like to find out what it is.''

He laughed. "Just think of how much more Mandala would like to stop you finding out what it is.''

"Yes, but I don't see why he has to know.''

"Don't you? Take it from me, he will.''

She rolled over onto her stomach, leaned over and absently kissed his shoulder. Her body inclined toward him in remembered gratitude.

"Well, I think I can be careful.''

He laughed again. "You can be a lot more than careful, Babe. You can forget all about it and leave it to the cops. Do you think they're going to walk away from this? It's stinking in everybody's nose.''

"They aren't saying much, if that's so.''

"No, and they won't. Use your head. The guy's got friends in high places. They can't say damn all about suspicion until they've got proof.''

"Or maybe they can't go looking for the proof at all.''

"Give me a break," said Johnny irritably. "How corrupt do you think these guys are?''

"Who? Politicians? About as corrupt as it gets."

"I meant the Mounties."

"I'm not talking about them being corrupt. I'm talking about them not being allowed to investigate properly."

"Uh-huh. And who's going to stop them? Mandala? Let me tell you something, Babe. There might be things you can buy your way out of, I'm not saying there aren't. But nobody is going to buy their way out of this one. Trust me."

"You said he has friends in high places," she said stubbornly.

"Not high enough for that."

"Anyway," she said, conceding the point. "I'm still mad at that man—who is it, Goldring—for not listening to me about Julie. I'd really like to show him."

He was shaking his head. "You'll show him, all right. You'll show him your dead body."

"No, I won't."

"No, you won't. Because you are going to pretend you never heard of your friend Julie or her friend Butch. Or Jerry Mandala. You're going to stop even thinking about this thing, right now. I mean it."

"Anyway, it's ridiculous to say he's going to kill me. That's murder, and I don't suppose you buy your way out of that, either."

He took a deep, impatient breath. "No. You just make damn sure it doesn't look like murder. What do you think Mandala had a guy like Stockton on his payroll for? To pick him flowers?"

She was shocked at that. "But he was his chauffeur!"

"Sure he was."

"Are you telling me that Butch did Mandala's dirty work?"

"Are you telling me he would have hired a chauffeur without checking to see if he had a record?"

"Oh," she said, as it sank in, and then in a different tone, "Oh."

"What?" asked Johnny, as her eyes met his.

"You're lying to me," she said evenly.

"I am not lying to you!"

"Yes, you are. A minute ago you said Mandala would have taken Butch's word for it that he was a pilot. Now you're saying he wouldn't have hired him even to be a chauffeur without checking him up since birth." She gazed at him. "What do you know, Johnny? Tell me."

He sighed. "What I know is that whatever this is, it is damned dirty and you have got to leave it alone. Can't you hear what I've been telling you?"

She said slowly, "It isn't possible that David Stockton was piloting that plane, is it? That's what you've figured out. Jerry Mandala would have checked him out thoroughly, and if he'd done that, the police would have the information. And if he wasn't flying the plane, then he may not be missing at all. He may be—with Julie." She looked at him.

"Damn it!" said Johnny feelingly. "I wish to hell you'd stop thinking!"

"That's what you've been trying to stop me from figuring out," she said accusingly.

He said, "Will you forget Julie! She is going to lead you into more trouble than you can handle! More than I can handle! One hell of a lot more!"

She said, ignoring him, "That's why Mandala offered me a job. He must figure I'm the only person who can put a face on David Stockton. The papers say the cops haven't been able to trace him at all."

"Mandala offered you a job?"

"One that will conveniently send me out of town," she went on. "The papers say there were too many David Stocktons in Vietnam and they haven't been able to trace him yet. But I know enough..." She trailed off, and looked up to find Johnny watching her expectantly.

"You've finally figured it out," he drawled. "Congratulations."

"And the only other person who knows is Julie Hastings. If I'm in danger now, she was in danger two weeks ago," Lou said through her teeth, fear somehow feeding her anger. "You figured that out, too, didn't you?"

He didn't reply.

"You were just going to throw Julie to the wolves, Johnny? Is that what you were going to do?"

He looked at her. "Do you expect me to care more about Julie than I do about you?"

"I expect you not to lie to me when a friend of mine is in danger," she said flatly.

"You can't do anything about it. All you can do is put yourself in danger, too. How will that help Julie?"

"I don't know," said Lou. "All I know is, you shouldn't have lied to me about it."

Johnny swore, sat up, and swung his legs over the side of the bed. He leaned over to pull his wristwatch from the windowsill. "Hell!" he muttered. "Six-thirty. I have to get going." He turned on the bed to look down at her. "Are you going to leave this alone? Can I trust you out of my sight?"

"Can I trust you out of mine?" she countered.

He dropped his hands onto his thighs in exasperation and heaved himself to his feet. He stood looking down at her for a moment, but all the loving camaraderie of the night had dissipated, and they gazed at each other in deep misunderstanding. He shook his head and bent to find his clothes, putting them on in silence.

Neither of them spoke a word till he was finished. Then he turned to her again. "Never mind me and what I've done," he said. "Just use your common sense, okay? Just think about it before you do anything. Take a long, hard look at what it means to be a threat to a man like Jerry Mandala."

She couldn't remember when she had ever felt so betrayed by Johnny, or so angry with him. She thought, it was too much of a risk, after all. We should never have taken such a risk.

"See you later, Johnny," she said quietly, and then sat listening as his footsteps crossed the sitting room and he let himself out.

Chapter 15

Is Sandy McMaster here?"

"Who are you, please?" The woman in front of her was a fairly standard example of a Burnaby housewife, overweight but pretty, unharassed. She probably took creative writing or pottery classes at the local community center, and if she wasn't entirely fulfilled, she had enough of a creative outlet to be happy waiting for more till the children were grown.

"My name is Lou Patch. I'm—"

"Oh, yeah, I *thought* I recognized you. Funny how much that little sketch over your column looks like you. I saw you on TV once, too. Hi! How can I help you?"

"It's actually your husband I'd like to speak to, if I may. Is he here?"

"He's here, but he's not well. Is there something I could help you with?"

Lou paused. "Yes, maybe you could. Would it be—do you have a few minutes?"

"Sure!" said Mrs. McMaster. "Come on, it's a lovely day, we'll sit outside." She came out on the front step, carefully closed the door, and led Lou down the walk and around the house to the patio at the back. There was something about the performance that disconcerted Lou, but she couldn't quite peg it. The backyard, although filled with the normal suburban detritus, was surprisingly pleasant—dotted with nearly mature trees and blossoming with all the climbing plants. There was a mixture of sun and shade, and a pleasant corner held the standard cedar table and chairs.

Lou was reminded of Kitsilano summers. Cookouts with hotdogs and roast corn on the cob, and the tent pitched for sleeping out. As she sank into a chair and accepted Mrs. McMaster's offer of lemonade, a child's voice cried out, and a small red-haired ruffian streaked out the back door and up to his mother, detailing in nearly incomprehensible language some outrage that had taken place within.

"Now, come on, Joey, you know you have to share your toys," said his young mother with tolerant firmness, and Lou was suddenly struck by the realization that Mrs. McMaster was a good seven years younger than she was. She watched as the mother crouched down now, reasoning with the still unhappy child in a low voice, and an unaccustomed pang struck her heart. She had left it so late.

Mrs. McMaster stood up with an order to her son to bring Rajib outside to play, because it was too nice to play indoors, and turned back to Lou at the table. "Oh, lemonade!" she reminded herself, in the act of pulling out a chair. "Hang on, I'll just get it."

Joey and Rajib came out of the house, restored to good fellowship. "And I'll go first, and then you can go!" Joey was assuring Rajib. They were attractive children, each in their own way—Joey was standard Canadian issue, with a shock of sandy-red hair, a snub nose, and all-over freckles; Rajib was dark-haired, smoky skinned, almost certainly a first-generation Canadian, with thick-lashed black eyes that melted Lou in her tracks.

"Hello." She smiled as this impossible gaze turned on her.

"Hello," returned Rajib. Joey was already running towards the swing.

"Come on," he called.

Rajib was a year or two younger than Joey, Lou guessed—he hadn't yet quite assumed the rowdy little-boy personality. Slowly he came to her side and held up a battered, much-loved soft toy. "My mommy gave me this," he said.

He leaned against her knee, and she bent over him in sudden protectiveness. "Did she?" she asked, thinking, how easy it is to love children. It's just instant. "What do you call him?"

"Fluff," said the child. "Because he's fluffy."

It had probably been true, a year or so ago. But now the fluff was flattened with wear and tears and a certain amount of dirt. Lou smiled and stroked it, unsure of its exact animal nature—cat? dog? bear? She was in a small reverie and came out of it with a start, to realize that she'd been guessing at the child's age, working out how old she had been when he was born, and trying to remember what she had done in the years between that was important.

Mrs. McMaster returned with a tray of lemonade and cookies. "Is Rajib showing you Fluffy? Come on, Joey," she called. "Time for cookies."

"Not Fluffy. Fluff!" explained the child.

"Fluff."

It took some time for her to settle the two little boys with their plastic glasses of lemonade and a cookie each, and Lou watched the operation from a position somewhere in the no-man's-land between pleasure and pain, between bitter and sweet. She could have had a child that age. Solly had wanted children. What had she thought so important that she had insisted on putting it off? It was very hard to remember.

Things that had seemed important then no longer ranked high on the list.

You'll be thirty-eight soon, an inner voice told her. I think you've put it off forever.

"I'm sorry about that," said Mrs. McMaster, but with the obvious self-assurance of a woman who knows that her concerns center on important things. She was not really sorry the children had demanded her attention. "Now, what can I do for you?"

"I'm trying to find out something about the man who flew Jerry Mandala's plane the day it went missing," Lou said. "I thought your husband might be able to tell me something."

"Well, he can't. The police have been asking him over and over. But he wasn't consulted in the hiring, he didn't even know a backup pilot had *been* hired until that day."

"That's interesting. What did happen that day? Do you know?"

"Well, only from listening to my husband tell the story to the police a few times. You're the first journalist, thank God, and I hope you're the last. He went to the airport to fly the plane up to Erehwemos, and got all the flight check done and all, but he just suddenly felt sick. He's still got it, it's that Yuppie flu or something, *I* think, because it just makes him so tired all day, he can't move."

"I've heard about that," Lou said in sympathy.

"Well, he went and called Mr. Mandala up on Erehwemos and said he wouldn't be safe to fly the plane, and Mr. Mandala said that Mr. Harrison was already on his way to the airport in the limousine, and that Sandy should tell the chauffeur that *he'd* have to fly the plane up. Sandy was really surprised. He didn't know anything about the chauffeur having his license. But he took Mr. Mandala's word for it, of course. So Butch—that's the chauffeur—got into the plane with Mr. Harrison, and Sandy drove the limousine back to the airport parking lot, and then took a bus home, because he felt so ill. He came in and just collapsed in bed for twenty-four hours. I didn't know what was wrong. The next day I had to go out to the airport and bring our car back. And he's been feeling low ever since.''

"That's too bad. I've heard it can last and last."

"Mr. Mandala's being very good about it. He's paying him full wages, and he doesn't complain at all. Some people don't believe in that Yuppie flu, you know. They say it's all in the mind. But it's real. Mr. Mandala says he understands completely, and Sandy should just concentrate on getting better. That's kind, isn't it?''

"Yes, it is. Especially in this day and age."

"Oh, this isn't the sixties, that's for sure," agreed Mrs. McMaster.

"I wonder..." Lou began hesitantly, "is your husband actually in bed with this?''

"What—now?" said the woman, and Lou caught the first flicker of nervous strain in her eyes. Something was bothering her. It hadn't taken any toll yet, but it was the sort of thing that would, given time. Lou nodded carefully.

"I was hoping I might just ask him one question," she said.

"Something I can't answer?"

"Just his opinion about a possibility." The woman opened her mouth to say no, and Lou forestalled her. "I'm not here officially as a reporter. It's personal. A friend of mine is missing, and she was a friend of David Stockton. I'm trying to find out if she—well, I thought your husband might have seen her with him.''

Mrs. McMaster jerked her head consideringly. "Well, he's not in bed, he's in front of the TV. That's about all he can do. I can go and ask him..." She paused. "Mr. Mandala said he shouldn't be disturbed." Lou said nothing. "Well, I'll go ask him. It can't hurt."

A few minutes later she came back and ushered Lou into the living room, where a sandy-haired, balding man sat slumped in a big easy chair, the channel-changer on the arm. The sound of the television had been killed. The picture showed a game show in progress, people screaming in silent excitement.

"Barb says you want to ask me a question," said the man quietly. He looked worn and frightened.

"Yes, I..." Lou hesitated, suddenly warily deciding not to ask him outright if he had actually seen Butch fly the plane. "It's about David Stockton. I think he is—was—the friend of a friend of mine. My friend left town suddenly— well, she disappeared, and I've been operating on the assumption that Butch...came and got her back. She'd left him. I was wondering—is there any chance that he took her aboard that plane?"

It was obvious that McMaster was wary. His eyes shifted away from hers to the television screen to her left. He thought for a minute. "There was nobody in the car. See, I'd know that, because I had to drive the car back from dockside to the airport parking lot. No, she wasn't there."

"Could she possibly have gotten into the plane after you left?"

"No," he said at once. "Well, I don't think so. It's a sea-plane, you know. We were out at the end of the dock."

"Did you see the plane take off before you left the airport?"

"Uh—" His eyes switched from hers to the TV screen again. "Wuh—I don't think so."

"Well, you were so sick, weren't you, Sandy?" Mrs. McMaster added from the doorway. Lou hadn't known she was there.

"Yeah, that's right. I was pretty far gone. I don't know how long it took me to get back to the car."

"The papers say the flight plan was filed by you and the change of pilots was never noted," Lou slipped in. "Shouldn't David Stockton have notified the tower about the change of pilot?"

"Oh, yeah, he should've. I told him to do it, before I left. I told him I was too sick to do it, he'd have to do it. I don't know why he didn't."

Something was wrong; something was making him nervous, making him lie. Lou could detect the lie in the tone, but not what the lie was. Not which of the many statements was the lie. She was nearly certain now that David Stockton had not been flying the plane, and if that were the case, nothing here made sense.

"And there was really nobody else on that plane except David Stockton and Gordon Harrison?"

"That's right."

"No girl anywhere around that you remember noticing? Julie's short and dark, long hair, pretty, very slim. You don't remember seeing anyone like that?" She was playing for time now, looking for questions that might shake him up, make him tell her the truth.

"Not that I remember."

"Did that plane have the capacity to fly to Hong Kong?" she asked abruptly.

"A Sea Otter? Of course not."

"Seattle?"

"Seattle? Seattle's closer than Erehwemos."

"And they could have caught a commercial flight there. Or gotten aboard a bigger plane."

"What are you talking about?"

"Are you absolutely sure it was David Stockton who flew the plane that day?"

"What are you suggesting?" His angry tone was half-hearted, as though he wanted to be indignant but didn't have the stamina.

"Julie never told me that David was a pilot." She waited. "I don't think he was. What really happened that day?"

Sandy McMaster had a can of beer tucked into his lap. Lou didn't notice it till it came flying at her head. She put up an arm to shield herself, and beer foamed out of the can and down over her neck and lap.

"You've been told what happened!" he said hoarsely, as she futilely tried to wipe off the foaming liquid. She hated the smell of beer. "And so have the police. Now get the hell out of here!"

"—ty-five thousand dollars!" roared the television, pressed into life.

Lou stood up. Barb McMaster was in the doorway, mouthing horrified apologies. Lou ignored her. "Did it ever occur to you that the plane might not have crashed at all?" she said, over the noise.

He stared up at her, riveted. "What do you mean?" he asked hoarsely. He knew something; for sure he knew something. What?

"Politicians do get kidnapped, you know. And my friend Julie saw Butch the day after the plane disappeared. So either he wasn't piloting the plane, or it never really went down. Which, do you think?"

"I think if your friend Julie saw Butch after the plane disappeared I'd like to know why you were asking me if she was on the damn thing!" McMaster said loudly. "Barb, get her out of here!"

"That was a pretty convenient flu you got that day. Did it ever occur to you that you might have been drugged with something, to make sure you couldn't fly?" Lou pressed.

He frowned. "No," he said. "No, that possibility never occurred to me."

"And did it ever occur to you that the simplest solution to all of this is that you did fly the plane yourself and you're now lying about it?"

The remote control crashed to the ground as Sandy McMaster got to his feet. He cursed her crudely. "If you don't get the hell out of here," he warned, "I'll personally—"

Barb McMaster, she noted without surprise, was crying. "Please, please, go away," she was saying, pulling at Lou, then pushing her toward the front door. "God, how much more do we have to take?"

"If I ever see you again, I'll break your neck!" she heard, as the door closed on her, and she was left standing on the step with the hot Burnaby sun beating down on her head.

Chapter 16

At home, Lou made a pot of coffee, took a pen and note-book, put her feet up, and tried to look at possibilities. It seemed to her the problem was that there were too many of them. If she was going to locate Julie, she had to narrow things down to the likeliest possibilities first.

Hypothesis one, she wrote. Julie was wrong about seeing Butch after the plane went missing. Butch was the pilot. The plane and Butch are missing. Julie got a job offer in Hong Kong, unrelated.

Problem: Butch not likely a pilot.

Hypothesis two: There are two identical-looking David Stocktons—a pilot, and Butch. Both of them work for Jerry Mandala.

Problem: Absolutely impossible.

Hypothesis three: The plane didn't actually go missing, but was taken somewhere deliberately. Kidnap. Butch flew the plane, came back later to get Julie.

Problems: no ransom demand yet, as far as we know. Why bother with Julie?

Hypothesis four: Same as above, but Sandy McMaster flew plane. Butch came and got Julie before doing disappearing act.

Problem: Why say Butch was flying plane?

Hypothesis five: Butch flew plane; it went missing. Mandala, knowing he wasn't legally licensed pilot, or worried about scandal if his past were revealed, grabbed Julie out of fear she would talk and got her out of the way. Maybe by offering her job in Hong Kong.

Problem: Sandy McMaster's reactions don't jibe with it. This scenario doesn't require lies from him.

Hypothesis six: Mandala wasn't on Erehwemos at all. He flew the plane in some variation of kidnapping plot.

Problem: Can Mandala fly? Why say Butch was flying?

Now that she had them down on paper, the possibilities seemed a lot narrower and easier to look at. Either Butch was flying the plane, or he wasn't; either the plane had legitimately crashed or gone missing, or it hadn't.

If Butch wasn't flying the plane, who was? If Butch wasn't flying the plane, why say he was?

Having written that, Lou sat back and gazed into space. That was really the question at the heart of the whole thing, because Butch, with his criminal record, would surely be the last person one would pick for a cover-up. Yet she was nearly convinced he could not have been flying that plane.

Was it possible the meeting with Harrison had been so urgent that Mandala had let Butch fly; that even though he had no license, Butch could fly a plane, and Mandala knew it, but he had run into trouble he couldn't cope with and now Mandala had to cover up his negligence?

Suppose Gordon Harrison were a pilot, but for some reason not allowed to fly? But Mandala wouldn't care about covering that up once the plane went missing.

Suppose Gordon Harrison had wanted to do a disappearing trick, like that English lord or Australian politician, or both, a few years ago? Suppose he'd borrowed

Mandala's plane to do it, and they bribed Butch to disappear... to Hong Kong?

But why did they need Butch at all? If Gordon Harrison could fly... if Gordon Harrison couldn't fly, and Butch couldn't fly, there had to be a pilot. Mandala? But if they were going to fake a missing plane, the pilot as well as Harrison had to disappear.

Sandy McMaster couldn't disappear. Not with a wife and kid in Burnaby to worry about.

Lou returned to the conclusion that kept recurring to her mind in spite of everything—the most likely circumstance was that Sandy McMaster had flown the plane. He had filed a flight plan. It had never been changed. The only witness to his return from the airport was his wife. His illness was nebulous, unprovable—Yuppie flu. Mandala was paying him to keep out of circulation. He was the only person involved whose ability to pilot was not in question.

Suppose Sandy McMaster flew Harrison somewhere nearby, then returned home, pretending he hadn't taken the flight. Suppose from there, Gordon Harrison disappeared.

Somewhere nearby. Jerry Mandala had talked about a gambling ship that cruised out beyond the twelve-mile limit. Suppose the plane had landed there, and Gordon Harrison had boarded in some kind of disguise, and was supplied with a false passport by Jerry Mandala, and the ship cruised down to Seattle, for example, and dropped him? Suppose they picked someone with not much to lose and bribed him to disappear at the same time?

But why Butch? Why not someone with an actual pilot's license? That spoke of hurry, grabbing whoever was to hand. Yet something like this would surely have to be planned well in advance. And why not say Harrison was flying the plane himself?

Where was the plane? Painted over with new numbers? Sold? Warehoused while the heat was on?

Even with all the drawbacks, this was the closest she'd come to a solution that seemed reasonable. It fit most of the parameters.

It meant Gordon Harrison had left himself open to blackmail with at least three people—Mandala, McMaster, and Butch.

But it fit most of the parameters.

At that exact point in her ruminations, Lou's phone rang. She leaned over the sofa arm to scoop it up.

"Jerry Mandala here," said his voice. "I was wondering if you're doing anything tonight."

"Not a thing," sang Lou.

"Is your bodyguard on duty?"

"I think I finally cured him of that."

"Well, what about dinner? Where would you like to go?"

"Well..." Lou said slowly, "this may be too much of a busman's holiday to you, but would you believe I've never gambled in my life?"

"I love busmen's holidays. Tonight you're going to gamble," promised Jerry Mandala, with more truth than she knew.

"You stupid cow!" Johnny shouted at her. "You stupid, witless—! What do you think you're playing at?"

Johnny had hardly shouted at her in her life. Lou stiffened. "Don't shout at me," she said coldly. "He asked me out for dinner. I thought it was a good chance to check out the casino ship. What do you want me to do?"

"I want you to say no! Do you have any idea what you're playing with?"

"Look, I came in to tell you about it so in case I don't come back you at least know where I am. If you'd rather not know, forget about it."

"You really think you've got this under control, don't you, Babe?" he said scathingly. He was sitting leaning over his desk at her, his fingers arched against the rough wooden surface, his arm stiff, the other on the arm of his chair. He tapped his fingers. He couldn't remember ever being so purely furious in his life. "'In case you don't come back!'" he repeated, brutally sarcastic. "You think it's a joke, don't you? Do you have any idea how close you'd really be to never coming back if you went with that guy tonight? God, women!"

Lou started a slow burn. "Don't talk to me like that, Johnny," she ordered. "I'm trying to tell you that what I think is that Gordon Harrison might have decided to—"

"You know what? I don't give a tinker's blast what you think. Because you damned well don't think. I am trying to tell *you* that the guy has serious Hong Kong Mafia connections. Does that grab you at all?" he demanded.

Lou gasped. "Mandala or Harrison?"

"Don't be so naive. Maybe that's your problem. You're too bloody naive."

"What do you mean?" she demanded, through clenched teeth.

"Lie down with dogs, get up with fleas," he said shortly. "And that goes for you, too."

Lou's face went white, then pink. "How dare you!" she whispered furiously.

His elbow on the desk, he pointed one strong forefinger at her. "I'm telling you now. You get involved with that guy, and you'll have blood on your conscience sooner or later. If not on your hands."

Lou jumped to her feet. "I have no intention of getting involved with Jerry Mandala."

"What you intend and what you get are often two very different things in this life. Or haven't you noticed?"

"Are you implying—?"

"Look," said Johnny roughly. "I'm not going to argue with you. I want you to cancel this thing tonight. Can I count on you to do that?"

Not now he couldn't. Not after the way he'd spoken to her. She stared at him, her jaw set. If she could have monitored her thoughts, she'd have discovered that what she was thinking was, sex ruins everything. I wish we'd never—

"Fine," said Johnny, interpreting her silence and the line of her jaw. "Allow me to tell you that they don't come any stupider than you're being right now. If you get out of this in one piece, give me a call some day. Right now, I have work to do."

He reached to pick up the phone, then his eyes met hers again. She had never seen them so darkly furious, not with her. But then, she'd never been so angry with him.

"If I get out of this in one piece," she said, "I won't speak to you again if you pay me!"

Johnny shook his head. "Oh, you'll be well above *my* touch, Babe."

She slammed his office door. On the other side, she had the satisfaction of hearing something fall.

Vancouver is a city of mostly casual dressers. Lou had few outfits smart enough for what she imagined the casino yacht would demand, and the best of those was the dress she had worn to Il Piccolo Mondo with Mandala. In a state of general dissatisfaction with everything, she tried on one or two other things, but at last decided that with different accessories the black dress would do.

It was a slim calf-length dress of pleated watered silk with no back. The last time she had put it on, Johnny had helped her take it off, but she was damned if she was going to think about that. High on the halter-style shoestring neckstrap, she pinned the amethyst and turquoise butterfly that she had worn before, but tonight, instead of the matching black jacket, she slipped around her shoulders a Chinese silk stole in swirls of purple, turquoise and blue. On her ears were amethyst earrings, on her feet, after some thought, she decided on low-heeled pumps. On a boat you never knew.

She looked like a woman dressed to kill. The butterfly had hinged wings that moved delicately when she breathed, catching the light, and naturally drew the eye to the smoothly tanned skin beneath, and then to the invitingly shadowed vale between her breasts. It was Johnny's favorite outfit on her. He had given her the butterfly brooch for her thirty-fifth birthday. In her mood of seething rage against Johnny, she assumed that she was wearing the outfit in spite of that fact, rather than because of it.

Jerry Mandala smiled when he saw her, and said in a low mellifluous voice, "I have to say it—I don't blame that fella."

Lou smiled questioningly. "What fella?"

"The one who wants to keep you all to himself. Is he going to be on our tail tonight?"

"Not if he knows what's good for him," Lou said with unconcealed animosity, and Mandala laughed.

They drove along the Upper Levels Highway toward Horseshoe Bay, where, she assumed, they would go aboard the yacht. Tonight there was no full moon, and no feeling of deep companionship on the journey. The last time she had been on this road, Lou thought, was her last night of uncomplicated friendship with Johnny. My God, she thought, what have we done? We didn't really give it two minutes' thought. And now it's too late. Even through her anger she knew that losing Johnny as a friend could kill her.

Jerry turned off before the Horseshoe Bay exit, and as he followed a narrow road down toward the sea, her heart set up a slow, frightening hammer beat in her temples. Where on earth was he taking her?

The small road ended at the water before she had time to think what to do. At the end of a single floating dock a small yellow seaplane rode gently on the water.

The first real inkling of how stupid and thoughtless she had been in undertaking this, how right Johnny had been, began to creep over her.

"What now?" she asked lightly, hoping he could not hear panic in her voice.

He glanced at her in surprise as he held open her door. "Now we fly to the other side of Vancouver Island, and pick up the yacht," he explained. She smiled at her own stupidity. He had told her before that they had to go beyond the twelve-mile limit for the gambling to be legal, and a trip like that by ship would have taken hours.

But the sense of unease remained. She could see, at last, that if Jerry Mandala did mean her harm, as Johnny so obviously thought, she really had delivered herself into his power. Remorse swept through her like a high wind. How stupidly foolhardy she was being, after all. And all because, she could admit it now, Johnny had made her mad.

As she climbed aboard the little plane, she comforted herself with the thought that no one was likely to kill her to protect a politician who wanted to disappear. It simply wouldn't be worth it. And threats she could handle: if they let Julie go, she would engage to shut up about what little she knew of Gordon Harrison's disappearance.

There was no pilot. Jerry Mandala settled behind the controls himself. Hypothesis six became possible. In fact, she was living out hypothesis six. She was actually in a seaplane, bound for the casino ship, just as she imagined Gordon Harrison had been, a couple of weeks ago. The thought gave her very little comfort.

She looked around. "Is this new?" she asked, shouting a little to be heard over the engine drone.

"No, this is my second plane," said Mandala. "I had two. I haven't bought a replacement for the other yet. It seems a bit premature—we're still hoping it will be found, though I can't say I imagine it'll be in one piece."

"I didn't realize you could fly yourself."

"I learned as a kid. But it's usually not practicable for me to fly myself. I only do it on occasion."

She looked over at him. "You know, I didn't realize I was putting you to so much trouble when I asked—"

Mandala shook his head. "Don't even think about it. I like to fly, keeps my hand in. And I like to visit the casino regularly. I haven't been for a while."

"Not since your plane—"

"A while before that, even," he said, and she reminded herself not to think she could ask pointed questions without making the fact obvious.

In a small plane, it was a long flight, the more so because the engine was noisy and conversation was a strain. "Just over an hour," Mandala explained once. "This thing cruises at about one fifty," and just over an hour was plenty of time for thoughts to come creeping back about where he might be taking her if he had something other than gambling on his mind. The last twenty minutes were an increasing strain, and she stared without seeing at the beauty of the sunset and the island scenery so close below.

"There she is," said Mandala at last, pointing, and Lou breathed an irrepressible sigh of relief that she hoped would sound like excitement.

It was a beautiful yacht, more beautiful because of all the time Lou had spent in the air wondering if she would ever see it. It was smaller than she had anticipated—clean, white and shining, with elegant lines, it rode lightly on the water, glowing softly golden in the rays of the evening sun.

"Like her?" asked Mandala, as, a few minutes later, he was helping her up the gangway from the dock.

"Beautiful!" Lou gushed, overdoing her real admiration and hoping she looked like a woman with money on her mind. "What's she called?"

"*Easy Money,*" Mandala told her. "Welcome aboard."

The casino was a huge room midship, beautifully carpeted and appointed, its roulette wheels glowing temptingly with the color of gold. Chatting in small groups behind the various tables, all the staff were young and attractive in tuxedos and red gowns, but although there were a few clients wandering around, also mostly in evening dress, no gambling was in progress.

"We don't open the tables till we're beyond the twelve-mile limit," Mandala explained. "Most of the patrons are in the dining room. Sherry?"

In the dining room they sat at a table by a large porthole that looked out to sea, and as the sherry was brought to them, she heard the sounds of casting off. Her heart kicked a little. She was now well and truly in the lion's mouth. Lou pushed the thought away, determined not to spend the evening nervous.

Over the meal she flirted openly with him, without trying to lead the conversation around to the missing seaplane or Julie Hastings. Mandala flirted back so determinedly that she almost believed he fancied her, and she thought suddenly, I wonder if there are bedrooms on board this thing, and whether he really expects to make the long journey home again tonight. After that she was less generous with her smiles.

Mandala tossed two hundred dollars across the table to the beautifully groomed girl behind the roulette wheel. "Fives," he said, and the girl counted carefully and her long bare arm moved across the felt and deposited forty round blue chips in front of Lou.

Lou lifted the clasp on her evening bag and opened it. "What's the—" she began, but Mandala covered her hand and snapped the bag shut again. "You're my guest," he said. "Go ahead."

She simpered at him. There was really no other way to look at a man who was throwing money at you, she thought wryly. "What do I do?" she asked.

"What's your lucky number?"

She thought of Johnny. "Eighteen," she said, for the years since the afternoon in Water Street.

He threw a handful of the chips to the girl. "Eighteen, all ways," he said. He leaned in to place more chips all around the number on the green baize that was being rapidly covered with chips of all colors.

The little white ball rolled to a stop in the wheel. "Twenty-seven," intoned the blond young man beside the girl, and a king's ransom in chips was slowly raked down a gaping hole in front of the pair.

"That was quick," said Lou, with a grin.

"No beginner's luck for you, I see," said Mandala, casually dropping more chips onto the number eighteen on the newly cleared table. All around the table arms waved out like seaweed in a swell that left in its wake another litter of chips.

"No more bets, please, ladies and gentlemen. No more bets." A few more chips fell as the little white ball was released. "No more bets."

The faces around her were spectacularly intense. Even between couples there were no smiles.

"Your coffee," said a voice behind them, and a small table appeared at her elbow with two delicate cups, a cream jug, a sugar bowl, spoons.

"Number six," said the voice, and the ritual repeated itself.

Lou's glance fell to the diminished pile of chips in front of her, then she smiled up at Jerry Mandala. "I think we should move on to your lucky number."

"All right," said Mandala, smiling. "But it's not good policy. When's your birthday?"

"August fifteenth."

He took the roll of bills from his pocket and exchanged two of them for forty blue plastic wafers. "Fifteen, all ways," he said.

It was nearly religious. Lou, not caught for the moment in this particular trap of greed, watched with detachment and noted the careful ritual, the grasping hands, the trancelike faces.

"Number eighteen."

Lou laughed. Mandala clicked his tongue. "Should have known better," he said. "Third time lucky." His chips disappeared down the hole and rattled into the tray below.

"Now I know what 'down the tube' means," Lou told him, still laughing.

He grinned back. His eyes held no trace of trance, and of course, the tube that swallowed the chips was feeding them into his pocket. Whether he won or lost on the table, it was all the same to him.

"Want to try something else?" he asked. "Blackjack?"

She was used to blackjack. Her father had run a blackjack table every Christmas, for herself and all her cousins. The stakes then had been Christmas candies, and the blue chips seemed hardly more desirable. But it might at least be more interesting than waiting for a ball to roll into a slot. "Great," she said.

At the blackjack table, once she was seated, he left her with a quick apology, saying he had to see to business, if she didn't mind. Lou didn't mind—now that she was here, she wanted to have a look around. For what, she didn't know, but Jerry Mandala's presence at her side had made it difficult for her even to people-watch.

She decided to lose all her money as quickly as possible, and then wander. So of course she had a wild run of luck— three blackjacks and no losses in seven hands.

Since she had bet wildly, she had, at a rough guess, upwards of four hundred dollars in chips in front of her. The atmosphere was casual around the table, and a few excited comments had been enough to summon one or two bored gamblers to the table. Recklessly, Lou pushed twenty chips onto the little square in front of her. The dealer dealt her a ten.

One of the men watching her was not bored, and he was not a gambler. Lou had noticed him before, but every time she glanced his way, he had looked away. Now, with the excuse of her luck, he had come much closer, and he didn't bother to look away.

The dealer dealt her another ten and drew a seven herself. "Pay eighteen," said the girl, pushing another pile of chips of equal size toward Lou. The onlookers groaned happily. They seemed to feed on luck—anyone's luck. Lou added the pile to the ones already on the square.

The dealer dealt her a nine and drew a queen herself. The table moaned in the expectation of calamity.

Lou drew another nine, chose not to split; the dealer drew an eight. Draw. Lou left the pile of chips. The dealer drew a king to her seven, an eight to her ten, and swept the chips away.

Lou stood up like a seasoned gambler who knew her luck had turned. The girl drew her chips in, counted them, and tossed Lou five one hundred-dollar chips. Lou slipped the chips into her bag.

She crossed into the dining room, which had a bar at one side, got up on a stool and ordered a drink.

"White wine coming up," said the bartender. Then Lou abruptly changed her mind.

"No, make that coffee, please. You're American," she said. He set a cup in front of her.

"Yes, ma'am."

"Where from?"

"Seattle."

"Have you been working here long?"

"Just a summer job. I'm still at the university. My mom's Canadian and I like to come up here for the summers. It's my first summer working like this, though. Usually I go up to the logging camps. Keeps you in shape."

And he was in shape. Lou watched his tanned arms under rolled-up cuffs with a detached erotic pleasure, as though he were a moving statue carved by a master sculptor. His hands were strong and precise, placing napkin and spoon in front of her, pouring the coffee. From detached erotic pleasure was a small jump to thoughts of Johnny, and how strong and precise his hands had been.

She said, "I flew in by seaplane."

"Oh, I guess you came with Mr. Mandala?" He brightened a little.

She nodded. "Do many people fly in like that? It seems a long way to come to throw your money away."

"A fair number," he agreed. Since he had no other customers he stayed by her, ready to chat. "We're a bit out of the way where we dock, but of course we have to be. Tonight there was just Mr. Mandala, though. We got a call to wait for him to arrive."

"What time will we get back to Tofino?"

"It depends."

"What happens if a customer loses all his money and wants to go home early? I guess he sits here propping up the bar and boring you all night?"

He laughed at that. "It's never a problem," he said politely, as though to assure her he didn't mind talking to her.

"So the plane never comes out here to take somebody off or land somebody, once you've set out?"

The young man pushed out his jaw consideringly. "I dunno. Might. I wouldn't hear about it unless there was trouble, I don't suppose." He picked up a rag and began rubbing the mahogany bar in increasingly large circles.

"Trouble?" she pursued.

"You know, if somebody got ugly, or sick or something."

She pressed, "But out here, it's so quiet, you'd be sure to hear the plane land, wouldn't you?"

He shrugged, moving off to polish down the bar. "Sir?" he asked.

The man who had been watching her at the blackjack table slid onto the stool two away from her own. "You got any beer?" he asked heavily.

The bartender smiled apologetically. "Sorry, sir, I only have wine and spirits."

The man grunted and pulled out a pack of cigarettes. "I'll have a coffee," he said.

"Yes, sir. I'll just make some fresh." He topped up Lou's cup and poured the dregs of the carafe away in the sink.

"You had a winning streak," the man observed, without looking at her, as he flicked his lighter into flame.

"Mmm," Lou agreed.

"Cigarette?"

"No, I don't smoke, thanks."

"Sorry, mind if I do?"

She shook her head.

"That table ate up all my money in the first half hour," he complained. "Bloody stupid habit, gambling, if you ask me."

She laughed aloud. "Haven't you tried it before?"

"Oh, yeah, a little. I like poker myself. But whaddya do on board a ship like this when your money runs out and you can't even get a decent beer?"

"There are films in the lounge," offered the bartender, coming back with a cup. "We have quite a selection on video, and it's a big screen."

The man swore grumpily under his breath. He did not look comfortable in the ill-fitting tuxedo he was wearing, Lou noted. He looked like somebody's uncle at a wedding, forced by his wife into what he would almost certainly call a monkey suit.

He seemed harmless, but he was definitely out of place, and he had been watching her. "Do you know Jerry?" she asked abruptly.

"Who?"

"Mr. Mandala. He owns the yacht."

"What, this boat?" He looked around at all the luxury. "I doubt it," he said gloomily. Lou laughed again.

She turned to the bartender. "When Jerry comes out to the yacht, does he stay the whole evening, or does the plane come and take him off early?"

The young man shrugged. "Sometimes one, sometimes the other."

"He said he had some business here. Does that mean I won't see him again till we dock?" she asked, in mock despair.

The bartender grinned again. "You'll have me," he said.

She thought idly how nice it was to be flirted with by a man young enough to be her son. She asked, without planning to, "What year were you born?"

"Nineteen sixty-nine," he joked. "But don't let that put you off."

"My God, you were just a toddler the year of the Gastown Riot," she said, and was amazed at how quickly the time had gone. For the first time in her life it struck her that if she had followed life's ordinary, millennia-old pattern instead of trying to carve out a new way, she might have had a son a few years younger than this...man. This afternoon, at the McMasters', she had had a moment of regret over a four-year-old, but this was different. This rocked her.

If things had been different, she might now have a son the same age as Johnny had been the summer of the Riot. And if Johnny had been the father...

Lou closed her eyes. What was the matter with her? Why was she thinking these thoughts now? She'd had her share of opportunities since then, both to get married and to have children. She had not wanted it. Why should regret over past choices be tearing at her like this now, so roughly that she felt she needed to throw up?

Well, she knew the answer to that one. She'd known ever since the night with Johnny, though she'd been running from it pretty hard.

She loved Johnny. One night of passionate loving with her best friend had changed everything for her, had opened her eyes to what had been possible between them all these years.

But unless Johnny had made the same discovery, and this afternoon's scene in his office made that possibility seem painfully remote, she had thrown it all away a lifetime ago— the summer this handsome young man had been two years old.

Chapter 17

Oh, there you are!''

Jerry Mandala came hurrying across the floor, his movements uncharacteristically graceless. "I've been looking for you in the casino."

He came up to her, nodding absently at the stranger on the other stool. Up close, she could see that he was sweating. He looked white.

"Jerry, what's wrong?" she breathed.

"What? Oh, nothing, nothing—" He took a swipe at his forehead and absently looked at his wet palm. "They're driving a hard bargain in there, that's all." He laughed without mirth. "Look, Lou," he said. "I've got a problem I didn't expect to have—the union people are, uh, making a lot of demands I wasn't expecting, and I can't leave the meeting. Look, there's a plane coming out in half an hour to bring some papers that were left behind. Tell the pilot I said he should take you back. I won't be able to go with you, or say goodbye. I have to get back in there. Do you mind?"

Lou looked into his face, her eyes stretching wider as she stared at him. He shook his head, as if she had communicated her fear. "No, no!" he said. He was deeply frightened. "It's all right. Please, get on the plane when it comes. Be there waiting, it won't wait. It'll be all right. I'm sorry I won't be able to—"

"I'll see the lady aboard the plane if that'll help," said the man on the stool behind Mandala. Jerry Mandala turned, staring fixedly at him.

"We've never met," he said. "What's your name?"

"Harry," said the man. "I just lost all my money at your tables in there." He jerked his head back over his shoulder. "So if it's all the same to you, I'll thumb a ride with Miss Patch here, eh?"

"Harry," repeated Mandala. "Yes, yes, that's fine. I'll leave you to make sure she gets aboard. Tell the pilot to fly you into Vancouver. All right? Don't land at Tofino."

"All right," said Harry. "Don't worry, I'll look after her."

Lou was badly shaken, not least because she didn't know whom to trust. Oh, Johnny, she thought. You told me you wouldn't be able to help me out when it got rough. I wonder if this is when it gets rough.

"Take her on deck now," Mandala said. "There'll be fireworks from the stern. There's a landing platform on the starboard side, about midship. You'll see how it operates." He turned to Lou, "Sorry about this." He tried to smile.

"That's all right, Jerry," she said, and he squeezed her arm and was gone.

"Like a turn around the deck?" asked Harry.

She hesitated, trying to calm herself down, thinking, even if they've planned something, they couldn't do it now. I've been seen by dozens of people.

"I'd like to talk to you," Harry said, in an urgent undertone.

She decided she wanted to hear what he had to say. "All right," she agreed quietly.

They crossed the bar to the door, where, oddly, he paused and looked up and down the deck before waving her through with a small flick of his hand. She threw a look over her shoulder to where the young bartender stood watching. "Thanks for the coffee," she called, and he grinned and waved. One person at least who might remember her if she went missing, Lou thought fatalistically, and stepped across the threshold and out into the wind.

"You're going to be cold," said the man named Harry.

It wasn't cold, just cool and windy. "I'll be fine," she said. "How long before the plane gets here?"

He shot his cuff and looked at his watch. "Twenty, twenty-five minutes," he said. He was jumpy, too. Lou took the inside position against the side of the ship. He made no effort to change that.

They walked up toward the bow. After a minute, he paused. "I guess this is where we board the plane, eh?" He leaned over the railing and fiddled with something, then lifted a section and swung it out over the water. Something clunked and clanged all along the side of the ship in the darkness below.

Lou opened her bag and surreptitiously removed her key chain. With her hand by her side, she shifted the keys so that they formed a knuckle duster, one key between each knuckle. It was a trick Johnny had taught her.

Harry stood by the space he had opened in the railing, looking down at the narrow flight of steps that now ran down the side of the yacht sternward to a tiny landing platform a foot or so above the water. It wasn't the gangway they'd come in by; it was obviously only used for boardings at sea. "Very neat," approved Harry. "Tucks right up against the hull when it's not in use."

Lou wondered if the last person to use the steps had been Gordon Harrison. "Let's get down there," said Harry casually, "and wait." He slipped out of his dinner jacket. Underneath he was wearing a strange vest that she couldn't see in the faint light. It looked shiny and yellow, and very bulky. Panic stirred gently in her stomach.

"You're cold," Harry said. She was shivering, but not with cold. She let him drape his jacket around her shoulders. "Let's go."

"I don't think so," said Lou mildly. "There's a lot of spray down there. We'll get wet. I'll wait here."

"Listen," Harry began. "I've got a message for you from—"

Suddenly there was the sound of happy voices on the wind. People were coming out on deck.

"Damn," muttered Harry, looking at her as if she were some kind of problem in logistics. The voices grew louder. He shook his head. "I'm sorry, I don't think there's time for explanations," he said quietly. "See, I have a funny feeling you won't be allowed to get aboard that plane."

He grabbed her without warning, imprisoning her arms against her sides under the enveloping jacket, and pushed her ahead of him through the opening in the rail and down the precarious staircase.

Lou gasped in the air to scream, and he slipped his hand up to smother her mouth. "If you scream, I'll throw you down," he muttered in her ear. "You'll either cut your head open on the landing, or go straight in the water, and I don't care which. I'll say you fell." The scream was choked off before it reached her throat. *Johnny!* she cried silently. Her anger, their argument meant nothing. All she knew was a terrible sorrow that now she would not spend her life with Johnny. Facing death, that was all she regretted.

"That's it," he said approvingly. "You stay calm, and neither of us'll get hurt. There's no time now."

He grunted with the effort of half carrying her down the narrow staircase. Her arms were securely pinioned, and she had lost both handbag and keys. One or two steps before the bottom, he let her slide out of his grasp to the landing, still covering her mouth and pulling her head back against his stomach. "All right," he warned in a low voice. "You keep quiet if you want to stay dry."

Behind her she felt him struggle out of the vest, then his arm swung out, and there was a sudden loud hissing noise. Lou leaped in panic, but she was held firm. She stared dumbfounded as a small rubber dinghy materialized in the darkness at the edge of the landing stage.

She could hear voices intermittently on the wind, and prayed that someone would see. Her blood was thundering in her brain, her heartbeat a wild thrumming in her chest, too strong and fast to sound as individual beats. But she had conserved her energy on the trip down. She went limp in his hands, and then, with a sudden surge, tore herself loose with all the panicked wild power of a small animal.

Harry swore and lunged for her. She caught the railing with one hand, braced herself against the ship's side, and swung her leg in a wild, sweeping arc up into his groin. She could feel it connect.

Harry cursed and fell forward, but he stayed on his feet, blocking the foot of the stairs, still coming for her.

There was only one place to go. Lou flung herself headlong off the platform toward the dinghy. It had floated a little sternward, but she landed with her arms securely around its fat sides that were still rapidly filling with air. The rest of her body hit the water with a smack, and the shock of its icy coldness made her lose all the breath she had. A wave smashed over her, drenching her, making her gasp.

Behind her, cursing like a madman, Harry made a wild grab at air, and overbalanced into the sea. She heard the splash, but wasted no time looking over her shoulder. She kicked off her shoes. The soft silk stole was all around her, like the cold, clinging arms of death.

She had no breath for screaming. Sobbing with fright, she dragged her wet dress up around her waist, freeing her legs, and hoisted herself over the side of the dinghy, tumbling into its protection in a heap.

He was a few yards away in the sea, cursing as the waves slapped over his head. Lou breathed in frightened relief, but she wasn't safe yet. The distance could be bridged by a capable swimmer, and she had discovered how strong a man he was.

Whimpering with fear and the need to hurry, she scrambled to the other end of the dinghy and leaned over the side to paddle away from him, forcing herself to make the calm, sure strokes that would take the dinghy out of his reach.

After a dozen strokes she looked back. He was stationary in the water, not swimming at all, but he was closer than he had been before. She gasped when she saw the reason—the dinghy was attached to a slender thread of fishing line in his hand, and he was pulling on it, bringing himself even closer.

She screamed in protest. Instantly, as if in response, a huge blue flare climbed into the sky from the stern of the ship and burst into a brilliant arc of blue and white stars. She stared skyward for a moment, thinking that someone aboard had given the alarm, before the glittering arc disappeared in a thunderous popping, and a pink flower magically was born from its remains.

Fireworks. They would not hear her screams now, so far away, nor would anyone look out in the dark water below while so much man-made beauty transformed the heavens.

Harry was now at the dinghy's edge, half drowning under the blows of the slapping waves, and she scrambled to him. He was trying to hoist himself into the dinghy. She punched at his face and his clutching hands with wrist-numbing blows, screaming and crying, panic and the animal determination to live giving her a strength she didn't know she had.

"Dammit!" shouted Harry, driven back but still holding on with one arm. "Dammit, Lou, I'm your friend! Johnny sent me! Lou, I work for Johnny!"

The name sank in under her panic, and she paused, staring at him, one fist above her head. "Johnny?" she cried in disbelief. *"Johnny?"*

"Will you let me aboard, for crying out loud? I'm freezing to death here!"

"Johnny?" she cried again.

"He gave me a password!" Harry shouted breathlessly as another brutal wave caught him. "He said, 'Truckstop.' Does that make sense to you?"

Even in this extreme, she felt the heat of memory warm her. "Johnny said that?" she cried stupidly.

Harry dragged himself aboard without answering, and lay slumped and gasping against the fat side of the dinghy. "He didn't tell me you had a right arm like a meat-ax," he said bitterly. "'You might have a little trouble with her,' he said. Ha!" He heaved another breath as they stared at each other. "God, woman, you nearly did me in."

"Serve you right!" muttered Lou. "What the hell was all that kidnap stuff? Why didn't you tell me Johnny sent you?"

He looked at her in the reflected glow of another firework, his face ghoulishly, effervescently green. "He said you wouldn't come willingly. I decided surprise would give me an advantage. People were coming. There was no time."

Both of them began to shiver simultaneously, as the cold that activity had earlier staved off suddenly made itself felt. "We'll die of pneumonia!" said Harry. "And those bloody fireworks—will he see a flare against that, do you think?"

She couldn't follow the logic. "Who?" she said stupidly.

"Johnny," he said briefly. He cursed again. "No one said there'd be fireworks!"

The ship kept increasing the distance between them, but the fireworks display was nearly overhead. "I don't know," said Lou. Then, "What do you mean, will he see? Where is he?"

"Right behind us," said the man named Harry.

From life-threatening danger to complete security within so short a time was more than her system could accommodate. Without warning Lou burst into sobs.

She was still tearful when Johnny found them ten minutes later. His spotlight fell harshly on them, huddled and shivering in the dinghy, but she looked up through the light toward his voice as if she could see him, and burst into sobs again, and Johnny cursed and swore all the time that it took him to negotiate the slapping waves and pull the dinghy in beside the small rental cruiser.

Lou stumbled aboard, her limbs awkward with cold, while Johnny struggled to keep the boat steady. The man named Harry followed behind her, holding the dinghy rope, and together they heaved it over the side.

"What the hell?" demanded Johnny, putting the boat into a hundred and eighty degree turn as soon as he could manage it. The yacht was a long way away, but the fireworks still exploding above lighted up the whole sea.

Harry was apologetic, even though he knew there was no reason he should be. "Sorry, Johnny, we got—we had a, uh—"

Johnny's laughter was sharp, brief and mirthless. He glanced at Lou. "Don't even bother," he said to Harry. "I know all about it."

Lou felt a certain amount of indignation at the implied injustice of that, but in relation to her other emotions, it was nothing. A few minutes ago—it seemed longer—she had thought she was facing death, and the only thing she'd regretted was not having had a lifetime to love Johnny. Indignation paled beside such self-knowledge as that.

She looked at him with a half smile on her lips. "I put up a pretty good fight," she said.

"I'll say!" agreed Harry feelingly. "I'm gonna have black eyes, you know," he told Johnny. "Not to mention—" He raised his eyebrows significantly.

Johnny laughed again. "I believe it." She couldn't read his mood at all. She frowned at him, puzzled. "You have a certain quality of Amazon about you, Babe," he said then, at the same moment that she realized she was close to completely naked.

The strap of her dress had broken sometime during the struggle to get aboard, and her breasts were bare, her dress having fallen to her hips and clung there. In the glow from the fireworks her skin had the look of marble. She supposed she did look like a Greek statue of some warrior goddess.

"Oh, for—!" said Lou, but after what she had been through in the past half hour, bare breasts, like indignation, were hardly world shattering. She laughed lightly. "Got a spare shirt?" she asked.

Johnny left the wheel to its own devices and picked up a blanket, shaking it out and wrapping Lou in its rough warmth. Harry grabbed a second one and pulled it around his own shoulders.

"Got any whiskey aboard?" he asked, shivering. "It's damn cold out there, when you're wet."

"Up by the wheel," Johnny said briefly. "Can you take it?" He began rubbing Lou down with the blanket, so roughly that she felt her dress give way altogether. A kind of lethargy gripped her with his touch, and she stood under the onslaught of his hands, letting the sensual warmth seep through from skin to muscle, and slowly her shivers subsided.

After a few minutes, he pulled off his jacket and the seaman's sweater underneath, and she stepped out of the cold huddle of her dress and the scarf, so that when he slipped the blanket from her shoulders she was nearly naked.

"Lift your arms," Johnny ordered, and flung the warm sweater over her upflung arms and her head, pulling it down over her hips and then crouching to pick up the blanket and rub her legs down. She looked down at his bent head and capable hands, and thought of the moment when she had known she would never see him again. She wished he would leave the blanket now and hold her.

"Drink," called Harry from the wheel, holding out the open bottle of Scotch. Johnny reached for it and handed it to her. Lou took a long pull of the liquid and it burned through her chilled body. She shivered in reaction.

"Get below, both of you," Johnny ordered, not offering to hold her. "Get some coffee into you and get warm."

No one said another word as they clambered down the companionway into the sheltered warmth below.

"Maybe not pneumonia," Harry remarked, when he had stripped off his wet clothes and wrapped himself in the blanket and was sitting at the table with her, drinking the thin-tasting instant coffee she had made. "By the jeez, I got cold out there! It's not healthy, you know, sitting in an open boat at night in wet clothes. Even in July."

"I didn't realize we were doing it for our health," Lou said dryly, and he laughed.

"You from the East coast originally?" she asked.

"Nova Scotia," he admitted, nodding. "Long time ago. You can still tell by my accent, eh?"

Lou nodded and dropped her head back against the seat.

"Think you'll grab some sleep?" he asked.

"I don't think I could," said Lou. She was weary, but too keyed up to let go.

"I've pumped enough adrenaline into my blood in the past half hour to last a year." He rummaged through the drawers in the galley like an old hand and produced a deck of cards. "How about a little real gambling?"

Lou nodded without speaking. She was exhausted but very tense. Johnny had seemed so businesslike and unapproachable. It took an effort of will to remind herself that since their last bitter argument Johnny had not had the kind of encounter with death that had so enlightened her as to what was really important in life. To him the argument was probably still an issue.

They heard the drone of an engine not long after.

"Airplane," said Harry, cocking an ear. "I guess they'll know soon that you're missing, if they don't already."

Lou thought of the young bartender and wondered if he would raise the alarm. If not, she couldn't imagine who would. Jerry had said he wouldn't leave the meeting to say goodbye. If he heard the plane come and go, he might just assume she was on it. "I guess it'll break up the union meeting if they do," she said.

"That was no union meeting," said Harry. "The union men I know don't wear tuxedos even if they are meeting on a yacht, which I doubt. And they don't look like a collection of gangsters."

Lou looked into his face in surprise.

"Who were they, then?" she asked.

Harry shrugged. "Gangsters," he said matter-of-factly. "I think our Jerry has got himself in pretty deep."

"What kind of gangsters?"

He shrugged again, and because it was too frightening to contemplate just now, exactly how narrow an escape she might have had, she asked, "Is your last name Thornton, by any chance?"

The sound of the plane had receded in the distance, and there was silence again, except for the chug of the motor.

"Yeah," he said, shifting his blanket more comfortably. "How did you know?"

"You were out at a house in Horseshoe," she said. Harry laughed.

"My brother-in-law's place. We had a good laugh over that, Johnny and me. Johnny told me I nearly wrecked his life when I came through that door. See, I thought the kids should be watched, but I couldn't do it myself in case George caught sight of me. I told my sister to call Johnny, eh?" He laughed. "I recognized his truck, but I couldn't risk walking up to it, in case George happened to be looking out."

"How did it nearly wreck his life?" Lou asked casually.

"Dunno. Just a saying, I guess. You were in the truck with him, I guess, were you?"

Lou nodded. "He was trying to tell me to leave Jerry Mandala alone." She grinned, telling herself that it was just a saying—"Wrecked his life." She was a little surprised by how much it hurt. "I wish I'd listened."

Harry laughed. "Yeah, it's usually a good idea to listen to Johnny," he said.

They didn't see Johnny again for the nearly two hours it took them to get to Tofino, and they sat yawning, mostly in silence, playing poker for matchsticks. Lou bet wildly on bluffs and lost heavily, and Harry had to keep giving her back half his winnings so they could keep playing. When at last they heard the motor rev down, they tossed the cards aside and ran to the companionway.

"Stay below!" Johnny called harshly. "The yacht's in port and there are lights all over it! Stay below, both of you!"

They turned out the cabin lights and ran to the portholes, pulling aside dust-caked curtains to stare out.

As he had said, all the lights of the *Easy Money* were burning brightly, and it was buzzing with activity. "Harry," Lou said, "they must have reported us missing!" Harry only grunted. "They must think we drowned! How are we going to explain?" The possibilities were just beginning to dawn on her.

They came back to the table and sat listening to the sounds of the cruiser being made fast to the dock, and the cry of gulls overhead. Lou looked at it every way she could, but all she could see was that she was going to look like an awful fool, however she tried to explain her disappearance. A broadcast journalist eating her press card would be nothing compared to Lou Patch diving off Jerry Mandala's yacht in the middle of the night because he had gangsters aboard.

At last Johnny came down the companionway steps, his feet in sneakers, his chest bare underneath his denim jacket, frowning. He poured himself a coffee, and leaned against the stove in the galley, watching them.

"What the hell happened? What went wrong?" Johnny asked. "How'd you get wet?" His voice was impersonal, and Lou threw off her weariness and sat up straight, all her emotions churning.

"That's what you're going to tell me, isn't it?" she said hoarsely. "What the hell happened? What did you think you were going to prove, Johnny, getting your hired gun to drag me off that ship so I thought I was being kidnapped, or murdered? What were you trying to do?"

"I was trying to save your life!" he said roughly. "Now will you—"

"Save my life?" she interrupted scornfully. "*Save* my life? You nearly killed me—and Harry, too! My life wasn't in any danger! I was—"

"That's a matter of opinion," Johnny said softly. He was standing with his arms folded across his naked chest, gazing steadily at her, sure of his ground. He seemed, for the first time in all the years she'd known him, like a stranger. It was like the moment when he had stood in front of her in his police riot gear, the moment before she had recognized him. A stranger.

"Yes?" she said. "A matter of opinion, was it? And whose opinion matters when we differ, Johnny, or is that a stupid question?"

"It is right now," he said levelly.

She asked, "How are we going to explain to whoever is over there why we jumped ship in the middle of the ocean? What are we going to say?"

"We're not going to say anything," he said. "We're getting out of here as fast and as quietly as we can."

For a moment Lou was speechless with surprise. "And leave them thinking we're dead?" she demanded, when she caught her breath.

"And leave them thinking you're dead," he agreed flatly. "I hope."

"Are you crazy? They'll have the search planes out next!"

"That's better than the alternative."

"What alternative? What do you think is going on?"

"I think Jerry Mandala and his buddies are trying to kill you," Johnny said. "I've already told you."

"Yes, you have, and for a while there I started to believe it, but now I think you're crazy! There's no reason whatsoever to think—"

"Isn't there?"

"There was a plane coming for me! We heard it flying over, Johnny."

"Yeah? Well, you might have been allowed to get on that plane, but I doubt it."

His calm matter-of-factness was more convincing than shouting would have been. Lou blinked. "Why? What makes you so sure?"

"They've got a good reason for wanting you dead, that's why."

"I'd like to hear it!"

"You're going to," said Johnny through his teeth. His tone was still level, but she realized suddenly that he was furious.

"I—" she began, but he overrode her.

"Know a guy named Sandy McMaster?" he asked. "I think you do."

That took her aback. "Yes," she stammered. "What's he got to—"

"Sandy McMaster had a fatal accident this afternoon, Lou," Johnny said. "He's dead. You were the last person he talked to. Did he tell you anything? No? Well, I believe it, Babe, I believe it. What are you betting Jerry Mandala does?"

Chapter 18

It was a long, weary journey home. Johnny wouldn't risk spending what remained of the night at any hotel in or near Tofino, and the pilot of the small aircraft he had chartered wanted to wait for takeoff till dawn, since it was so near.

"Near" was a purely subjective judgment, and to Lou the time of waiting was nearly intolerable, spent, as it was, huddled in the darkened plane, talking in low voices about Sandy McMaster, what she had learned from him and how he had died, with a constant eye out for the pilot, who could not be allowed to overhear anything, and who wandered up and down the dock, kicking his heels and reassuring them from time to time that takeoff was imminent.

At last they were in the air, and later, a long, cold time later, since a chill had gripped both Lou and Harry—on the water near Vancouver, and finally in the welcome warmth of the big Bronco and heading home.

Then, finally, sometime after seven o'clock in the bright morning of another glorious summer day, they stopped outside Harry Thornton's house.

Johnny said, "Harry, we're gonna keep this completely quiet."

"All right," said Harry, who was nearly at the breaking point of fatigue and exhaustion, and looked it.

"From everyone," Johnny said. "I want them to keep thinking Lou's dead as long as possible."

At that, Harry's eyebrows went up, but he only nodded briefly, and said again, "All right."

"I don't understand why," said Lou.

Johnny looked at her. "Because if they think you're already dead, they won't be trying to kill you," he said. He was tired, too tired to be anything less than brutal, though he didn't realize how brutal he had been till he saw the dull shock reflected in her eyes.

Lou was too tired to protest, but in any case there was nothing to say. She had thought of nothing in the past few hours except the awful central fact that Sandy McMaster was dead, that Joey had no father, and that Barb McMaster's life must seem a blackened, unrecognizable ruin of what it had been a day earlier.

The next time she opened her eyes, they were parked in front of a familiar building, but it took her a second to recognize it as the one where Johnny lived. She nearly cried out at that. "Johnny, can't I go home?" she begged.

"No," he said. "Come on."

The face she saw in Johnny's bathroom mirror was pale and drawn, her makeup grotesquely smeared, her hair damp and stringy. She looked old, and she thought, Well, that's all right, I feel old. I am old. She climbed wearily into the bath, and its heat at last killed the chill in her bones that had been a part of her for what seemed a lifetime.

She didn't stay long in the warmth. This morning it had lost its power to comfort her—she felt a lost soul, and her soul would not be found here.

When she reemerged, Johnny was in the kitchen, smoking and drinking a cup of black coffee. He hadn't changed;

he had merely put on a shirt under his jacket. Wrapped in his bathrobe, with a towel still around her head, she sank into the chair opposite and picked up the cup he poured for her.

Then he butted his cigar where he stood, and shoved the pack and his lighter into his jacket pocket.

"I'll be back," he said. "I don't know when. Try to get some sleep. You're going to be talking to the police, and you'll have a long day—"

But she jumped to her feet, nearly crying. "Oh, God, you're not leaving?" she said, her voice hoarse with desperation. She pressed herself against him, knowing that whatever he thought about things, here was where her comfort lay. She couldn't stand to have him leave her now. He wrapped his arms around her, and when she lifted her face for his kiss, he bent to kiss her, and the touch was pure solace.

"Johnny," she begged, when he lifted his lips again. "Don't leave me. I need you. Please, I need you."

The pages of time flicked slowly by as they looked into each other's eyes, and she thought—I thought I'd understood, but I hadn't. Not till this moment have I understood. This—God forgive me—*this* is how he felt then.

He said nothing, merely gathered her in against his chest and half led, half carried her to his bedroom. Beside the bed he took her face in his hands and kissed her again, then bent to pull back the covers. He eased the towel from her hair and his robe from her shoulders, dropping both at his feet, and gently put her into bed. For the space of a moment she was frightened, but when he pulled off his jacket she sighed, like an animal released from a trap, and waited for the moment when his naked body slipped in beside her and enveloped her in his comforting heat.

His arms wrapped tightly around her, pressing her to him, and his kiss was hungry with need, and already his body was hard against her thigh.

There was no skilled teasing now, nor did she want it. What they both wanted was to be joined, to be one. He pressed his way there, because though her body was not ready, her spirit was; and she welcomed the soft pain of his entrance because it made his presence in her body real and immediate, not softened by her body's honey, nor clouded by her mind's desire.

His entrance stirred her more deeply than she had expected, and she felt the suddenness of her own response as her body melted all at once into welcome, and eased his passage toward her soul.

He lay over her, raised on his elbows, his hands cupping her head, his body thrusting rhythmically in and in, a steady knocking at some door within, while all the time she felt her response behind that door, a surging need to open to him and meet with Johnny in the deepest part of her self. The need rose up through her being—a being neither body nor soul, but some strange melding of both that was locked in this strange moment of time and space, but did not belong there; and under his persistent request, the door burst open, and then all disappeared; time, and space, and self, and door, and knocking; and she stood with Johnny on the threshold of the vast sea of belonging, and awestruck, they entered and were swept into the Nothing that was the All.

She was crying. Not the gentle tears of a heart touched by beauty, but deep, racking sobs of understanding and acceptance that shook their bodies and the bed that was, somehow, again beneath them. Johnny's hands touched her cheeks to wipe away the flood of tears that poured from her eyes, and the knowledge of the marvelous piece of creation his hands were, rushed through her with a joy that was nearly too great to bear, and she sobbed again.

He was crying, too. She lifted trembling arms to touch his cheeks, and smiled on a sob, and his arms slid under her as she wrapped her own around him. They lay in that tight, wordless embrace, filled with light, and in startled gratitude for the richness of their union.

Lou thought she hadn't seen so many cops in one place since the Gastown Riot. There were, in fact, only six, but they seemed crowded into the little room, sitting, standing, leaning against the walls, and she was the focus of their attention. It seemed like more.

"All right, we'll just take you through it again, Miss Patch, if you don't mind, for the sake of the Staff Sergeant Williams," said the detective sitting across from her. Staff Sergeant Williams was the big gun from the Mounties who had just entered the room with another man, presumably a smaller gun, since his name hadn't been mentioned. Everyone was in plain clothes, but they were all pretty unmistakably police officers.

For all she still joked with Johnny, Lou was long past the age where she had considered the police her enemy. In spite of all the recent noise about their secret files on blameless citizens, when she heard the word "Mountie" now, what she thought of first was the image she had learned at school, of brave men in red coats who always got their man. And of—"The Musical Ride," she said to Staff Sergeant Williams. "Did you ever ride in that?"

A small grin flickered across his face. "As a matter of fact, yes," he told her, and she rode the horse of memory back to the first day she had heard the story of The Royal Canadian Mounted Police, and the film in social studies class, where brave, handsome men rode proud, handsome horses and there had been an aerial view of a field of riders that suddenly formed into a perfect red-and-black X on a field of green. She could recall the kick of wonder and pride her eight-year-old heart had felt, and she smiled now, shaking her head, and said, "That X, that was terrific." For her it had been, in fact, a sudden awareness that to be Canadian was to be something special.

Everybody laughed, and the atmosphere lightened in the room so that the air was breathable again.

"All right," said the Vancouver officer, who had been in charge ever since she and Johnny had walked through the door of the Vancouver police station. "Let's start from the top."

She started with Julie, and her boyfriend Butch, and led them through the car Winnie had seen, and the receptionist's blunder, and Mandala's reaction to her questions—through everything she had learned about them all in the past week, including the night just past. The only thing she left out of the recapitulation was the fact that Johnny had been given David Stockton's record and his last name by his friend Brent, because they decided there was no point getting the man into trouble. She said that the description given her by Jenny, the receptionist, had convinced her. A while ago they had shown her a bunch of photographs, and she had unhesitatingly picked out Butch, and a sigh had gone around the table.

Johnny sat beside her throughout, reminding her of things that she forgot, and he was still there as Staff Sergeant Williams put her through it all again.

"Now, are you certain about the day Julie saw her friend outside her building?" he asked, when she had finished.

She said, "I know it was the Tuesday before she disappeared. I wasn't in the restaurant the next day, and she didn't come to the beach that afternoon. I went in on the Thursday, and when she wasn't there I asked her boss where she was. He said she hadn't come in."

"And that Thursday was the eighteenth?"

"Absolutely."

"She couldn't have seen Butch on Monday, and delayed telling you till the Tuesday? You appreciate that the plane went missing on Monday."

She said, "I only know what Julie told me. She came down to the beach on Tuesday and said, 'I saw Butch this morning.' I remember that clearly."

"Now, yesterday you went to see Sandy McMaster." A look passed over his face as though he thought it was a pretty stupid thing to have done, but he didn't express it. "Would you like to tell me about that again?"

She did. "And he was nervous and reacted very strangely when I asked him if he thought that maybe the plane hadn't really crashed at all," she finished.

Staff Sergeant Williams nodded. "And what time did you leave the McMaster home?"

She bit her lip. "Two-thirty, I think. What time did he—?"

"Let's leave those questions for now." She hadn't learned much of anything from them. They were devoted to getting information, and were entirely uninterested in giving any.

"At what time did Mr. Mandala phone you and ask you out to his yacht?"

"I don't remember. About four, perhaps."

"Did he mention Mr. McMaster to you at all?"

"No."

"He never mentioned that he knew you had been to see him?"

"No, nothing like that."

He made another note. "Do you have the postcard you were sent from Hong Kong?"

"It's at my apartment. I haven't been back there, but it's there."

"We'll have an officer go out and pick that up, if you don't mind." Lou nodded. "What's the name of the woman who saw the car in the alley?"

"I only know her as Winnie. She lives in apartment 306. Julie was in 304."

"And she saw that car, with the license plate MONEY, on—?"

"She wasn't sure of the day. Late the week that Julie disappeared," she said.

"An old lady, I understand."

"A very sharp old lady."

The questions went on and on, over and over the ground, without any hint that Lou could read as to what the man was looking for.

"Can you tell me why you haven't come to the police before this?"

"I did come to the police. I came to report that Julie was missing and that I thought Butch had come and gotten her. But I wasn't allowed to file a missing person report because I wasn't family."

"Yes, I understand that. But once you learned what you did about some possible connection with the missing plane, you didn't come back?"

She shook her head. "I really didn't know what to tell anyone. I didn't have any proof. I thought you'd think—I don't know." She shrugged. "To be honest, when I told Staff Sergeant Goldring what Julie said about Butch and the Burnaby Mall murder, he acted as though I was making it up to impress him. I didn't feel like going through that again."

"Yes, it's under wraps at the moment, but we think we've got that guy. It's almost certainly not this man Butch," said Williams.

"Oh. Well, I didn't know that, and I could just imagine his face if I told him the man I'd told him was the Burnaby Mall murderer had kidnapped the Solicitor-General, too."

"Why do you think he was kidnapped?" asked one of the Vancouver officers, in a tone that suggested she herself might be responsible if she knew so much.

She looked at him. She could never understand why professional people always assumed that laymen couldn't reason around their particular specialization. She said, "Isn't it obvious? If David Stockton was the pilot, and he was seen the day after the plane went missing, then it's not very likely the plane crashed, is it?''

"But you don't think he was the pilot?'' pressed the same officer. Lou thought, with sudden detachment, your real reason for asking that question isn't to get information. It's to show your colleagues what a brilliant questioner you are. The insight fascinated her.

She said, "I told you, I don't think Julie's boyfriend was very likely a pilot. Are her boyfriend and Jerry Mandala's pilot the same man?''

"Why don't you think he was a pilot?'' Staff Sergeant Williams asked, ignoring the question.

"I've already explained that I know he was in and out of prison a lot. He was in prison when he was supposed to be in Vietnam getting his pilot training. Unless you're dealing with two different men.''

"We have no reason to believe we're not.''

For a moment she was stunned into silence, believing them. Then her tired brain recovered. "Then why have I been here for the past—'' she looked at her watch, but the inside of the crystal was clouded with water droplets and it had stopped at 2:00 a.m. "—two or three hours answering your questions?''

No one answered.

"If there's no reason to believe so, there's no reason for me to be sitting here,'' she said, irritated. "If you don't mind, I'll go home.'' She pushed back her chair, but Williams raised a hand.

"Please bear with me,'' he said. "Don't assume—''

"Please don't *you* assume I'm a fool,'' she responded tartly. "You have a lot of reason to believe they're the same man, and so do I. You just asked me why I didn't come to you earlier. If there's no reason to believe that Julie's boyfriend was Jerry Mandala's chauffeur, why did you ask that question?''

He merely nodded, looking through his notes.

"You asked Sandy McMaster whether your friend Julie might have been a passenger on the plane. Why did you think she might have been?" asked the eager Vancouver officer.

She was tired, too tired to guard her tongue. "Because she was a member of the Baader-Meinhof gang," she snapped sarcastically.

They all looked up, startled into attention. "She was—" began Williams.

Lou said, "Give me a break, okay? Obviously I *didn't* think she might have been once I'd gotten the dates worked out. I asked him because I wanted him to lower his guard. It sometimes helps to ask naive questions," she finished dryly. "As you're doing now."

Williams shoved back his chair and tossed down his pen. "All right, I think we've got all we need for the moment, Miss Patch."

Johnny spoke for the first time since Williams had come into the room. He said, "Has Lou been reported missing from that yacht?"

Williams looked to the Vancouver officer in charge. He cleared his throat. "Yes, she has. She was reported missing by the yacht's radio shortly after midnight. A search plane went out at dawn. An unknown man was also reported to have disappeared from the yacht at the same time. I believe someone's coming in today to file a full report."

Johnny said, "Are you planning to call off the search and announce that Lou's been found?"

Williams made a face. "I don't like to do it, but I think we'll leave the search going for now. It would be a good idea if you didn't go home, Miss Patch. We don't know how much they think you know."

A chill climbed up Lou's spine. She had expected them to pooh-pooh Johnny's idea. To think that she was in danger herself was one thing. To have a room full of police officers agree was unexpectedly frightening. She looked around. "Do you mean I have to let everybody think I'm dead?"

"For a day or two."

"But I have a family, friends—a job..." she trailed off helplessly, knowing her deepest objection wasn't this, but a frightened rejection of the fact that they all believed her to be in such great personal danger. They were saying that Jerry Mandala would try to kill her if he knew she was alive. She didn't want to believe it. "If he knows I've spoken to you and told you everything, what would be the point?"

"He may not know exactly what you do know. He may imagine you're a material witness," the officer pointed out gently. "Once we've made some arrests I imagine you'll be out of danger."

"What'll happen—what do I have to do?"

"Just don't talk to anybody. If absolutely necessary, you can tell your family, if you think they're capable of keeping it to themselves." He looked at Johnny. "We'll keep the search plane up there till sundown. Everybody knows no one could survive in that water more than a few hours."

Lou looked at Johnny. "All right," she said. "You'll just—tell them I haven't been found?"

"It would be wise," said Williams.

They all pushed back their chairs and got to their feet, so they missed the sound of the knock on the door. A voice outside called, "Did you say he's in D?" and the door opened.

The Vancouver officer called sharply, "This room is in use!" But the door was already open wide. *"Lou!"* they heard someone call in sharp surprise, and everyone in the room turned and stared at the two men in the doorway.

Jerry Mandala was frozen to the spot, staring across the room at Lou. Behind him, all unconscious, Staff Sergeant Goldring said, "Ah, sorry to interrupt. Mr. Mandala's here to file a report on those people who went missing from his boat, Phil. I thought you might like to sit in."

Chapter 19

Johnny drove home in a frighteningly controlled rage, keeping rigidly to the speed limit and obeying every rule of the road as though to break even the least important by-law would let the lid off a full-blown anarchism within him. Lou was afraid to speak until they had pulled up in front of his building again. Then she said tentatively, "Don't you think I may as well go home, Johnny?"

"No, I damn well don't think you may as well go home," he said, in soft violence, his voice nonetheless unnerving for being pitched so low. "I think I'm going to have my work cut out keeping you alive as it is."

He slipped the engine into park, pulled out the keys from the ignition, then turned to her. He said, "Here's what happens now—we get out of the truck. We cross the road quickly and get into the building. We go upstairs by way of the stairs. You'll stand by the stairwell door until I've checked out the apartment. You'll stay there till I come and get you." He handed her the truck keys. "If you hear any- thing suspicious, you will not come to investigate, you'll turn around and go quietly down the stairs and drive back to the police station as fast as you can. If you hear someone coming after you, you'll go to the super's apartment on the ground floor at the front—101—and ask them to let you call the police. Otherwise you'll wait at the stairs till I come and get you. Understood?''

This was a nightmare. "Understood," she said.

"Right. Let's go. Don't get out till I open your door. Don't get ahead of me."

In spite of everything she felt protected with Johnny's huge bulk so close to her as they crossed the street and went inside and up the stairs, Johnny's eyes as restless as a secret-service agent she had once seen protecting the Prime Minister. At the top of the stairs she stood half in and half out of the doorway, listening as he strode through every room of his apartment. Then he was beside her again and at last they were inside and the door was closed.

She said, "I'm sorry, Johnny."

"It's not your fault, what are you sorry for? That jerk Goldring hasn't got the brains of a—"

She said, "You're always protecting me. I never get a chance to pay you back, and when I do, I mess it up. I've never realized before what a selfish cow I've always been in this relationship."

He was at the tap filling the kettle. He turned and looked at her in surprise. "What are you talking about?" he asked roughly.

Lou dropped her eyes. "That night—after Marianne died . . . I wish I'd—"

"Don't be stupid," he said roughly. "That was my fault. I had no right to ask that of you, certainly not that way. I knew it as soon as I said it. I should have apologized to *you*."

"You did," she said quietly. "But that doesn't change the fact that—"

"Look," he said. "It was years ago. It's long since under the bridge. Why are we talking about it now?"

"Because this morning I understood how you felt that night. You were there for me. I've never been there for you."

"Hogwash," he said briefly. "What about the year we were in grade five? I've always owed you."

"What? What did I do for you in grade five?"

When the kettle boiled, he made a carafe of coffee while she stood watching. He dumped cream and sugar and spoons on the table, and at last she jerked into action and fetched two mugs.

He said, "Your class was treating me like some kind of leper, don't you remember? It was a closed group, most of you had been together since grade one. All my friends were in grade six. No one in your class was even friendly. Remember?"

Lou put sugar in her cup, though she didn't normally like sweet coffee. "Sort of," she said.

"The worst thing was always being chosen last for any team," he said. He sipped his coffee and made a face at memory. "I don't know if there's anything more shaming than that for a kid that age."

She said, "But you were good at sports. You were the captain of the class baseball team, weren't you?"

"Afterward, I was. But in the early days I couldn't play right. I got chosen last, and I played up to everyone's expectations. There's no humiliation like it."

"I believe you."

"You were the most popular girl in the class," he said. "One day we were chosing teams for a baseball game at lunchtime. You got named one of the captains. We were all standing around, and I was on the outskirts of the group, as usual, looking down and wishing I were somewhere else. Suddenly I heard you say, 'Johnny,' and I looked up and everybody was looking at me. I walked through them all and over beside you. I was your first choice. Nobody said anything, it was as though they didn't really think it was anything important. But I played a great game that day, and that was the day everything changed.''

"I do remember," Lou said. "You got a home run, didn't you?"

He grinned. "Something like that."

"And our team won. I remember now." She remembered more than the game. She remembered what had led up to her choosing Johnny first that day.

She and her mother had been in the grocery store on Saturday, standing at the meat counter, when a voice beside her said tentatively, "Hi, Louise."

She turned to see Johnny Good standing beside her, waiting with his mother. "Hi," she had said neutrally, and turned away, for she and her coterie were ostracizing Johnny as much as the rest of the class. As they walked away, her mother asked softly, "Who was that, Louise?" and she'd airily explained that he was a boy in her class that no one liked.

"He looks like a very nice boy," her mother said. "Why doesn't anyone like him?" Lou had explained about his failing the previous year, and being "a jerk."

"Why is he a jerk?"

"He never says anything in class, Mom. We think he'll probably fail again. We think he'll be in grade five all his life, like that guy in the song who doesn't have a nickel to get off the train. You know—'The Man Who Never Returned.'" Lou laughed at the joke.

"That doesn't sound very friendly," said her mother. "That doesn't sound like the Louise I know."

Lou had been shocked at the gently chiding tone. "But, Mom—!" she'd protested. "He doesn't belong in our class. All his friends are in grade six. . . ."

Her mother said, "Do you remember that cat you found last year that some boys had shot with a beebee gun?"

"Yes...." She had wanted to save the cat, but it was too badly damaged, and weeping, Lou had accompanied her father to the vet and had it put to sleep.

"That was an alley cat. Did it make any difference to you that it was dirty and didn't have a home?"

"No."

"That's the Louise I know. If an animal is in pain, you get very concerned. You always have. And I'm sure you care about people as much as animals."

"But Johnny's not in pain!"

"Isn't he? I think it hurt him when you wouldn't speak to him just now."

"I said hello," Lou protested mulishly, but she blushed with shame, and her mother wisely said no more. It was the following Monday that the lunchtime game had been played.

She had forgotten all about it. It had all happened in the first few weeks of school, and after that Johnny had been her friend and part of her crowd, and that was the Johnny she'd always remembered.

"God, kids can be cruel," she said now.

"Yeah," Johnny agreed. He pulled out his little cigars and lit one.

She said, smiling, "And that's why you've been looking after me all these years?"

"It's not, and you know it. But don't start thinking this has been a one-way rel...friendship, because it's not. When Marianne and the baby died, I'd have gone crazy if it hadn't been for you."

"Really, Johnny?"

"My God, woman, you sat with me every night for weeks, don't you remember?"

"Yes, I remember."

"I could have killed myself for asking you what I did that night. I was afraid it would spoil everything. I wanted to apologize afterward, but I didn't know how to bring it up, and you didn't seem to change, so I settled for being grateful."

She said, "I've felt guilty about that for ages. I really didn't understand."

"I was crazy that week. It was the week that Ben got killed."

"Your partner! That's right, I'd forgotten."

"I thought if I lost your friendship, too, I'd go out of my mind. I think that night was the worst I've ever spent in my life." He knocked the ash from his cigar, looking at her. "This isn't a one-way street. It never has been. Or if it is, it's all the other way."

A load of guilt fell from her shoulders, and she shook her head, smiling. She desperately wanted to ask him what he felt now, how he felt things had changed. But she was afraid. So she said instead, "Tell me about last night. Why were you so sure last night that I would be in danger on Mandala's yacht? And how did you get there so fast?"

"I've been doing some checking on Mandala. It's starting to look as though he's being financed by some very dirty money."

"The Hong Kong Mafia?"

He nodded. "After you told me you were going on Mandala's yacht I grabbed Harry Thornton and went out and chartered a plane to Tofino. On the way to the airport Brent phoned to tell me that Sandy McMaster had been killed. We got there just before you did. Harry went on the yacht and I rented the boat. It was a bloody narrow squeak."

"It's hard to believe he was going to kill me that night. Wouldn't that make the police even more suspicious?"

"You may be right. It wasn't a risk I was willing to take. Frightened people do crazy things. It was crazy to kill McMaster, but that didn't stop them doing it. And it was always possible that whoever Mandala was involved with was looking to get rid of him, too. Having him go down for your murder might have been just what they wanted."

Lou closed her eyes. "It's all so hard to believe. It's so hard to believe that someone you've just talked to is dead. Do you think..." She took a sip of coffee. "Do you think it's because I talked to him, Johnny?"

He shook his head. "Brent told me they've been leaning on McMaster pretty hard. They figured he was the weak link and he'd been getting a lot of pressure."

"The weak link in what?" she asked. "What happened to that plane?"

"That's what they don't know. But there's far too much cover-up going on. McMaster was out at the aircraft, and he reported in to air traffic control. The controller thought McMaster took the flight, but the airport records have disappeared."

She gaped at him. "Are you serious?"

He shook his head at her. "I've been trying to tell you, Babe, you don't know what you're getting mixed up in. Whatever it is it's serious."

"Has Gordon Harrison been kidnapped, then? Has there been a ransom demand?"

"Not according to Brent."

She gazed at him. "So the plane really went missing?"

"They're beginning to think it didn't. But they haven't found any sign of it anywhere."

"I don't understand. Are you suggesting that the plane landed on Erehwemos and that Jerry Mandala killed Gordon Harrison?"

Johnny shrugged. "But it doesn't make sense!" she protested. "Why would they want to kill him? What would anybody gain from it? He was Mandala's friend, wasn't he?"

"He was his political friend," Johnny said, stubbing out his cigar and standing up to pour them more coffee. "Mandala made a lot of contributions to the Harrison campaign during the election. It's possible he made more than was strictly legal, and I've already told you where the money came from."

"So Gordon Harrison's campaign was paid for by the Hong Kong Mafia? Why?"

"There's a lot of money coming out of Hong Kong right now. Vancouver real estate is being heavily bought up by Hong Kong interests. They want to get their money out, and they want a place to come to in 1997. The crooks as well as the legitimate business people want to get out." He shrugged. "Maybe having the Solicitor-General in your pocket is helpful for getting on the top of the list for Canadian passports."

"But killing him doesn't make sense. I can't believe this adds up. Don't you think it's possible that he thought the Mounties were taking an interest in his campaign funding and decided to disappear before things got hot?"

"Cabinet ministers in this country have a way of riding out that particular kind of storm," Johnny said cynically. "I don't see that it would be worth his while to go and start somewhere as a nobody even if he knew for certain he was being investigated."

"But what possible reason could they have for killing him?"

"You keep asking me the same thing, Babe, and the answer is, I don't know. But it's pretty certain they killed Sandy McMaster to keep him quiet about something, and your friend Julie has disappeared, and Jerry Mandala has been keeping a damn close eye on you, and offered you a job that would get you out of town for the duration. I don't have the answers. I just know the questions are ugly."

She shivered. "How long am I going to have to stay here?" Johnny shrugged.

"As long as it takes. Is it going to be so bad?" He smiled at her.

She smiled through her worry. "Could I go back to the flat to pick up some things, do you think? I feel a bit sloppy in your clothes." She had dressed in a pair of his blue jeans and a cotton sweater to visit the police station that morning, and by no stretch of the imagination did they fit.

"I guess we can risk a quick trip. But no more than five minutes in there, okay? No dawdling. You grab some clothes and we get out."

On the way he stopped and bought the morning papers. The *Sun* had headlined a different story, but her own paper, the *Province* screamed, Lou Patch Missing From Mandala Yacht!

"'Search for *Province* columnist looking hopeless,' say police," Lou read out, aghast. "My God, Johnny, I didn't realize it had hit the news! I have to call people!"

"Yeah," he said. "Well, don't worry. The next edition will say you've been found."

"But my parents! And Tom and Dorothy! I have to call as soon as we get back."

"Just so long as you don't try to call from your place."

He pulled up in front of her building and escorted her in as before, using his plastic card on the entrance door because her keys, along with her evening bag, were somewhere at the bottom of the Pacific.

At her own door, however, the card was unnecessary. The door opened as he touched it, and Johnny hastily waved her back to the protection of the stairwell before he went in. A minute later he came to get her, and it was obvious Johnny wasn't the only person in Vancouver who went uninvited through locked doors.

It wasn't all that chaotic, once she got over the initial shock of realizing that someone had searched the place. They hadn't cut into cushions, or dumped drawers on the floor. Mostly they had confined their interest to the area around her desk, and the mess was mostly the reams of paper that had been pulled from her desktop, drawers and filing cabinet and thrown around. But her computer had been smashed beyond recognition, and all her floppies had disappeared.

So had the postcard from Julie that she had put beside the little cat sitting on the coffee table.

Chapter 20

Her mother was crying when Lou called to tell her she was safe. "I'm sorry," said Lou, "I didn't know the papers had gotten hold of it already."

"The police phoned us early this morning," said Mrs. Patch. "It's been the worst day of my life, thank God you're safe."

"I'm sorry," Lou said again.

"Darling, what happened? How did you fall off that ship?"

She said, "It's a long story, Mother. And I'm exhausted. I haven't been to bed yet. Can we save it for another time?"

"All right, dear. Your father is here. He wants to speak to you."

"Hi, Dad."

"Hello, Chook. Good to hear you're safe. Are you all right?"

"I think I'm getting a doozer of a cold, but I'm okay."

"You did fall off the yacht, then? It wasn't a false alarm?"

"It wasn't a false alarm, but I didn't exactly fall off. I more jumped."

Her father laughed, and she heard a small choke that meant he had been crying, too. "I'm sorry I didn't think to phone earlier. It's been pretty hectic."

"Are you in trouble, Chook?" he asked, in the direct way her father always had.

"I can't talk about it now. I've been looking for... I'll come round in a few days and tell you all about it."

"In a few days? Lou, what is going on? You *are* in trouble!"

"Johnny's looking after me. Which reminds me, I'll be at his place for a while, if you want to get in touch with me. But please don't tell anyone else that. Not anyone at all."

This was followed by a pause. "Is Johnny there now?" her father asked.

"Yes, he's here."

"May I speak to him?"

Rolling her eyes, but not objecting to this masculine impulse to get the straight goods from another male, she passed the receiver over.

"Hello, Craig," said Johnny, very man-to-man. Light-headed with lack of sleep, Lou merely giggled. When all was said and done, it wasn't unpleasant to have her troubles taken over by two strong, loving men.

"Yes, I'm afraid so," said Johnny. "She's got to be kept in hiding for probably a few days. I'll keep her here unless that looks dangerous—if so, we'll find somewhere else."

They talked for a few minutes, but she hardly heard. She had been yawning uncontrollably for the past twenty minutes, and felt nearly asleep on her feet. When Johnny passed the phone to her, it was her mother again.

"Men," Lou muttered, with a grin at Johnny. He laughed.

"You take care," said her mother. "I don't like the sound of this."

"I'll take care."

"You're with Johnny. You listen to what he tells you. Don't go running wild, dear."

"No, Mommy," she said.

"It's all very well, but we're worried," said her mother, responding to the implicit message in that. "I'd insist on your coming here, but you'll be safe with Johnny."

If he wants me, I will be, Lou thought. If he doesn't, I don't think I'm safe anywhere. "Yes, I'll be safe with Johnny," she said aloud.

She hung up and called Dorothy, and then her editor. Dorothy said tearfully, "Did someone throw you overboard? I was sure that was it."

"Not quite," said Lou. "Say hi to Tom for me? I'm really tired."

"Get some sleep," ordered the ever-practical Dorothy. "Thanks for phoning. We've been really worried."

"Thank you," said Lou.

"See you at the beach," said Dorothy. "We're awfully glad to know you're all right."

Lou looked out the window at the streaming sunshine, and suddenly felt an overwhelming desire for the beach and her ordinary life. "As soon as I can," she promised.

She didn't tell Dorothy, or the features editor, where she could be reached. Her editor had already gotten the news that she was safe.

"Good thing, too," he said. "Not that it wasn't a great headline. But the next one will be even better. George wants to know if there's going to be an exclusive story in all this."

George was the news editor. "Might be," she said, realizing for the first time that it was a distinct possibility. "Think he'll offer me a job if it's a good one?"

"Is it?"

"Might be," she said evasively. "Bye now."

She put down the receiver and turned to Johnny. "I'm on the verge of collapse," she said. They hadn't slept after their lovemaking that morning. They had decided to go straight to the police. "You must be, too."

"Get to bed," he said. "I'll wake you in a few hours for dinner."

"Aren't you coming, too?" she begged. "You've had as little sleep as I have!"

"Sorry," said Johnny, "I'll get Harry to come over later and grab some sleep then. But right now, I want to be awake."

She was too tired to argue. "It's not fair," she protested, staggering into the bedroom.

"Life isn't fair," Johnny said briefly. "Get to bed."

In the bright bedroom he undressed her, tucked her in and pulled the blinds. Then he settled in a chair with the newspaper. Sleep came up to claim her, pulling her down through layers of consciousness like the sea. Images of horror and comfort wrestled before her eyes, and she struggled with unconsciousness for a moment, wanting the comfort to win.

From the toils of a dream that was just beginning, she asked thickly, "Johnny, do you love me?"

"I love you," his voice said, and she smiled and accepted the dream's embrace.

Johnny awakened her at six with a cup of tea, the late editions, and the news that there was no news. "What are they waiting for?" she demanded groggily, sipping her tea and feeling as if he'd pulled her from a region near death. Johnny shook his head.

"Something certain, maybe. There's no easy proof that Butch and the pilot are the same man. They've got to have that before they proceed."

"Why don't they show Jenny a picture of Butch?" she said.

"Maybe they have. Brent says there's one hell of a lot of activity."

"You're getting a lot of news from Brent these days."

"It's the male club, Babe. When a man's woman's life is on the line, your buddies have to pull for you." He was grinning, but it was only half a joke.

She looked into his eyes while sleep suddenly fled, leaving her brain clear and filling with too much blood. "Does Brent think I'm your woman?" was the closest she could come to it.

He grinned. "Yup. So do I. What do you think?"

She said, "I think I love you."

Johnny nodded once. "I guess that'll do," he said. "You hungry?"

She wanted to say she thought she'd been blind for eighteen years, but she didn't know how. So she said, "Yes, starving. Have we eaten today? I forget."

"There was a sandwich at the police station, but you can't call that eating. It's ready when you are," he finished, leaving her to go back to the kitchen.

Johnny's woman got up and went to the bathroom for a quick wash, then threw some clothes on and followed him. The table was set casually, but the food smelled divine.

"Mmm." She sniffed appreciatively. "Did you get any sleep?"

"I grabbed a couple of hours when Harry came over. He's gone home to sleep now. He'll be back at midnight to take the night shift. Steak okay?"

"Perfect," she said. "Does this mean you won't stop cooking?"

He threw an amused look at her as he set a steaming plate of food in front of her. Baked potatoes with sour cream and string beans sat beside a steak and freshly sliced tomato. "Forgive me if the truth is cruel, Babe," he said, sitting at his own place, "but if my chauvinist principles are going to mean eating your cooking every day, the chauvinist principles have to go."

She wondered if they would joke their way right into marriage. "I cook some things very well," she said defensively.

"And you will," he said, attacking the steak with an appetite that looked the equal of her own. For a few minutes there was silence as they ate, and then, once the edge was gone, they sat back and smiled at each other.

"I suppose it won't be so bad," she admitted, mock-grudgingly. "Though I don't know who I'll phone in future when I'm in trouble."

"That's easy," Johnny said, chewing. "You won't phone. You'll nudge me."

They laughed. She couldn't be sure they were serious. She wondered if he could. Were they really going to live together? She'd lived in the same apartment for three years, and she loved it, but it was too small for—

"Oh, my God!" she said suddenly, remembering. "My apartment! My *computer*!"

"I wondered when you were going to remember," he observed.

"Johnny, they even took my floppies! I've lost everything—all my research notes for future columns, the Janet Smith stuff—ages of work!" Now that she'd remembered, she couldn't believe it had left her mind for one minute. "What am I going to *do*?"

"Right now, you're going to forget about it and finish your dinner," he said. "There's no use worrying."

"Can I go back there? Can I go and see how bad the hard disk is? Maybe it's not as bad as I thought."

He said, "Let's wait till Jerry Mandala is arrested before you show your face, okay?"

"There wasn't one thing on that computer about Jerry Mandala!" she exclaimed irritably. "What do you suppose they imagined I was writing?"

"An exposé? The info is easy enough to get hold of."

"God, and just for that I will! I can't wait to get my teeth into him and his phony poverty. Upper Canada College, did you say? Do you think his family is from back East?"

Johnny shrugged. "You'll find out, I'm sure."

"I'm going to phone George first thing in the morning!" she promised wildly. "I'm going to ask him to let me have the story. Do you think I can write about the Hong Kong connection without getting into a libel suit?"

"I think when the lid blows on this it'll be open season on Jerry Mandala."

"Johnny, what do you think happened to Gordon Harrison? Is he alive or dead?"

He looked serious. "Dead," he said flatly. "Otherwise Sandy McMaster wouldn't be."

She shuddered. "And you think they were really planning to kill me last night?"

He shook his head doubtfully. "It would have been a pretty stupid thing to do, right from his yacht, but I wasn't going to risk it."

"But *why*?"

"Because you'd made the connection about David Stockton. The same reason they nabbed your friend Julie. And as Williams said, they couldn't know what else you knew."

That sobered her, but she couldn't ask the question. She wanted to go on believing that Julie was alive.

"And is that why they killed Sandy McMaster?"

He shrugged. "He knew something, but I doubt if it was the same piece of information."

"Something to do with how the plane went missing. But the biggest question is, why kill Gordon Harrison? What advantage could that possibly give them? It doesn't make sense!"

"No, it doesn't," Johnny agreed. "It's as crazy as all hell. But I'm sure of one thing—Jerry Mandala is no master criminal. He doesn't have the brains, and he doesn't have the nerve. I don't believe he organized this.''

She said, ''I noticed the same thing last night. He was sweating, you know, when he told me the plane was coming. He said it was union troubles, but Harry said they weren't union men.''

''They weren't. We saw them go aboard.''

''I'll be so glad to get to the bottom of this,'' said Lou.

She tried to do just that over the next few hours, sitting with notebook and pencil making notes while she and Johnny went over the events of the past weeks. At ten, they stopped to watch the news. There was nothing, not even the story of Lou's brief disappearance, but since it was *The National* and came out of Toronto, this was hardly surprising. Later the local station broadcast made a brief mention of it, saying Lou had fallen off the ship while watching the fireworks and a passing fishing boat had rescued her.

''Did the reporter make that up, or is that the story the cops are putting out?'' she demanded. ''I sound like such a fool.''

''Which isn't too far off the truth, Babe,'' Johnny observed mildly.

She laughed and threw a cushion at him. ''I suppose I'll never live this down?''

''All depends. You might get a medal.''

''Or a job as reporter, if I play my cards right. I wonder if I'd like that.''

''Would you?''

''No,'' she said after a moment. She liked the independence of being free-lance. And besides, if she wanted children, she had better start soon. She looked at Johnny again, remembering the way he had been in grade five, and thought, yes, I suppose that's what I've been waiting for. To have children who look like Johnny.

''Good,'' he said.

"What about you?" she asked. "Are you happy being a detective?"

"Not really," said Johnny. "Now that I've got my degree I thought I'd have a look around."

"Your degree? What—have you got your B.A.?"

"I will have, as soon as I write my last exam."

"Terrific! I didn't know it was so close! Why didn't you tell me?"

"I'm telling you now."

"It's taken a long time," mused Lou.

"Yup," he agreed.

"Johnny, why was it you didn't go to university right after high school? You could have applied for the government grant and loan program."

"I had to start earning. It wasn't just a question of looking after myself. My mother was too ill to support herself anymore."

She looked at him. "Did you ever really enjoy being a cop?" she asked softly.

He shrugged. "Not really. I didn't think it was a bad choice. But even then I wanted to be a lawyer. A cop seemed like the next best thing."

"Is that why you quit in the end?"

He shook his head. "I quit because of Ben."

"Oh," she said, remembering.

"I couldn't forget that Ben was killed by a man I could have had behind bars three months earlier if the department had given me a lousy two thousand bucks to pay an informer. And I couldn't forgive it."

"Why wouldn't they pay? I've never understood that."

Johnny shook his head. "Just bureaucratic foot-dragging. It happens all the time."

"It's pretty horrible."

"It was enough for me, for sure. There's nothing more frustrating than being a cop." He grinned at her, dispelling the gloom. "Unless it's trying to keep you out of trouble."

"And now you'll enroll in law school at last."

He shrugged. "It's what I planned, but it would mean three years full-time, so that's out."

"Why is it out?"

He looked at her. "If you don't know the answer to that, Babe, I can't tell you."

She dropped her eyes. "I don't want to be the cause of you losing a dream."

"Balls," said Johnny, without heat. "There are dreams and dreams."

"What are your other dreams?"

"Right now, I have two. I'd like to start a family pretty soon. I'd like to have some kids around before I'm too old to enjoy them."

Her heart skipped a beat. "And the second?" she asked.

Johnny glanced down at his watch, then his eyes looked into hers. They were laughing. "I'd like to get into the bedroom with you before Harry gets here to take the midnight shift," he said.

Chapter 21

Tuesday morning it was announced that Jerry Mandala had been taken in for questioning by the police. It hit the province like a small bomb: the premier's golden-haired boy was being asked questions by the Mounties about kidnapping and murder. The press could scarcely rein in their delight as they prepared to feast on the still-kicking carcass.

Brent phoned to tell Johnny an hour before Lou heard it on the noon news at Johnny's office. "Does this mean I'm out of danger?" she asked. It didn't suit her at all to be sitting here doing nothing much while Johnny worked.

"I wish I knew," said Johnny.

"Can I go home for a couple of hours, at least, and look at that computer?"

Johnny sighed. "Can you wait till I can go with you?"

"How long?" she asked. The thought of the total loss that might be represented by that smashed computer wasn't letting her rest. She wanted to know the worst.

"Hour, hour and a half," Johnny promised, and he made good on the promise. By two o'clock they were parking in front of her building.

Johnny followed all the bodyguard rituals again, getting her into the apartment, but they met no trouble, and the apartment seemed untouched since last time. She carefully dismantled the smashed housing of the computer and looked inside. "The mother board's in ruins, and so's the floppy drive," she told Johnny. "But the hard disk itself looks kind of okay. Maybe we could take it out to Syd's later."

"It's all Greek to me," said Johnny.

Syd was her cousin and a computer expert. It occurred to Lou that the art of a comfortable life was collecting experts around you, so that in any extremity someone you trusted had the information or capability you needed. She passed this observation on to Johnny as he helped her lift the hard drive out of the wreckage.

"I suppose that's the principal behind marriage—and government cabinets," he said. "Then you get the problem of the Prime Minister's experts—or the spouses—offering their services around to others, and when the crunch comes they can't provide support in both directions. I wonder if Gordon Harrison had a little problem of conflict of interest?"

Which meant he hadn't stopped thinking about him. "But where?" Lou said. "I mean, do you kill a man because he doesn't provide your friends with passports?"

"Anyway, that's not his responsibility," Johnny said. "It's the Immigration Minister who deals with exceptions to the Immigration Act."

They were halfway to the door when Lou stopped dead. "You're right!" she said. "I've been thinking along completely mistaken lines. What's the Solicitor-General responsible for?"

"Prisons and corrections, mainly," said Johnny. "The Parole Board, Gaming, Transportation of Dangerous Goods...."

"How do you know so much about it?" Lou demanded.

"I took a couple of courses in Canadian government in second and third year," Johnny said smugly.

"And you remember all that?"

"I looked it up this morning when you were in the shower," he confessed. She hit him on the arm.

"You ever thought of running for public office?" she joked. "You seem to have the necessary urge to duplicity."

"Nope," said Johnny.

"You could run for municipal office. That wouldn't be so awful, would it?" She'd been joking, but now she'd said it, it didn't sound so bad an idea.

"Babe," he said gently, "those people are bureaucrats. They do things by committee and by consensus. And committees never do anything, and consensus is never reached. You think I could handle that?"

"No," she agreed. "You'd start tearing up desks after the first week." In the way the human brain has, she suddenly heard what he'd said. "Transportation of Dangerous Goods," she repeated slowly. "You think Jerry Mandala's been getting ministerial approval for moving dangerous—" She stopped suddenly. "Did you say Gaming? Does the Solicitor-General run the Gaming Branch?"

"Yup."

"He's got a casino ship. You think there might be something in that?"

"It does kind of leap to the eye."

She suddenly noticed her answering machine lying half-hidden under a scramble of papers. The message light was on.

"It seems like days since I've listened to my messages," she exclaimed, crouching down over the little machine and pressing the rewind button. "I guess it's really not that long, is it?"

There were nearly a dozen hang-up calls, probably people who had heard the news of her disappearance off the yacht yesterday, and were unable to believe it. These were followed by a message from George. "Does this mean you're back home today?" he asked. "And why the hell are you being so lazy when you should be writing up something for us on Mandala? Don't you realize the lid's coming off? Call me, please."

"What's he talking about?" asked Johnny.

Lou shook her head. Two more beeps indicated hang-up calls. "My outgoing message is out-of-date, I can't change it." She rewound the tape. "Which reminds me—do you think we could drop down to the beach for a few minutes? I'd like to say hi. They must have all thought I was dead for a while."

Johnny knew all about her community of summer friends on Bikini Beach—the group of people she saw nearly every day in summer, but, with a few exceptions like Tom and Dorothy, only rarely in winter. He called them her "fair weather friends."

"All right," he said. "But only a few minutes, okay? I've got work piling up."

They drove to the beach in the truck, though walking would have been faster, and parked not far from the long spit of rocks that marked the place the locals called Bikini Beach.

Lou climbed out of the truck, and the walk across the grassy ground at the edge of Stanley Park was like a homecoming. The sun beating its welcome down on her head, the distant noise of the surf, the sound of a quiet radio off to her left, the kite high in the sky that marked the position of the fruit-juice stand down the way, and the gulls were a welcome confirmation that normal life was still going on in spite of the past few frightening days.

They walked slowly down to the seawall and along to th
spit. Away to the left the broad curve of sand around En
glish Bay was covered with bodies even on a Tuesday after
noon, but just below them now was the small, less popula
beach, sheltered by the spit and overhung by a large tree
that she and her friends had chosen. "It's a real commu
nity," she had told Johnny once. "We all know each other
and if strangers do come, we make sure they obey ou
rules."

"Like what?" he'd asked.

"Like, no radios, and clean up your dog-do." She'
laughed, telling him of the day that Dorothy had led a small,
determined delegation of indignant sunbathers down to the
water's edge, where they had forced a dog owner to take hi
Lab's intended contribution to the ocean's coliform coun
with him in a bag instead.

The beach lay about six feet below the level of the path
and the small cliff that bordered it was faced with rocks
Lou stood for a moment above the heads of the sunbath
ers, picking out the bodies she recognized, and, almost im
mediately below, the sun beds that marked Tom and
Dorothy's little territory.

"The tide's a long way out," she observed sadly. It was
always nice to sun when the tide was out, because there was
so much room. "I wish I could st—"

She broke off suddenly as Dorothy looked up and waved,
gesticulating wildly at the small figure sitting beside her on
the sand. Lou stared for a breathless moment, taking in the
slender body, the tiny build, the long dark hair.

"Julie!" she cried incredulously. "It's Julie!" She started
to scramble down the path over the rocks.

"I'm so glad you came," Julie said. "I really didn't know
where to go. I phoned you from the airport, and your mes
sage said you'd be here, but Dorothy said she didn't think
you'd be down today. I was just wondering what to do."

"What happened?" Lou said. "Where did you go?"

"Butch took me to Hong Kong. Golly, it's been weird. I don't know what's going on. We were in a big hotel, and he made me stay in the room most of the time. He wouldn't let me out of his sight. One day he got a phone call and made me write a postcard to you. Did you get it?"

"Yes," said Lou. "I've been so worried about you!"

"Before that he wouldn't let me write any letters or anything. I couldn't figure it out."

"Why did he take you there? Did he tell you?"

"He was bragging that he'd killed someone really important. I didn't believe him. Is it true?"

"Butch? He said *he* killed him?"

"Who was it?"

"Gordon Harrison. The Solicitor-General," Lou told her, and Julie's eyes got wide.

"Oh, my goodness!"

"Why did he kill him? Did he say why?" Lou turned and waved up at Johnny, still on the bank above her head, his eyes restlessly watching. She thought, they can't find us here, we're safer here than anywhere, unless— "Do you think you were followed from the airport?" She interrupted suddenly.

"No. I don't even think Butch knows where I've gone. Anyway, I ripped the important pages out of his passport when I took my own. He really killed the Solicitor-General?"

"I guess so. But why?"

"He said it was a mistake. They were only supposed to scare him, but he died. Butch thought that was pretty cool."

"Then what did they do with the body—and the plane?" Lou asked, without expecting an answer.

"They sank it," Julie said.

"*What?*"

"Yeah, up near some island. I forget the name."

"Erehwemos?"

"That sounds right. Is that an Indian name?"

"I think it's 'Somewhere' spelled backward," said Lou.

"Weird," said Julie. "They sank it so people would think it had crashed—that's what Butch said. And then Mr. Mandala said Butch would have to disappear and get a new identity." She lifted a handful of sand and let it trail through her fingers. "Butch thought that was really great. He thought it made him a real international criminal. He kept saying, 'You're looking at a world-class criminal.' He really scared me when he talked like that. I think Butch is crazy."

Someone threw a stone, and it churned the sand a few yards away, making it spray wildly up. Lou frowned. She'd never seen a stone do that before.

"But you—"

"Lou!" she heard above her head. *"Lou!"*

The sound of warning in Johnny's voice electrified her, and she leaped to her feet. "Get her out!" cried Johnny. Behind him, two men in dark suits were standing on the hill above the beach, pointing in their direction. Johnny turned in their direction. "Two targets!" he shouted back over his shoulder to her. "Give them two targets!"

She grabbed Julie's hand, pulled her to her feet, and started running.

"What's going on?" Dorothy demanded, sitting upright on her bed. Then, in an altered voice, "Who's *that*?"

The water had never seemed so far away. Lou thought wildly that she would never be grateful for low tide again. The sand sprayed up in front of them again as another bullet went wide, and belatedly she understood Johnny's message. "We have to give them two targets!" she panted to Julie. "Run zigzag! Get under the water."

With that she let go Julie's hand and veered right, toward the long spit of rock that lay pointing out to the ocean, almost entirely out of the water. If the tide had been higher, they could have swum underwater around the point and hidden against the rocks, but it offered no such protection now, as the two girls staggered their separate ways down the long stretch of gluey sand to the water.

Behind them, on the beach, their two dark clad pursuers now ran to the edge of the small cliff overlooking the beach, and one of them scrambled down while the other stood to take aim at the running figures below. Neither of them seemed to spare a thought for the inhabitants of the beach. In their experience, perhaps, guns frightened bystanders into quiescence. But the inhabitants of Bikini Beach were more than bystanders. They were a community.

At the top of the small cliff, Johnny hammered the man who was shooting with a body blow that took them both clear of the rocks, and they smashed down onto the beach below, landing among towels and picnic baskets and sending a plastic bowl flying, the cherries inside spraying in all directions. Johnny, winded, lay for a moment on top of his quarry, watching in stupefaction the small war that was erupting around them on the beach.

A tall, slender man of sixty sprinted over to where Johnny lay, put his foot sharply on the dark-suited man's right wrist, and bent to relieve him of his gun. "All right, got it," he told Johnny, and stood guard while Johnny dragged the man's arm up behind his back and made him immobile. Johnny suddenly recognized the older man as Tom.

Behind him, a large, tanned red-haired woman smashed the second man in the teeth with a wickedly swung chrome-plated beach bed as he tried to negotiate his way down the precarious rock face. He lost his balance and fell back among the rocks, swearing and lifting his gun hand, but a younger woman in a black bikini and another in blue heaved a metal picnic cooler into his face, while other tanned bodies rushed up to pelt him with rocks or whatever was handy, including food, dishes, a Frisbee, and the end of a whipping towel.

Along the beach a few yards, someone was screaming for the police with a voice like an air-raid siren, while a mother and her two sons were flat behind a log, the two boys appearing at intervals to throw stones at the much beset man against the rocks.

A white-haired man of seventy rushed up with the umbrella he had ripped from his beach chair, and started smashing the man's gun hand against the rock. Everybody was screaming encouragement and orders at everyone else, and Johnny noted without surprise now that the brown bodies running on all parts of the beach were heading toward, and not away from, the scene of the action.

A bullet twanged against rocks, making people gasp. "Get his gun!" the cavalier with the umbrella grunted to a man wearing a ridiculous straw hat. "Get his bloody gun!" His voice held a tone of pure military command. He pressed the man's wrist cruelly against the rock with the point of the umbrella while the man in the hat obeyed. He met with no resistance from their stunned victim.

The white-haired ex-officer dropped his umbrella to snatch the gun from the man in the straw hat and leveled it at the man against the rocks. "Get up, you swine," he ordered, in an English accent, the tone of his voice giving no ground to the fact that he was dressed in baggy red swim trunks. "Get on your feet."

I'm in a war movie, Johnny thought. This is the citizenry capturing the Nazi infiltrators. He put his head against the poor slob beneath him and gave in to laughter.

Chapter 22

"They must all be crazy."

Lou laughed. "I guess so," she said. The speaker was Brent, and he was talking about her beach friends. "But everybody in Vancouver is a little off-the-wall."

"Take on two armed men?" Brent shook his head. "You're lucky none of you were killed or seriously hurt. Never challenge a gun. Never."

"If my friends had followed that advice," Lou pointed out reasonably, "Julie and I and probably Johnny, too, might have been killed. We've got to start taking these people on somewhere."

"Well, not when they've got guns," insisted Brent.

"Not when they've got guns, and not when they're going to rape us—when *do* we get to fight back?" Lou asked. "I'm grateful for what they did. I think it was very brave."

"So is the department, of course. But—"

Johnny was silent, listening to the quiet argument between them. Julie was sitting opposite him, also silent. She was staying in Lou's apartment until she got settled, and tonight Johnny had asked Brent over to give them the scoop on Jerry Mandala's confession.

"I'll say one thing," Julie interrupted suddenly. "Butch is the kind of guy who used to mug people and all that, and I'll tell you, he always despised people who gave in. He despised me, too. He'd say, 'Why don't you stand up to me?' I think he used to run away if people stood up to him. But I never could."

"You're a very tiny woman," said Johnny quietly. "He was over six foot. Why did he expect you to be able to stand up to him?"

She shook her head. "Yeah, I guess you're right. But he always made me feel like a coward."

"That's all right," said Brent, in a sudden surge of revulsion. "We get him extradited back here, I'll give him a little message from you he'll remember. I'll show him coward. Oops," he said, glancing over at Lou. "You never heard that," he warned.

Lou didn't think a police beating was the answer to anything, but she held her peace. In his rough way, Brent was trying to show Julie she was important. And if she'd had Butch in front of her, Lou would have been tempted herself to give him something "from Julie."

"I knew a guy used to say, after he finished creating it, God picked up Canada by one edge and shook it, and all the loose screws and nuts rolled down to the other end and got caught in the mountains. And that's why we have so many kooks in B.C.," Brent said, reverting to the argument. "Still, I'd like to have seen what happened on that beach. Those two perps must have been the most surprised guys in the world." He laughed.

"I don't understand who they were, or why they wanted to kill us," Julie said.

"Ah, it's a long story," said Brent.

"And you're going to tell it to us," Johnny pointed out with a grin.

"I *thought* I might have to sing for my supper." He reached for the can of beer Lou had set within easy reach, and snapped it open.

"Why don't you tell us what happened to you," Brent suggested to Julie. "And then I'll fill in what's missing."

Lou looked at him. Johnny had said he was going to give them the details of Mandala's confession, but she hadn't really believed it.

"Well," said Julie. "All I know is, I was pretty sure I saw Butch outside my apartment one day. I was really worried but I didn't have time to do anything, because the next night he was waiting for me when I got home."

"Was that on Wednesday?" asked Lou.

"Right. Wednesday. He said he was going to be rich and start a whole new life and had to go to Hong Kong, and I was supposed to go with him. He said I knew secret things about him and there were people who didn't want me talking, and that if I didn't go with him, my life wouldn't be worth shi—" She looked around apologetically. "Sorry, but that's what he said."

"Crude, but probably true," observed Brent. "They had to get you out of circulation one way or the other."

"But what did I know about him?"

"You knew he wasn't a pilot, for one," said Lou. "And you knew he wasn't American and hadn't been a soldier in Vietnam."

"No, I didn't," said Julie. "I didn't know him like that—all about his past."

"But you knew he'd been in Oakalla instead of Vietnam in the early seventies. And you knew he was alive after the plane went missing, because you saw him in the car."

"Yeah...but the funny thing is, you know, I heard about that plane, and I thought it was funny the names being the same, but I never thought of it being Butch."

"I have a feeling," said Johnny, "that Butch might have lied to Mandala about how much you knew so that he would be allowed to take you with him."

"He said he was really mad when I ran out on him. He went crazy looking for me," Julie said. "It's not me. He just hates to think anyone else has won. If he let me get away it would mean I'd won. That's the way Butch thinks."

"So you left the apartment on Wednesday night?" asked Lou.

Julie shook her head. "Butch said he had to lie low. The plane to Hong Kong was leaving in the morning, and we waited in my apartment till a car came and picked us up to take us to the airport. We sneaked out the back way to the alley. I thought it was because they'd found out about that Burnaby Mall murder that he had to get out of town. But I was afraid to ask. We argued all night, but he said he'd kill me if I didn't go with him, and I was afraid he meant it."

"We think we've got that Burnaby perp, but we'll be asking Butch questions about it, just in case," Brent told them. "No point locking the wrong guy up if the right one is right there." He laughed.

"So on Thursday, one of Mandala's men went back to your apartment to pay the rent and the other bills, I guess," said Lou.

"Yes, they made me give them the keys. Butch hardly let me take anything with me. I wonder what they did with all my things?"

"They threw them out," said Lou. "I've salvaged your little cat, but that's all."

"Oh, that's all right. I didn't have a lot of good things or anything. Butch said he'd buy me new stuff in Hong Kong. He did, too. It was one of the few times I got out. It was great because Chinese women are small, too, and all the nice styles came in my size. But I left it all there."

"We'll get you some clothes," Lou said.

"Oh, I'm not worried about clothes! I'm just really grateful to be here. I don't even understand why you started looking for me."

"Well, because I was worried. I thought for sure that Butch had come and grabbed you and forced you to go with him. I went to the police, but they wouldn't do anything, so I had to do it myself, with Johnny's help." She remembered the day she had gone to ask for it. Not very long ago, yet so much had happened it seemed as if a lifetime had passed since then.

Julie shook her head in disbelief that anyone should care so much. "Boy," she said.

"Lou really stirred up the ant heap," said Johnny. "Just when they must have been thinking they might get away with it, Lou went to Mandala's office and told him that *she* knew David Stockton had been in prison when he was supposed to have been a soldier." He shook his head. "If I'd known then—when you look at it, it's amazing they didn't kill you immediately."

"But why?" demanded Julie. "I mean, why did Butch have to disappear? Because he killed someone important?"

"It's looking like it," said Brent. "Very important."

"The Solicitor-General?" Julie pressed, trying to believe it.

"That's right."

"But *why*? What was going on? I never believed him when he said he'd killed someone important," she muttered as an aside. "I thought he was just bragging. But if he did, why didn't they just have him arrested? Why did they let him hide and give him money?"

"It wasn't as easy as that," said Brent.

"Jerry Mandala was trying to get favors from Gordon Harrison in return for a lot of support at election time. Financial support, and also a lot of publicity stuff," Lou began.

"He'd bought his politician and now he wanted to know he owned him," Julie said, nodding. "Why did he want Butch to scare him? Harrison didn't want to pay up?"

"It wasn't Mandala who wanted him scared," said Lou. "It was—I think first we have to backtrack a little." Lou glanced at Johnny to see if he minded her stealing his thunder, but he waved her on. "Okay—in the first place, as you know, there are a lot of people in Hong Kong who want to get out before it reverts to mainland China's possession in a few years. They're taking their money with them, and naturally they're looking for places to put it. And some of it, naturally, is crime money. Crime has to relocate the same as businesses do, especially if they want to go on making money into the future. Am I explaining this clearly?"

"Yes," said Julie after a moment. "It's pretty awful, when you think about it, isn't it? That's *really* crime looking for a place to happen."

They laughed a little, lightening a mood that had been growing imperceptibly gloomy.

"Johnny did a lot of research on Mandala's background, and what he found out is that the whole 'Mandala Success Story' is a crock. Jerry Mandala's success all started when some Hong Kong people started investing in him. Period. That was about five years ago, and they've spent those five years building up Mandala's reputation as a business genius. Most of his money was coming straight from Hong Kong."

"That's pretty smart, when you think of it," said Julie. "If you want a rich front man, make your own."

"I like that," said Johnny. He flicked a glance at Lou and their eyes met in understanding. He was seeing in Julie what Lou had seen.

"Among all the real estate and other investments," Lou went on, "they bought some casino cruise ships. At the same time all this was giving him a pretty solid reputation as poor-boy-made-good and simon-pure and all that. He had to look clean, and he had to get government contacts. They made up a whole past for him that gave him credibility with the public and with people like the Premier."

"You mean, Jerry Mandala was a complete phony?"

Lou nodded. "From the poverty-stricken background on up. Jerry Mandala's father made his money in tableware back East. He wasn't poor at all. The family he was supposed to be a 'poor relation' of was his own family."

"But why didn't they realize people would find out?"

Brent said, "I get the feeling that it was Mandala's own brainchild. His friends didn't really understand Canada and didn't realize how much of a lie he was telling, or how dangerous it would be if a journalist got hold of it. I think Mandala really believes those free enterprise dreams, and wanted to believe himself that he was a poor boy making good on nothing but his own hard work."

"That wouldn't surprise me," Johnny said, nodding. "The guy's always struck me as a little too far off the ground."

"Yeah, well, he came down with a bump, all right."

"So there he is with his money and his connections," said Julie. "Then what?"

"His Hong Kong backers wanted to get into the B.C. scene in a big way," put in Brent. "They picked a couple of politicians who looked like good bets and started financing them through Mandala. Gordon Harrison was one. When it paid off with him nabbing the Solicitor-General's portfolio in the reshuffle a while ago, they started to make plans."

"You mean, they started to look at what the Solicitor-General could do for them?" Julie asked, and Lou glanced at Johnny with another little smile. Julie was no fool.

"That's right," said Brent approvingly. "The Solicitor-General's office runs the Gaming Commission in the province. And the Gaming Commission licenses casinos and bingos and raffles."

"And I don't suppose they were interested in bingo," said Johnny.

"They were interested in getting a license for a couple of big casinos," said Brent.

"Casinos aren't legal in B.C., are they?" Julie asked. "Or not very."

"They are," said Brent, "but they have to be run for charity. Fifty percent of the win goes to charity."

"That's true," said Johnny, "all over the country. It's a federal statute. But the number and size of the casinos in any given province come under provincial jurisdiction."

"Now, this is where you know more than I do," said Brent dryly. "All that legal education."

"Just Business Law and Canadian Government 301," Johnny grinned. "It's within the powers of each individual province to license casinos and decide on the size of the casino and the size of the maximum bet, as long as that fifty percent of the win is going to charity. All right? And Gordon Harrison was the guy, now, who'd have that responsibility. So Mandala's friends took a quick look at the scenery, and decided they wanted to put their money into gambling. Jerry Mandala started asking Gordon Harrison for some action on increasing the number and size of the casinos he'd license, and making sure Jerry Mandala got a license to operate."

"Is that how he got the casino ship?" asked Lou.

Johnny shook his head. "That operates outside the twelve-mile limit. It's not subject to the licensing laws at all. They could run as many of those as they wanted, but they're expensive to run and awkward for business, and you only get a certain segment of the gambling population that way. And you can't gamble in rough weather, for example. These guys wanted casinos on the mainland, and they thought Gordon Harrison should make it easy.

"But again they must have been reckoning without a clear understanding of the local political climate. The number of casinos in the province is limited to eighteen, and Gordon Harrison couldn't change that by himself. Nor any of the other laws these people wanted changed. He had to take it to the Cabinet. Unfortunately, there he ran into the Premier's position on gaming.''

"So he couldn't come up with the goods," said Brent. "Mandala understood that, but he couldn't explain to the Hong Kong Mafia what the Premier's religious stance had to do with them getting their casino licenses. They'd paid for action, and they wanted action. And they are people who are used to threatening people to get what they want.

"And that's why Gordon Harrison was flying up to Erehwemos that day, according to Mandala's confession. It wasn't a fishing holiday at all. He was being called in to talk to the big guns."

"Oh, my God," said Lou. "They were going to *threaten* him? Are they crazy?"

"Ah, you know the Hong Kong Mafia, Babe. They all sit around watching old Jimmy Cagney movies. They think that's how it's done with politicians."

"Well, and maybe it is, for all we know," Lou said. "Now that I think of it, what do we really know?"

"I know what happened next," said Julie. "Butch was on the plane with him, because Mr. Mandala had told him to soften the guy up. And instead, he killed him. It was a mistake, he said he didn't know his own strength. He really doesn't," she added, with a matter-of-factness that made them shiver.

"Mandala was more scared of his friends than Harrison was," Brent added. "He hoped by scaring Harrison to take the heat off himself. He says he never ordered violence, but I guess we won't know the truth of that till we get Butch over here. What Mandala says is that the seaplane arrived at Erehwemos with Butch, Gordon Harrison's dead body and a hysterical pilot aboard.

"Mandala panicked. His Hong Kong bosses weren't due to arrive till the next day. He couldn't wait that long. The best he could think of was to get Sandy McMaster to take the plane out and scuttle it with Gordon Harrison's body aboard. Then he reported the plane missing, and flew straight down to Vancouver. Mandala's a pilot himself, and he told police he flew down alone looking for signs of the plane. In fact, of course, Butch and McMaster were also aboard that flight, and as soon as it arrived Butch went into hiding, and McMaster went home and told his wife to tell everybody he'd been sick in bed all day."

"But why did they say Butch was the pilot?" asked Julie. "That doesn't make sense, does it?"

"I'll bet Sandy McMaster refused to be listed as the pilot since it would have meant he'd have to go missing," said Lou. "He had a wife and family to think about."

"Oh, right!" said Julie. "I never thought of that. Too bad they didn't say Gordon Harrison was flying the plane himself."

"They should have had you there."

"Well, but maybe he didn't have a pilot's license, either, and that would have been easy to prove." Julie was thinking aloud. "Yeah, I see their problem."

"Not many people really want to go away and start over as someone else," said Brent. "It's a very painful life."

"Butch didn't mind," said Julie. "He thought it was great."

"Mandala gave money to Butch and told him to fly to Hong Kong, where he assumed his friends could supply Butch with a new identity and a false passport. Butch insisted on tracking you down, Julie, telling Mandala you were crucial to the success of the plot. With Mandala's connections behind him, of course, it took less than twenty-four hours to find where you were."

Julie shuddered. "It's awful to think you can't get away from people if you want."

"I'm afraid this is the modern world," said Brent. "What Mandala was planning for Butch was going to be more expensive and complicated than he knew. It's not easy to disappear, even if you change your identity. You really have to undergo plastic surgery to make it stick at all. People travel too much these days. There's a lot of risk."

"Yeah, Butch didn't want any plastic surgery." Julie grinned. "He liked his own looks too much. He had an argument on the phone about that, with Mr. Mandala. Mr. Mandala was really nervous."

"But he thought he might carry it off until Lou arrived on the scene, I suppose," said Johnny. "Lou scared them all. She had to be stopped."

"That's when I knew someone was worried about me," Julie said. "Butch got that phone call, and made me write that postcard to Lou. Up till then I thought nobody even remembered who I was. I was so depressed."

"Just in case the postcard didn't work, Mandala also had someone phone me with bribes and threats. He even offered me a phony job that would send me out of town."

"Actually," said Brent, "Mandala says he wasn't behind the threats. He was frightened, but according to him, he didn't intend to kill anybody. He said he had offered you a job, but he didn't know about anyone phoning to buy you off. He figured he could catch you with honey faster than vinegar, to use his own phrase. He thought if you figured he was interested in you, you'd lay off trying to expose him."

"Charming," said Lou. "What a little self-interest can do, eh?"

"We're assuming, not that it'll ever be proven, that the Hong Kong end arranged that phone call independently."

"Which would explain the sheer stupidity of it," said Lou.

"When you went to visit Sandy McMaster, McMaster phoned Mandala to tell him he couldn't face any more and was going to confess. McMaster didn't know about the

Hong Kong connection, or he might have been more careful. We'd been giving McMaster a pretty hard time," Brent admitted. "We figured he was the weak link, and he was being ridden pretty hard."

"Weak link in what?" asked Lou. "Did you suspect there was something funny about the plane?"

"Are you kidding? The thing stank like rotting dog dirt," said Brent. "Excuse me, ladies. The Mounties were putting everything they had into it, and some VPD detectives—me included—were seconded over to them for extra manpower. We could smell cover-up a mile away."

"Have you found the plane yet?"

Brent nodded. "Only a couple of hours ago. Mandala's friends had got it covered up with underwater military camouflage, but he identified the place for us. Gordon Harrison's body's been recovered. No autopsy report yet, of course. That'll take a while."

"So Sandy McMaster called Jerry, and Jerry called me," said Lou. "And I walked right into the lion's mouth." She smiled ruefully at Johnny, who grinned back.

"Of course, after this, Babe, you'll listen to me every time," he said.

"Mandala told his friends that McMaster was cracking, and why. They told him to ignore McMaster and arrange a meeting with Lou. He arranged it on board the casino yacht. It was when he talked to them on the yacht that he learned what had happened to McMaster. And that they wanted to kill Lou, too. That's when Mandala cracked. He didn't want any part of it."

"Oh, my gosh!" breathed Julie.

"So they really did plan to kill me?" Lou asked calmly. She had gotten used to the fact that she had been cold-bloodedly chosen as a target; it no longer shocked her as it obviously shocked Julie now.

"Yes, but Mandala didn't know where, or when. He was sick of the whole thing, and he wasn't having any more deaths on his conscience, he says. He got out of the meeting and arranged to get you off the ship. He'd finally figured out that he might be expendable, too. In which case they wouldn't worry about having you disappear off his yacht. Up till then, he said, he thought you were safe, since so many people had seen you with him. But if he was going down the tubes, you weren't safe.''

"That's what I'd figured," said Lou. "That I had to be safe on board, because he couldn't risk another scandal."

"Well, you might have been right," said Brent. "But I'm glad Johnny got you off. There's no saying."

"Cursing your stupidity all the way," said Johnny. "Did your ears burn, Babe?"

She smiled lazily at him.

"Mandala didn't know what had happened to you," said Brent. "He thought they were lying to him. He'd figured you were safe with a stranger, but when you disappeared, he imagined that Harry Thornton had been one of their hired guns."

"And all the time he was one of mine," Johnny reminded Lou dryly.

"When we brought Mandala in to make a statement about your disappearance, he saw you and realized his mistake before he could talk."

"And how is Staff Sergeant Goldring feeling these days?" Lou asked sweetly.

"Well, let's say he ain't exactly happy," temporized Brent. He obviously didn't intend to talk about internal matters, whatever else he talked about.

"Has Mandala been charged yet?" asked Johnny.

"Yeah, we got him without bail on conspiracy to murder and a few others. Fortunately the judge listened to us. A guy like that could disappear in five minutes. We'd never see him again."

"And what about all these Hong Kong people? Have they been arrested, too?" asked Julie.

"The two on the beach have, but they're just cheap help. As far as the others go—they're pretty shadowy people when it comes to grabbing them," said Brent. "We know who a couple of them are, but I'm afraid that part of it isn't so easy. It'll take time."

"What about Butch?" asked Julie.

"Thanks to you, he's been arrested in Hong Kong. We're in the process of extradition now."

"Why thanks to me? Because I wrecked his passport?"

"We haven't heard about that bit yet," said Johnny inquiringly.

"He kept me with him all the time, but I saw where he had the tickets and passports. He used to carry the wallet with him, but one night I got up when he was sleeping and took mine out of the wallet and hid them. I tore the ID page out of his passport, too. The next day he didn't check the wallet, he just took it and went out. He always left me in the room without any money. He knew I couldn't go anywhere. I knew he'd be gone all day. I'd been taking a little money from his pockets every day. So when he left I just took a taxi to the airport. I left all my things in the room. I didn't know what I was going to do if I didn't find Lou. Her answering machine said she was at the beach."

"Butch must have called someone when he found you'd gone," said Johnny. "They must have figured you'd run to Lou."

"But how did they find us at the beach?" asked Julie. "Did they follow me from the airport after all?"

"If they did, they didn't have to. Lou told them where to look, same as she told you," said Johnny.

"What?" said Brent, his head snapping forward.

"Lou's answering machine had an old message on it," said Johnny dryly. "It said something like, This is Tuesday and I'm at the beach, though she never bothered to tell me that when she was saying how much she wanted to see all her friends."

Brent slapped his head. "How d'ya like that!"

"That was an old message?" asked Julie.

"Yup," said Johnny.

"Well, it was lucky for me, wasn't it?"

"Who did they want at the beach? Julie or me?" asked Lou.

"Until they talk, we can only guess," Brent said. "My guess is both."

Another little pall threatened to settle over the room. "And then those crazy lunatics started their own Beach Blanket Brawl," said Brent, laughing. "I wish I'd seen that!"

They all laughed a little, but Lou was suddenly remembering Joey McMaster, and wondering how Barb McMaster was getting through the night.

"I suppose if I hadn't done anything, Sandy McMaster might still be alive," she said. "And Julie got away on her own."

"Well," said Julie, "I thought I was pretty well helpless until Butch made me write that postcard. I don't know why, but somehow knowing that someone somewhere cared about me made me want to fight. Up till then I felt kinda like a nobody, you know?"

"Look, Babe, McMaster knew what he was doing when he scuttled that plane and agreed to the cover-up. That was his choice."

"Oh, yeah," said Brent. "He was on the breaking point with you or without you. His mistake was phoning Mandala to announce it. I have to get going," he added, slapping his thighs and getting to his feet. "Please remember, ladies, I haven't spoken to you about any of this. This is strictly a favor."

Lou and Julie nodded.

"I'd like to go home with Johnny tonight," Lou said to Julie quietly, under cover of the two men chatting. "Do you mind staying alone?"

Julie shook her head. "I'll be fine," she said.

"Don't bother with the mess. We can do that tomorrow," said Lou at the door.

Julie hugged her. "I really meant what I said," she said. "It made a big difference to me, knowing you were worried about me. I have a lot to thank you for. More than I can tell you."

Lou felt tears burn her eyes. "Okay," she said. "Believe me, you're welcome."

Brent walked with them to the truck. "Just remember I wasn't here tonight, okay?" he said to Johnny.

"There's no way anybody's going to be able to keep the lid on this," said Johnny. "Are they going to try?"

"Don't think so. But some of what I said is supposed to be kept under wraps for a while. It's gonna get out, as you say. I just don't want it traced back to me."

Johnny nodded, and as Brent disappeared down the softly lighted street, they climbed into the truck and Lou asked, "Why did he come tonight and tell us all that stuff?"

"Ah, he owed me," said Johnny, revving the motor into life.

"Did he? What for?"

"I tipped him off that the David Stockton whose record he pulled for me was the pilot. He's smelling pretty sweet around the department right now."

"Did you? When?"

"As soon as I knew it, Babe. You had a grudge against Goldring, but I wasn't going to sit on information like that. Anyway, I was hoping they could trace the guy and find Julie for you, and then you'd be out of this mess."

"You mean, you thought Julie was with Butch, after all?" It was late; the streets were quiet outside the truck windows.

"Nellie was pretty strong for that viewpoint."

"Good old Nellie. I notice you didn't tell me."

He pulled up at a red light and yawned without answering. She was too tired to joke suddenly, and she leaned against his arm, feeling the comfort of twoness.

"I'll be glad to get home," she said, without thinking. In the darkness of the truck, she didn't notice the glance Johnny threw down at her, or the way that he smiled as he pulled away from the light.

Chapter 23

Johnny's apartment was warmly comforting as they entered, and Lou unconsciously relaxed. Since the break-in, she hadn't felt easy in her own place, and she'd needed this feeling of being at home more than she realized.

"I suppose it's going to take a while before I feel right about my own place again," she observed. "I hate the way they've made me feel about my own home."

"I think you'll get over it after a while," Johnny agreed. She followed him into the kitchen and he pulled out a saucepan. "What do you want to drink?"

"Some decaf, if you've got it. I've had a lot of wine tonight."

"I'm having a cup of hot chocolate."

"Oh, yeah, that sounds much better." She watched in silence as he poured milk into a saucepan, then sat at the table and looked out over the soft Vancouver night.

"What are *we* going to do, Johnny?" she asked, after a moment.

He turned from the counter and looked at her. "Whatever you want, Babe."

Could it really be as simple as that—whatever she wanted?

She said sadly, "There was a young kid on Jerry's yacht, working behind the bar. I looked at him and thought, I could have a son nearly his age, if things had been different. Somehow I can't figure out now why I made the choices I did. Even with Solly, I can't figure out why I thought my career was so important. Sandy McMaster has a boy about five. I don't know why I kept turning my back on having children. What have I done instead that's so important?"

He stirred the hot milk into the mugs in silence. He said, "Babe, I don't think regret's any good. You just have to go on."

"I keep thinking that if we have what we have *now*, we could just as easily have had it *then*."

"Maybe." She stood up and followed him into the sitting room, where he set the mugs on the coffee table. She curled her feet up on the sofa, and he sat beside her and took her in his arms. "But we didn't. And maybe if we'd had it then, we wouldn't have it now. We've both been through a lot of changes, and I think we'd have had to go through them, married or not. But marriage has a way of not surviving those pressures in the modern world."

"You don't think we'd have made it through?"

"I don't know. What I do know is, I know what I want now and I know how to get it. And I'd a damn sight rather have you now for the rest of my life, than have had you for a few years when I was young and lost you."

"You make it all sound so right."

"Babe, it isn't right or wrong. It just is. It's life. We don't have a teenage son. But if we want to, we can have one in fifteen years."

"And is that what you want?"

He bent his head to look into her face. "It's what I want. What about you?"

She started to cry. "Yes, it's what I want, Johnny. I don't know why it's taken me so long to realize it."

He touched her wet cheek. "Stop blaming yourself. Maybe you didn't want it before. Just because you know you want it now doesn't mean you always have. You had a chance to have children with Solly, and you didn't. I don't accept that it was because you were blind. I think you just weren't ready."

"I don't regret not having children with Solly," she said, sniffing. "I don't know why, but I don't."

"Well, don't regret not having children with me, either," he said. "It's a waste of time."

"All right," she said, smiling through her tears. She knew he was right. She hadn't wanted children before. Now she did. It was simple enough, if you didn't try to rewrite history from the point of view of the present.

He put a hand under her chin and gently kissed her. "Have I told you how grateful I am to you for being so pig-headed about looking for Julie? Sometimes I wonder if this would ever have happened for us if it hadn't been for the shock of that night in the truck."

She laughed. "Harry told me you said that night nearly wrecked your life!"

"Ah, that's just man-talk, Babe," he said comfortably.

"So what do we do now?"

"I'd like to get married. Do you want to get married?"

"Yes," she said.

"And I'd rather not live in the West End if we're going to start a family. I'd like to buy a house."

She nodded. It was all so strange in its normality. Like a homecoming when she'd hardly realized she'd been away. "Not too far out," she said.

"Not too far out," he agreed. "How about right close in? Shall we look at something in Kits? Would you like to be near your parents?"

She realized that she would, only as he said it. "Yes, I think I really would. We could send the kids to our old school. My mother says it still has a pretty good reputation."

"Well, let's start looking."

"Johnny, can we afford Kits? It's so expensive these days."

"We can afford it if I sell the agency. I don't think that'll be too difficult."

It seemed so odd to be having this conversation with Johnny. As though her life were a ball that had been thrown into the air, had reached the apex of its curving flight, and now, in this incredible way, was going to ride back down to its roots.

"Do you want to sell the agency?"

"Yeah, I've about had it with that life."

"What will you do?"

He shook his head. "Take some time off to think, maybe."

"My parents could probably lend us some money, if you don't mind that."

"I don't mind that. I don't think it'll be necessary, though."

"Probably we could manage law school for three years, you know. If you're going to sell the agency..."

"No, not law school. I think that's a dream that's run its course. It would take years afterward before I was earning any real money, and anyway, I don't really believe anymore that law will be any less frustrating than the police force was.

"What about you?" he said. "What do you want to do about your career?"

"Could you stand it if I said I'd like to be mainly a mother for five or ten years?"

Johnny sighed. "Yeah, I'd like that. Let's have more than one, okay? Let's have at least three."

She nodded in content. "Who would have believed we could get so reactionary in our old age?"

He laughed. "I was never a revolutionary, Babe."

"No," she agreed. "You've always just done whatever you saw as right, haven't you? You don't get swayed by trends the way I did."

"Well, with trends, you see one and you've seen them all. Hula hoops did it for me. Things like hula hoops and revolutions just come and go. It's life that matters."

She laughed. "Oh, you're comforting to be with! It all used to matter to me so much."

"I know it did," he agreed.

She said, "Anyway, I can go on writing while we're raising children. I don't have to stop, really, just slow down a bit. Maybe for a while I could work and you could stay at home and be a father, too. I don't think it's right that I should grab all the fun."

He kissed her. "Sounds good to me."

She said tentatively, "Johnny, back in the early days, after the Riot, did you—were you disappointed that we never made anything out of our friendship?"

"For a while, I was."

"It seems to me now that I must have loved you then, but just didn't know it."

He shook his head. "It doesn't pay, Babe. What have we missed, that we can't have now? We've had years of good friendship—the best friendship. I don't regret anything. And I don't accept that we were both unconsciously missing something. When the chance came, we were lucky enough to see it, that's all. We've got something to start with in marriage. I don't think I'd want to start from scratch with someone now, not at this age. When we were both ready, it was there for us. What is there to regret in that?"

"You're right. It's just my romantic nature, wanting to believe that we were both secretly in love all that time."

"Well, we weren't. And a pretty poor pair we'd be, if neither of us had had the courage to make a move in eighteen years."

She laughed again. "You make it all so simple."

"It is simple. Isn't it? It's just life, and you make of it what you can."

"I want a baby soon," she said.

"You won't get any argument from me," said Johnny. He set down his empty cup. "Shall we go to bed?"

As they walked to the bedroom, she asked, "Do you remember that story in grade five or six, I forget which, about the little boy who used to go to his grandparents' house around a hill?"

"Remind me."

"He figured the path around the hill was the long way, and couldn't understand why it didn't lead over the hill. He thought that would be shorter. So one day he decided to go up and over and get home faster. But the hill was high and it took him forever, and when he finally got home he understood the reason for the path."

"Vaguely," said Johnny, sitting on the bed and pulling off his boots.

Lou set her earrings on his dresser between a pile of spare change and a bottle of after-shave. "The moral of the story was, 'Sometimes the longest way around is the shortest way home,'" she said.

Johnny tossed his shirt onto a chair and grinned. "And what's the moral of the moral?"

"Just what you've been saying to me in there. We've taken the long way around, but maybe it really was the shortest way home."

Naked, he slipped between the sheets, where the soft light of the lamp fell on his strong chest, his black hair, his amazing grace.

"Maybe it was," Johnny agreed. Raised on one elbow, he patted the sheet beside him. "Come to bed, love," he said softly, more softly than she had ever heard him speak. "Let's make a baby."

* * * * *

COMING SOON...

For years Harlequin and Silhouette novels have been taking readers places—but only in their imaginations.

This fall look for PASSPORT TO ROMANCE, a promotion that could take you around the corner or around the world!

Watch for it in September!

★